THE
LAST
LEGACY

ALSO BY
ADRIENNE YOUNG

Sky in the Deep

The Girl the Sea Gave Back

Fable

Namesake

THE
LAST
LEGACY

A NOVEL

ADRIENNE
YOUNG

WEDNESDAY BOOKS
NEW YORK

First published in the United States by Wednesday Books, an imprint of St. Martin's Publishing Group

THE LAST LEGACY. Copyright © 2021 by Adrienne Young. All rights reserved. Printed in the United States of America. For information, address St. Martin's Publishing Group, 120 Broadway, New York, NY 10271.

www.wednesdaybooks.com

Design and case stamp illustration by Devan Norman

Library of Congress Cataloging-in-Publication Data

Names: Young, Adrienne, 1985– author.
Title: The last legacy : a novel / Adrienne Young.
Description: First edition. | New York : Wednesday Books, 2021.
Identifiers: LCCN 2021015904 | ISBN 9781250823724 (hardcover) | ISBN 9781250823731 (ebook)
Subjects: CYAC: Fantasy. | Family secrets—Fiction. | Self-actualization (Psychology)—Fiction.
Classification: LCC PZ7.1.Y74 Las 2021 | DDC [Fic]—dc23
LC record available at https://lccn.loc.gov/2021015904

Our books may be purchased in bulk for promotional, educational, or business use. Please contact your local bookseller or the Macmillan Corporate and Premium Sales Department at 1-800-221-7945, extension 5442, or by email at MacmillanSpecialMarkets@macmillan.com.

First Edition: 2021

10 9 8 7 6 5 4 3 2 1

For River

Make your own fate

ROTH FAMILY TREE

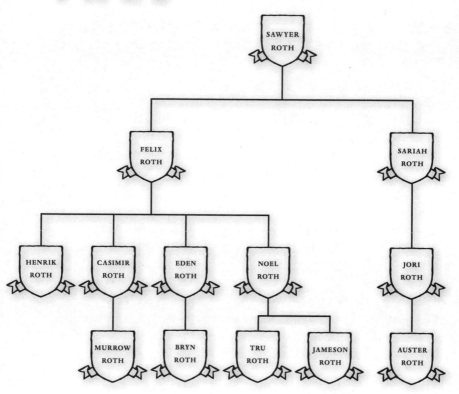

THE
LAST
LEGACY

ONE

The docks were no place for a lady.

My great-aunt Sariah's words fell with the beat of the heavy rain as I snatched up my skirts, realizing the hem was soaked through. It was one of many lessons she'd imparted to me in my years beneath her watch. But while my great-aunt was many things, she was certainly no lady.

A rivulet of water rippled down the steps, where I stood beneath the harbor's entrance, trying to stay out of the downpour.

I pulled my skirts up higher, looking again to the street. The city of Bastian was gray, its pointed rooftops cloaked in a thick, white fog. I'd arrived on the *Jasper* on schedule, but despite my uncle's claims, there'd been no one waiting to receive me.

I shifted to the side when a cluster of men barreled past me and their eyes cut back, raking me from head to toe. The ridiculous frock Sariah had me wear was completely out of place among the hucksters, fishermen, and trading crews who filled the docks. But I'd spent my life not belonging anywhere and all of that was about to change.

The wind picked up, stinging my cheeks and pulling strands of hair loose from where they were tightly pinned back. By the time Murrow showed up, I'd look like I'd been hauled up out of the water in a fishing net. My skirts were growing heavier by the minute.

I cursed, reaching into my pocket for the letter. It had arrived on my eighteenth birthday, as expected. From the time I was a tiny girl in a ruffled frock learning to hold my teacup without spilling, I'd known about the letter. It was a harbinger that followed me through every one of my memories in Nimsmire.

The morning I woke to eighteen years of age, I'd come down the stairs of the gallery to find it sitting unopened on the breakfast table. My great-aunt sat beside it, spectacles propped up on the tip of her nose as she read the morning reports from her many enterprises. As if it were any other day. As if the very air we breathed hadn't shifted the moment that wax-sealed envelope was delivered.

But it had.

I found the softened edges of the parchment, pulling it free. It was worn from where I'd unfolded it over and over. And though I had the words memorized, I read them again.

Bryn,

It's time to come home. I've booked you passage to Bastian on the Jasper *out of Nimsmire. Murrow will be waiting at the docks.*

Henrik Roth

It wasn't an invitation or a request. My uncle was summoning me home—part of a deal he'd made after my parents died. The penmanship was almost flawless, the script slanted in perfect black ink on pearl-white parchment. But there was an unruly flick of the quill at the ends of the words that was unrefined. Brutish, even.

The thought sent a chill up my spine.

I refolded the letter and slipped it into my cloak, gritting my teeth. He'd called me back to Bastian from Nimsmire, but he hadn't had the decency to show up and greet me himself. From everything Sariah had told me about her nephew, it didn't exactly come as a surprise.

Ahead, the great city I couldn't remember hid beneath the mist, stretching along the rocky shore and disappearing into the hills. It had been fourteen years since I boarded a ship in my great-aunt's arms and she took me from this place. She'd made me a promise as a child—that she'd never lie to me. Through the years, she'd answered my questions with a darkened gaze about the family we'd left behind here. But her answers often left me wishing I'd never asked. Because though I was the niece of one of the most respected aristocrats in Nimsmire, there was one thing I'd never been able to wash myself clean of: my name.

Bryn *Roth*.

I'd never had a choice in the matter. It was a truth as simple and as evident as the fact that I had brown eyes or that there were five fingers on each of my hands. While the girls in Nimsmire's merchant families were being matched and given their own business ventures, I waited for my uncle's letter. I'd known all my life that one day, I'd go to Bastian. I'd even hungered for it, longing for the day that I could disappear out from under Sariah's attentive gaze and escape the dismal fate of my peers.

The harbor bell rang out, signaling the opening of the merchant's house. There was already a long line of traders waiting to pick up their inventories before they set out for the next port city on their routes. More than one of them glanced at me, eyeing the trunk at my feet. It was filled with frocks and shoes and jewelry—things Sariah had packed for me. *My armor,* she'd called it. All the things she said I'd need if I was going to be of use in Bastian. That's why I was here, after all.

I stared at the trunk, considering whether I could carry it. Certainly not in these blasted, heavy skirts. If no one was coming for me, I'd have to hire someone to deliver the trunk to Lower Vale. If I did, I figured I had about as much chance of seeing it again as I did of getting the mud out of the hem of my frock. For a moment, I thought maybe that wasn't such a bad thing.

"The long-lost Roth!" A smooth voice carried on the cold wind, finding me. "Come home at last."

I dropped my skirts and turned in a circle, searching the

faces on the street until I spotted him. A young man with a fine wool coat leaned against a lamppost ahead, one foot crossed over the other as he watched me. His hair was shorn to the scalp on both sides, but its top was a mound of dark, loose curls.

I scowled as he grinned up one side of his face. "Murrow?"

He smiled wider. "Bryn."

"How long have you been standing there?" I snapped, climbing the stairs and abandoning the trunk.

He had a sharp, handsome face, but it was his eyes that caught my attention. They were a pale, silvery gray that caught the light in a flash. He nodded in greeting and stood up off the post, sliding his hands into the pockets of his jacket.

"Long enough." He walked toward me slowly, and it was only when he was standing a few feet away that I realized how tall he was. He towered over me, tilting his head as he looked down into my face. "It's good to see you, cousin."

I glared at him. "Henrik's letter said you'd be waiting for me."

"And so I am."

Sariah had told me about Murrow. A rascal, she'd called him. He'd been a boy when she left Bastian for Nimsmire, but the entire family tree was etched into my mind, each of the names that lived there branded into my memory. To me, the tales of the Roths were like the fantastical myths of the sea that the traders lived by. Except these tales were true.

"Sariah didn't come with you?" he asked, absently checking his pocket watch.

"No." In fact, Sariah had refused to come. She'd sworn when she left Bastian that she would never step foot in the city again and that was another promise she intended to keep.

"Just as well." He breathed out a sigh. "Come on." He jerked a chin toward the entrance to the harbor and started up the docks without me.

"But my things." I turned back, only to find the trunk that had been sitting at the bottom of the steps was gone. When I searched the street for Murrow's head bobbing above the others, two men were striding ahead of him, my trunk poised ungracefully on their shoulders.

"Wait!" I called out, rushing to keep up.

Murrow slowed just long enough for me to fall into step beside him, pulling his hat low over his eyes. The rain beaded on the dark gray tweed like tiny diamonds and the chain of his gold pocket watch glimmered as it swung from his vest pocket. At first glance, he was as elegantly dressed as any of the young men in Nimsmire, but there was a roughness to his countenance.

Murrow tipped his hat at a man passing us and the man promptly frowned, edging a step away.

Murrow laughed, clearly amused. "He won't like it if we're late."

"Who?" I looked back at the man, confused.

"Henrik." Murrow said his name with a finality that made me pause.

My uncle Henrik was the patriarch of a generations-old trade in fake gemstones. He'd inherited the business from his father, Felix, my great-aunt's brother. When my parents were killed in a scheme gone wrong, Sariah struck a deal with Henrik. If he let her raise me in Nimsmire, away from the dangers of the family business, he could have me back on my eighteenth birthday. He'd kept his end of the deal. Now my great-aunt had kept hers.

"How was the journey?" Murrow picked up his pace.

I hauled up my skirts as we plowed into a puddle, dodging a rickety cart of red plums on the walk. "It was fine."

I'd been on the ship only one night and hadn't slept, instead staring at the stars out the window of the private cabin Henrik had paid for. I'd been thinking of Sariah. How she'd pulled me close and kissed me on the cheek before she let me go. It was a rare show of affection that had made my stomach twist with dread. Her soft skin had been cold against mine and fleetingly I had thought, *This could be the last time I see her.* Even so, I'd parted from her without so much as a single tear. In addition to teaching me how to read, write, and name every gemstone, Sariah had also taught me to behave. And there was no one so unbecoming in her eyes as someone who refused to accept their fate.

"You don't remember me, do you?" Murrow said suddenly, coming to a stop in the middle of the street.

I stared up into his face, my eyes searching his. I didn't. There were moments when I thought I remembered the time before Nimsmire. I'd wake from a vivid dream, with distantly familiar images dissolving before my eyes. But they always slipped away just as I reached for them, lost to the past once more.

"No," I answered. "Do you remember me?"

Murrow's eyes narrowed, as if he was sifting through his memories. "Maybe."

Without another word, he turned onto the next street. A half-bewildered laugh escaped my lips before I followed. He might pass for well-bred in appearance, but Murrow was a different creature than the ones I'd been brought up with. There was a sly humor about him, and I wasn't sure if I found it a relief or an irritation.

I followed him beyond the iron archway ahead, where a knot of tangled streets lay between the rows of buildings. The filtered light cast a glow over the rooftops, reflecting on the hazy glass windows. In every direction, the walkways were filled with people, and the smell of seawater and baking bread was thick in the cold air.

It was nothing like the small, quaint city of Nimsmire, with its well-groomed thoroughfare and small harbor. And for the slightest, fractured moment, I had the feeling that I *could* remember this place. As if I could see myself standing there at four years old, pulled along by Sariah's hand, toward the docks. But again, the threads of the image were frayed, unraveling each time I tried to hold them in my mind.

Ahead, Bastian unfolded like a book and a small smile lifted on my lips. It was a city of stories. But not all of them had happy endings.

TWO

The house wasn't a house at all. Not the kind I was used to, anyway.

Murrow stood before the narrow slab of brick wedged between two other buildings down an alley paved with cracked cobblestones. The rain had finally stopped, but it still dripped from the corners of the roof overhead, where three rows of windows looked out over the street. It was the ancestral home of the family, first inhabited by my great-grandfather Sawyer Roth. According to Sariah, there would never come a time when the Roths didn't live beneath its roof, but compared to the estate in Nimsmire I'd grown up in, this was a hovel.

My hands fisted in my skirts as I studied the face of the dark row house. It was the subtle shift of a curtain in one of the windows that drew my eye. But behind the glass, there was only darkness.

Murrow drew a key from his pocket and it clicked as he turned it in the lock. My trunk had been waiting beside the steps when we turned the corner and I'd instantly frowned, disappointed that it hadn't been carried off to the market. Its contents were like a chain around my ankle, keeping me from venturing too far from the role I'd been born to play.

This end of the alley was empty, tucked away from the busy main street of Lower Vale, and the mud wasn't pocked with footprints. It was apparent that there weren't many who passed by this way, and there wouldn't be. Those who had business with the Roths weren't the kind of people who'd knock on this door in the daylight.

It opened with a sharp creak and a small, scowling face peered out of the darkness. A smile broke onto the boy's lips when he laid eyes on Murrow and he opened the door wider. But my brow furrowed as I looked him over. He couldn't be any older than ten years, but he was dressed in the same tailored jacket and trousers that Murrow wore, his made of a deep blue tweed instead of gray. Even the boy's white shirt was spotless and unwrinkled.

"Is this her?" His wide eyes moved over me from head to toe, like I was a tea cake waiting to be eaten.

"Yep," Murrow answered, mussing the boy's perfectly combed hair as he pushed inside.

The boy groaned, pushing him off, and I hesitated before I took the steps. With the door hanging open, the house looked like a beast, mouth open and tongue unrolled.

"You coming?" Murrow didn't wait for a response, disappearing into the shadowed hall.

I glanced up and down the alley again. For what, I didn't know. The Roths weren't just residents of Lower Vale, they were its keepers. There probably wasn't a safer place in this part of the city than under this roof. So why did I feel like I was crossing a dangerous threshold?

The boy closed the door behind me as I stepped inside and I unclasped my cloak, letting it slide off my shoulders.

"I'm Tru." He watched me with a bright grin, thumbs hooked into his suspenders. Aside from the playful twinkle in his eyes, he looked like a miniature man.

Tru. I found the name in the mental register I kept of the family. He was the eldest son of my uncle Noel. "I'm Bryn. Nice to meet you."

"Don't you have work to do?" Murrow arched an eyebrow at him, unbuttoning his jacket so that it fell open more comfortably.

Tru gave a sigh before he turned on his heel and reluctantly went up the stairs. They curved as they rose and he disappeared, leaving only the sound of his footsteps beating behind the walls.

The house was cold, pricking over my flushed skin as my eyes trailed across the entry. Old wood paneling reached up the walls like the cabin in a ship, but the hallway was papered in a rich garnet. It rippled with the damp and curled at some of the edges along the ceiling, where a few oil lamps were lit on brass mounts. They badly needed polishing.

"You're the same, you know," Murrow said, suddenly. He held out a hand for my cloak.

I gave it to him, feeling the heat come up into my cheeks. "So, you do remember me?"

"Oh, I remember you." He gave me another wry grin,

hanging the cloak on one of the pegs in the wall. "Remember that temper, too."

I frowned. If Sariah were here, she'd give me a knowing look. My temper was the one wrinkle she hadn't quite ironed out of me.

I didn't like the idea that Murrow might know me in a way that I didn't know him. I'd grown up with tales of the Roths, but what stories had they heard about me? Maybe none. My great-aunt hadn't spoken to the family since we left, except for essential correspondence with Henrik about their overlapping business.

Her residence in Nimsmire and her ability to run her family stake away from Bastian was a privilege granted by her brother, Felix, but now that he was gone, it was sustained by Henrik. From what I could tell, she knew better than to tempt my uncle's wrath by refusing him anything. It was the reason she hadn't hesitated to pack my things when his letter arrived. That said more to me about the Roths than the whole of what she'd told me over a lifetime.

Murrow led me down the dark hallway, past the kitchen, where a small woman stood at a butcher block kneading a round of dough. Strands of icy-gold hair fell into her eyes as she glanced up at me, but Murrow didn't stop, breezing past the opening. I followed him around the corner, and he waited before a set of doors that were painted black and fitted with bronze handles.

It wasn't until that moment that I realized how quiet the house was. It didn't have the feeling of being lived in or a sense that there were people between its walls. It was unsettling, as if the rooms had been empty for years, the hearths cold. When Murrow reached for a handle, I stopped him, setting two fingers on the crook of his arm.

"What's he like?" I asked, trying to keep my tone more curious than wary. The truth was, I was half-terrified. And I wasn't even sure why. I'd been invited here, but the unfamiliar atmosphere of the house made me feel like an intruder.

Murrow let go of the handle and he turned toward me, his face only half lit by a beam of light coming from a high window. "Henrik?"

"Yeah."

For a second, he looked almost suspicious of the question. His head tilted a little to one side, but when his mouth twisted, I realized he was really thinking about his answer. "He's . . . serious. Resourceful. Intelligent. Nothing matters more to him than loyalty." There was a calm honesty in the words that almost put me at ease. But when he reached for the door again, he hesitated. "But, Bryn?"

I looked up into his face, smoothing my hands over my skirts. "What?"

The muscle in his jaw ticked. "Don't ever, *ever* cross him."

A stone sank in my stomach as the door swung open and the heat of a fire came rolling out into the hallway, wrapping me in gooseflesh. The room was a study, with a polished wooden desk set before an illuminated fireplace. Stacks of unused parchment were neatly arranged at one corner of the desk, a quill and pot of ink at the other. At its center was a small leather book.

The light didn't quite make it to the edges of the room,

leaving everything slightly dark despite the roaring fire, and the mantel was littered with pipes and mullein boxes, a trinket left here and there. But my gaze was pulled to the wall behind us as we stepped inside. Portraits in gilded frames hung on the short wall, clustered together like a chaotic constellation. The most prominently placed among them was a painting of my great-grandfather Sawyer, who had built both the house and the business that was run in its workshop. To its left was a portrait of his children, Felix and Sariah. Sariah's son Jori was beneath it, her only child who was lost at sea as a young man. But the place on the wall next to that portrait was missing, leaving behind a discolored circle on the wall.

The painting that hung over the fireplace was the most recognizable to me. Three young men and one young woman were posed together, the tallest of the boys standing behind the others. I guessed it was Henrik. The others had to be Casimir, Noel, and my mother, Eden.

Henrik, the oldest, was followed in age by Casimir and then the youngest of the three brothers, Noel. Eden had been the only daughter, born third in line.

There was something about those faces that felt familiar, but I wasn't sure if it was because I recognized them or because I wanted to. Everything I knew about my mother had been spoken from Sariah's lips and only in reverent whispers. When her son, Jori, died, Sariah had taken to Eden and they'd been close when she died. Sariah had once told me it felt like losing another child.

In the portrait, Eden was dressed in a green frock with her brown hair unbound and falling over her shoulders. I took a step closer when I spotted the tattoo on the inside of her arm. The ouroboros, two entwined snakes eating one another's tails. It was the same mark every member of the Roth family bore. Even Sariah. Only one of the snakes' heads was visible in the painting, the rest hidden against her frock.

There was no portrait of my father. Only those in the direct bloodline had a place here. In the same way, I'd been given my mother's name instead of my father's. It didn't matter which side of the parentage you had, anyone born in this family was a Roth.

The door on the other side of the study opened and Murrow straightened beside me, clearing his throat. In an instant, he lost his easy, lazy manner and his chin lifted in the air, his shoulders pulled back. Impossibly, he looked even taller.

Across the room, a man I would know anywhere was framed in the open doorway. Not because I remembered him, but because his presence flooded the study around us, filling its dark corners like black ink. His cinnamon-colored hair was combed and tucked behind his ears, his face cleanly shaven except for a thick, curling mustache. His sharp gaze focused as he surveyed me.

"Jacket, Murrow." His gruff voice was too loud for the small study.

Murrow immediately reached for the buttons of his jacket, rebuttoning them. "Sorry." He cleared his throat.

A rag was clutched in Henrik's big hands, and I bristled when I saw the knuckles of his right fingers. They were covered in healing cuts, the skin red, as if they'd recently landed blows on someone's face.

I stood silent, waiting for him to say something. I knew how to take my cues from others. How to match my behavior to theirs. But this man was difficult to read.

After several agonizingly silent moments, a small smile lifted beneath his mustache. It lit his eyes, changing their shape. "Bryn." He said my name as if it was heavy on his tongue, but it wasn't without affection.

I let out the breath I was holding.

He finished wiping his hands and dropped the rag onto the desk before pulling the leather apron he wore over his head. Underneath it, he, too, wore a crisp, white shirt and his shined shoes caught the light. He handed the apron to Murrow, who stepped forward to take it and hang it on the wall.

"I'm glad you're here," Henrik said, reaching out to shake my hand. On his third finger, a merchant's ring for the Narrows looked up at me. It was set with a polished round of tiger's-eye.

I glanced to Murrow, confused by the sudden shift in his temperament, but he stood silent against the wall. I took Henrik's hand and he covered my fingers with his, squeezing. He didn't let it go. "Back where you belong."

When he finally released me, he leaned into the desk, crossing his arms over his chest. "It's been a long time."

"A very long time," I echoed. I wasn't sure what the rules were for a greeting like this one and Henrik wasn't giving me any indication of his expectations.

"How is my aunt?"

"She's well." I didn't tell him that she'd sent her regards, because she hadn't. I had a feeling it would come as no surprise to him. Henrik and Sariah seemed to tolerate each other, at best.

He nodded. "I am happy to hear that. And your journey? Your cabin on the *Jasper*?"

"All very well," I answered. "Thank you for arranging everything. I'm grateful."

Another silence fell over the study as he curiously looked me over. His eyes studied my hair, my frock, my boots. The shimmering bracelet around my wrist. "Murrow will show you to your room. I'm sure you're very tired. You'll meet the rest of the family tonight at dinner."

There was a subtly commanding air in the words, but I relaxed slightly. When I opened my mouth to speak again, Murrow was already opening the door. I looked between them, realizing that Henrik wasn't giving a polite suggestion. He was dismissing me.

I forced a polite smile. "I'm glad to finally meet you," I said.

At that, Henrik seemed to stiffen. "I suppose it feels that way to you."

My smile fell a little. I wasn't sure what he meant. Maybe that to him, it didn't feel like a first meeting because he'd known me as a child. Or maybe that I didn't feel like a stranger to him. Either way, he didn't exactly look angry and I took that as a good sign.

"I'll see you tonight," he said, straightening from where he leaned on the desk. He turned toward the fire, reaching for the small leather book, and I watched him over my shoulder as I stepped back out into the hall.

The chill that hovered outside of the room was a relief.

I was too warm beneath my frock from the study's blazing fire.

"This way." Murrow gestured to the stairs behind me that Tru had taken.

I followed him up, each step creaking as we climbed their winding path. When we reached the next floor, a bit of sunlight was coming from a high window on the topmost level. Outside, the gray sky had brightened to a soft blue.

Murrow led me around two turns before he stopped in front of a closed door. More light spilled into the hallway as he swung it open. Across the small room, the single window was cracked, letting a breeze skip through the air.

Murrow tapped the top of the trunk sitting at the foot of the bed. Someone had brought it up from the street, along with my cloak that now hung on the hook at the back of the door.

I looked the space over. There was a simple dressing table, a bed, and leaning in one corner was a long mirror with a porcelain washing bowl on one side and a chair on the other. The walls were painted the palest shade of green, but it was chipping, revealing the white plaster beneath.

It was bare and modest, but it had the feeling of once being lived in. I liked it.

In Nimsmire, I'd always felt like a roughly cut jewel set into a shining brooch. My edges were too sharp. My anger too swift. Sariah had done her best to make me into one of the girls from prominent merchant families who would be matched like shoes to a handsome frock, but I'd never fit seamlessly among them. I'd never wanted to.

In that way, Bastian was more than my destiny. It was my chance at freedom from charades and displays and diplomatic marriages.

"Whose room was this?" I asked, eyeing the tortoiseshell comb on the dressing table. "Before, I mean."

Murrow's expression shifted just slightly. "Someone who's not here anymore." He stepped back into the hallway. "Welcome home."

He left me alone, and I took the three steps to the window, reaching up to close it. Outside, the rooftops of Bastian were still glistening with rain as the sun burned off the fog. It was only then that I got a glimpse of just how big the city was. A sea of buildings rolled over the hills in the distance, edging along the shore for as far as I could see. In comparison, the small port city of Nimsmire that had been my whole world seemed tiny. The thought made me feel small in that window.

I went to my cloak and reached into the pocket, removing the two envelopes inside. The first was Henrik's letter. It was still badly creased, but the other was crisp, the corners sharp. It was the letter Sariah had given me before I left. The envelope was sealed, the wax pressed with her initials, *SR*. I hadn't yet had the guts to read it.

I opened the top drawer of the dressing table and dropped them inside before I sat down on the bed and kicked off my boots. I pulled my legs up beneath my skirts and hugged them to my chest, shivering. The quietness of the house returned, like the sound of a cavern. Empty and hollow.

Back where you belong. Henrik's voice crept through my mind.

I'd never belonged anywhere. Not in Nimsmire. Not with Sariah. But there was a faint, whispering voice that had found me as I crossed the threshold of the house tucked back in the dismal, forgotten alley of Lower Vale. It had snaked its way through me, echoing that single, terrifying word that Murrow had spoken.

Home.

THREE

I wouldn't write to her. Not yet.

In the hours since I'd arrived in Lower Vale, I'd unpacked my things into the few drawers and wardrobe. I'd set my jewelry into the little glass box on the table and paced the floorboards in front of the long mirror. After I'd spent a good hour at the window, watching the distant water darken in the falling light, I finally sat at the desk and pulled a piece of blank parchment free.

The scribble of the quill was a chaotic flurry of half thoughts and admissions, but the moment I signed my name I'd torn it up, feeding the pieces to the single flame on the candle.

Sariah would see it as weakness to receive word from me so soon. She'd know exactly what lay beneath the prompt message—uncertainty, fear. Worst of all, she'd know that I needed her.

Sariah had never been particularly warm, and I'd always

thought it was because I was destined to leave her. Or that the pain of losing her son and my mother haunted her so much that she'd never really let herself grow too attached to me. But there had been an ache that woke in my chest as I stood on the deck of the *Jasper,* watching her grow small on the docks as the ship left port. Like the tether between us had finally been cut. And for the first time in my life, I was drifting.

I stood at the top of the stairs, listening to the sound of glass clinking and boots on the hollow floors below. Laughter. The house was full of people, missing the emptiness from that afternoon. For a fleeting moment, I thought it stirred a memory somewhere deep in the back of my mind. The smell of lamp oil and mullein smoke. The golden glow of a fire and the sparkle of crystal.

My skirts brushed along the walls of the narrow stairwell as I came down and I paused on the other side of the entrance to the dining room. Shadows moved over the walls and the light cascaded, reflected by the chandelier that hung from the ceiling. It was a piece too beautiful for the rundown house.

I pasted on my softest, most proper smile before I stepped through the open doorway. My fingers tangled together at my lower back and the voices promptly silenced when the family saw me. I counted seven pairs of eyes, all glistening in the firelight. Among them there was only one woman, a slight, dark-haired figure with a toddler on her hip. She was the only one who didn't look directly at me, absently tucking the little boy's hair behind his ear.

"Ah." Henrik stepped out from behind the others, a grin spread wide on his face.

He clapped his hands together and walked toward me as I stood frozen, unable to move beneath the heavy stares. He took his place beside me, wrapping one arm around my shoulder, and I tried not to go rigid. The smell of leather polish and spice enveloped me, distinctly male scents that rarely filled my home in Nimsmire.

"Bryn, I'd like to introduce you, once again, to your uncles." He lifted a hand toward the man standing beside Murrow. He had the same straight edge to his shoulders, but he wasn't quite as tall as his son. The greatest difference between them was the pensive look on his face. Murrow had a perpetual humor in his eyes. "This is Casimir."

The man lifted one of his hands from where it was tucked into his elbow in a silent greeting.

"And you know your cousin Murrow," Henrik added.

Murrow gave me a nod and he looked as if he was about to laugh, making me feel embarrassed. I probably looked as uncomfortable on the outside as I felt on the inside.

"This is Noel." Henrik pointed to a shorter man on the other side of the fire. He was younger and handsome, with wide, open eyes and a gentle set to his mouth. "He and his family live in the flat on the third floor."

"Hello," he said, quietly.

"His wife, Anthelia," Henrik continued. "And their sons, Tru and Jameson."

The young woman finally did look at me, but her eyes dropped almost as quickly as they found mine. The young boy, Tru, who'd answered the door that afternoon, poked his head out from behind her, formally tipping his hat as if he were a grown man.

"I'm sure you will all join me in welcoming our Bryn back to Bastian."

Our Bryn.

The words put gooseflesh on my skin again.

Henrik clapped me on the back suddenly, sending me forward just enough so that I had to take a steadying step, and the room erupted with laughter, making me blush. Their manners were as confusing as their empty expressions. I couldn't tell if they were happy to see me or if they were going to set me on a platter and have me for supper.

"All right." Henrik moved to the head of the table and almost in unison, everyone broke from the fire, lining up behind the empty chairs.

A hand touched my arm, and I glanced up to see Murrow motioning me to the seat beside his. I was grateful. There was no decorum about these people. No apparent order. They were smartly dressed and groomed, but something about them had the look of feral creatures who'd been tamed. The only thing that seemed clear was Henrik's leadership over the rest of them.

Everyone stood, waiting patiently, and I eyed the chair across from mine. It was the only one that was empty.

The table was set with fine china and silver, crystal goblets and linen napkins. There was a roasted pig in the center, wreathed in herbed potatoes and cooked apples. It was a familiar scene to me, except for the dark glass bottles that were poised at each end. Rye. Never in my life had I seen rye served at a proper dinner. It was the drink of filthy taverns and surly ship crews.

Henrik pulled out his chair to sit and the others followed, taking their seats in what looked like a choreographed movement. The fire was at his back, illuminating the small leather-bound book that sat at his right, the very same I'd seen on his desk.

"That chair's been empty too long," he said, giving me a smile.

I realized then that it must have been my mother's seat at the table. The thought made me feel uneasy, but it was quickly followed by a sense of grounding. That's why I was here, after all. To take her place. Carve out my own stake in the family. Help Henrik bridge the gap between Lower Vale and the guilds.

Murrow picked up a basket of bread and passed it to me. I stared at it, unsure of what he wanted me to do, and he stifled another laugh, plucking one of the rolls from inside and setting it on my plate. "You look like you're about to crawl under the table," he murmured, reaching over me to hand the basket to Noel, who sat at my other side.

"Sorry." I attempted a smile, unfolding my napkin in my lap and at the same time watching the way everyone else left theirs crumpled beside their plates.

Heat crept up out of the collar of my frock, stinging my skin. I didn't know how to act. What to do. And everyone but Murrow and Henrik seemed to be watching my every move, sending me side glances every few bites.

A door opened and closed somewhere in the house and I

felt a shift in the warm air, as if someone had come in from the street. But no one seemed to notice, refilling their glasses with rye and roughly cutting into their food. Boots sounded through the doorway and a figure appeared, slipping into the dining room without a word. My eyes followed him as he moved around the table, finding the empty chair across from me.

He was a young man, dressed in a clean, white shirt and suspenders, with a dark brow set over even darker eyes. He was cut from a different cloth from the others entirely, with smooth, pale skin and defined features.

"You're late," Henrik said, his voice heavy and deep with reproach. He didn't even look up from his plate, but the air in the room went cold.

"I apologize" was his only reply. He took his seat, sitting straight-backed, his eyes pinned to his plate.

The young man picked up his fork, serving himself silently as Murrow reached across the table to fill his glass. My grip tightened around the stem of my goblet when I noticed a patchwork of silver scars tracing over his hands. They wrapped around his knuckles and fingers, disappearing beneath the cuffs of his shirt.

"Don't be rude, Ezra," Henrik spoke again.

The muscle in his jaw clenched before he cleared his throat and finally, he looked up, his eyes catching mine. They were so focused that a flash of heat raced over my skin, making me swallow.

Ezra. A name I didn't know.

"Pleased to meet you." The words were polite, but they

were missing any semblance of sincerity. And as soon as they left his mouth, his gaze dropped back to the table.

"Pleased to meet you," I echoed, stabbing an apple with my fork. It hovered over my plate as I studied him.

There was something different about him, and not only in his features. I was sure I'd never heard his name from Sariah, but he looked about Murrow's age. Maybe two years older than me. If that was true, he wasn't blood. But if he was sitting at this table, then somehow, he was considered family.

"Ezra is our silversmith," Henrik said, sensing my curiosity.

I looked down to his hands. That explained the scars. They were from the forge.

Henrik took another too-large bite of roast and chewed, setting his fork down on his plate with a clatter, and everyone looked up, dropping their own silver. My other uncles settled back in their chairs, pulling out small books from inside their vests, as if waiting for something.

I followed suit, setting my knife on the edge of my plate neatly and folding my hands awkwardly in my lap.

Henrik opened his book, flipping to a page filled with markings. From where I sat, it looked like a ledger.

"Casimir?" he began, picking up his quill.

There was a tense silence and I looked up to see more than one person looking at me. Whatever was being discussed, they were uncomfortable with me hearing it.

"Cass," Henrik said, impatiently.

Casimir set his elbows on the table, shooting me a quick

glance before he answered. "Are we discussing business to-night?"

"Is that not what we do at every family dinner?" Henrik shot back, not bothering to hide his annoyance.

"Surely Bryn doesn't want us to bore her." Anthelia smiled, but it was stiff on her lips.

I wasn't stupid. It was clear that not everyone was happy to have a new face at the table, even if I was Eden's daughter. And I couldn't blame them. To them, I was an outsider.

The silence pulled taut, filling the room with a choking tension that coiled itself around me and squeezed. I bit the inside of my cheek nervously.

Henrik set down his quill, turning to me with what looked like an attempt at patience. "Are you bored, Bryn?"

My lips parted as I looked around the table, my face aflame. "No."

"Satisfied?" Henrik's attention swiftly returned to Casimir.

Casimir let out a heavy breath, relenting. I watched as he opened his ledger, following the numbers with the tip of his finger and reading them off. "Forty-three to Drake's apprentice and one hundred and twelve to the helmsman of the *Emerald*," Casimir answered.

Bribes, I guessed. The family business relied upon sensitive information and that required coin. Sariah did the same thing in Nimsmire, paying off traders for ratting out helmsmen or reporting to her what was going on at other port cities. There was nothing delicate about it and I kept my eyes on the fire, careful not to show even the slightest bit of interest. Too many people at this table didn't want me listening to

this conversation and I wasn't going to give anyone reason
to notice me.

"And the rye?" Henrik murmured.

"Fourteen cases from the Narrows coming in on the *Alder*
day after next."

"You'll be ready?" Henrik looked up.

Casimir answered with a nod, closing his book.

"All right, what about you, Noel?"

"Sounds like Tula has a new ship. The *Serpent*. She'll be
looking for a merchant to contract with and expanding her
route to the Narrows. I'm guessing Simon will make a play
for it."

Henrik grunted. When traders expanded their routes
and added to their fleets, it opened doors for merchants. But
this was an opportunity Henrik wasn't eligible for. The ring
on his finger gave him permission to trade in the Narrows,
but not in the Unnamed Sea.

"I'm heading to the tavern tonight to see what I can find
out," Noel said. "There won't be any shortage of merchants
trying to land that contract."

Henrik's head tilted to one side as he looked up from the
book. "And the harbormaster's logs?"

"Being copied as we speak. They'll be ready for delivery
tomorrow."

Each member of the family had a stake in the business—a
scheme or trade that put coin in the coffers. It sounded like
Casimir's was a rye side trade and Noel's had something to
do with the harbormaster. According to Sariah, my mother's
stake had been a tea house that never opened. The only advice

my great-aunt had offered me when I left Nimsmire was to build my stake as soon as possible. The sooner I was bringing in copper, the sooner I'd earn their trust.

Henrik scratched another set of numbers into the book. "And the inventory, Ezra?"

He was the only one who didn't pull out a leather-bound book, answering from memory rather than notes. "Six crates of bronze bricks and eleven barrels of mullein. There will be silks next week and a few gems to choose from. Other than that, it's the usual."

"What do you think?" Henrik paused.

Ezra thought about it for a moment before he answered. "I'd say the bronze."

"All right, the bronze it is," Henrik said, making another note.

He finished going around the table as the food on our plates went cold. Each of them gave their cryptic reports as Henrik notated them with a careful hand, asking questions and assigning tasks. It sounded mostly like ship cargos and merchant goods, many of which they shouldn't have if Henrik wasn't a merchant with a ring to trade in Bastian.

"Has the invitation from Simon come yet?" Noel leaned forward, eyeing Henrik.

There was that name again—Simon.

Henrik's mustache twitched as he snapped the ledger closed. Whatever Noel was talking about, it had clearly struck a nerve. "No."

A quick hush fell over the table and Casimir and Noel

shared a look before they picked up their forks. Just like that, talk of business was over, and with it, there seemed to be a collective relief. Not another word was said about it and everyone finished eating, growing more relaxed with every glass of rye that was poured. Everyone except for Ezra.

Every time I thought I could feel his eyes on me, I looked up to find him staring at his plate. He'd barely spoken, answering Henrik quickly each time he was asked a question but offering nothing more.

I picked at my food, grateful that no one acknowledged me for the rest of the meal. Henrik had summoned me to Bastian to take my place in the family. But it hadn't occurred to me that some might not want me here.

The sharp scrape of chair legs over the floor made me blink and I looked up to see Henrik standing. As soon as he tossed his napkin to the table, Jameson slipped from his mother's lap and ran down the hall. The others followed, leaving their places at the table but taking their rye glasses with them. I'd barely touched mine, but Murrow refilled it anyway.

"Congratulations," he said. "You've survived your first family dinner and not a single punch was thrown." He snickered.

I almost laughed, picking up the little glass and taking a sip. I winced as I swallowed, my lips puckering. The rye would take getting used to.

The others had flooded into the kitchen, gathering around a long counter as the small woman I'd seen earlier set out platters of pastries. No forks or plates. They simply picked up the cakes with their hands and took bites between laughter, speaking with full mouths. I couldn't help but smile. They may be missing the manners of the guild society, but they were also missing the cold cordiality.

I watched them from the doorway. They had a rhythm with one another, something that I could only assume came from growing up in a family. It was something I'd never had before, and I found the noise and lack of decorum comforting. There was a warmth among them. And despite the awkwardness of the dinner, I found that there was something I liked about these strange people.

I slipped back down the hallway once they were lost in conversation and went up the stairs, finding my room. The second floor was drafty and quiet and when I reached for the latch, I noticed a thin beam of moonlight beside my feet. The door beside mine was cracked open and I could see flashes of white in the darkness as I took a step toward it, gently pushing the door open.

It was another bedroom that looked almost exactly like mine. The bed was made, the wardrobe shut up tight, and the window was shimmied open, letting the night air inside. But it was the wall above the small desk that caught my attention. It was covered in pieces of parchment, fluttering in the breeze. Each one was filled with scrawling handwriting. Stacks of books and papers covered every inch of the desk beneath it with a kind of orderly chaos.

On the dressing table beside the doorway sat three dice that looked like they were shaped from a pale moonstone. They were the kind of dice used to play Three Widows, the unsavory game of chance that had filled my great-aunt's parlor on many late nights.

A soft creak sounded in the hallway and I turned, sucking in a breath when I saw Ezra standing behind me. So close I could reach out and touch him. His scarred hands were tucked into his pockets, the top buttons of his shirt undone, and he looked down at me in the dark with narrowed eyes. I hadn't even heard him come up the stairs.

"Stay out of my room." His deep voice filled the space between us.

He stepped around me before I could speak, the door latch clicking in the silence as he disappeared behind it. Soon after, the glow of an oil lamp illuminated beneath the door, touching the hem of my skirts.

I wasn't a fool. I'd known when I got off that ship at the docks that joining the Roths wouldn't be as simple as taking my mother's chair at the table. I'd counted on the fact that to them, family was everything. It was the net that would catch me if I made a mistake or if I fell from grace. But there was a clear line drawn between those who belonged and those who didn't. It would take more than blood to cross it.

FOUR

y room was filled with the smell of the sea.

I opened my eyes to the first of what would be many mornings in Bastian, drawing the damp air deep into my lungs. The footsteps of little feet trailed across the upper floor, where Noel's children were waking, and the room was cold, making me burrow deeper into the quilts as I watched the birds outside the window. Their feathers were puffed against the early chill, their pale colors almost vanishing in the fog.

I shared a wall with Ezra's room, and though I'd heard him late into the night, parchment rustling and footsteps heavy against the floor, now there was only silence. Daybreak was lifting over the city in the distance and once the sun rose just enough to paint the floorboards, I finally willed myself up and out of bed.

My trunk had been meticulously packed by Sariah's servants, complete with the silver brush and jeweled hair combs she'd gifted me. I'd never liked decadence the way she had, but in my sometimes pathetic attempts to gain her approval, I did myself up in a way that I knew she liked. Among the Roths of Bastian, the pretense felt silly. But it was no secret what Henrik and Sariah wanted from me. I was the polished stone among them, and my uncle would make use of that.

I chose the simplest of my frocks, a dark purple with a full skirt and long sleeves that buttoned at the wrists. The fabric was warmer than the ones Sariah usually had me wear and raw silk would draw less attention out on the streets of Lower Vale. After fourteen years of being paraded before the elite of Nimsmire, I liked the idea that I could disappear.

The boots I'd brought with me were perhaps the only practical items in my trunk. They'd take the uneven cobblestones and keep my feet dry. I laced them up, keeping the cord symmetrical as I tightened them, and knotted the ends above my ankles. When I stood, I turned in front of the mirror, eyes falling down my reflection. I almost looked like one of the girls I'd seen out on the street yesterday. Almost.

The smell of freshly baked bread was thick in the air as I came down the stairs. The dining room was empty, but the kitchen was busy, and the sound of voices pulled me down the long hallway that led to an open door. A small square-shaped chamber was tucked into the corner of the house, where the fresh air from outside was coming in through propped-open windows that completely lined the walls. At its center, Henrik, Casimir, Murrow, and Ezra were seated at a round table. They looked up almost in unison as I appeared.

"Breakfast is at *seven*," Henrik said, abruptly.

My cheeks bloomed hot and I reached up to the collar of my frock, fidgeting with the lace. "I'm sorry. I didn't know."

The stern look in his eye melted into a smile as quickly as it had appeared. "Well, now you do." He pointed the bread in his hand at the empty chair beside him and Murrow gave me an encouraging nod.

Anywhere else in polite society, one of them would have stood to pull the chair out for me, but they kept right on eating. I may be of use, but I wasn't a precious thing to them, I realized. And I found that I liked the idea as much as it made me nervous. I wouldn't be handled gently in this house.

"Have you got a watch?" Henrik asked, still chewing.

It took a moment for me to realize that he was still speaking to me. "I—I don't."

"You'll be sure she gets one. Take her to the watchmaker's shop," Henrik said to Murrow, who answered with a grunt. "We like things tidy and timely, Bryn. That's what keeps this family running."

"Of course," I answered, carefully unfolding my napkin into my lap. I felt like a child being scolded, but the others didn't look fazed by the reproach.

Across the table, Casimir's attention was on the running yolk of his egg as he wiped it from the plate with his bread. But Ezra was watching me over the steaming teacup clutched in his hand. He didn't hold it by the delicate handle. Instead, his fingers wrapped around its rim and he lifted it to his mouth, taking a sharp sip.

I dropped my eyes, placing a piece of cheese onto my plate.

"I want those deliveries made before noon, Cass," Henrik said.

"It'll be done," Casimir answered.

"The bronze, tonight."

Casimir nodded.

I wondered if they were talking about the bronze that Ezra had mentioned at dinner. It had sounded like they were discussing a ship inventory that was headed to port and Ezra was making his recommendation on what to lift from their hull.

It was the kind of job they pulled again and again, and it kept the coin coming in. It was also the same kind of job that had gotten my parents killed.

Casimir wiped his mouth before dropping his napkin onto the table. He stood, draining his teacup as the woman from the kitchen came gliding in, a fresh pot of tea in her hands.

She scowled at Casimir. "Now, wait just a minute. You've barely eaten a thing!"

He set the cup down on the little saucer, giving her a smile. It was the first one I'd seen on his face and it made him look more like Murrow. "I've had plenty. I've got work to do down on the docks."

She gave Henrik a disapproving frown, as if expecting him to agree with her, but he ignored the exchange, cutting into the egg on his plate with his fork.

"A belly of tea will do you no good, Cass!" she called after him as he left the room.

When he didn't answer, she set the pot of tea down with a huff.

"Sylvie, Bryn." Henrik spoke without looking at either of us. "Bryn, Sylvie."

The woman set both hands onto her hips, giving me a look over. "I see." She smiled. "Welcome to Bastian, honey. Don't let these brutes scare you off." She let a purposeful gaze fall on Ezra, who looked thoroughly irritated by the sudden attention.

"I won't." I smiled.

"Messages?" Henrik grunted.

Sylvie shook her head. "None."

A muscle in Henrik's jaw ticked before he took another bite.

She left the room and my eyes trailed from Henrik to Murrow as I ate. Noel and his family were nowhere to be seen, so I could only guess they took breakfast at a different time. Many households did when there were children underfoot.

I didn't dare look to Ezra, though I could feel his gaze every few minutes. Sylvie had made her quip at him with humor, but a clear truth was in the words. There was a balance of scales in this house and until I had some idea of what they were, I wasn't going to take any chances with him.

"Ezra, I'd like you at the tavern tonight," Henrik said, wiping his mouth with the back of his hand.

"The tavern?" Ezra set down his cup.

"That's right."

Ezra propped his elbows onto the table, his brow pulled. "I have a pickup for the harbor logs tonight."

"No, you don't." Henrik leaned back into his chair. "Bryn is going to do it."

Murrow and Ezra caught each other's gaze across the table and my knife froze in midair over my plate.

"What?" Ezra's voice was careful.

But Henrik looked to me. "There's no better way to learn than by doing. Wouldn't you agree?"

"That pickup is *my* route. Every week." Ezra's voice took on an edge, but if Henrik noticed, he didn't show it.

I looked between them. It was obvious that Ezra didn't want me here. From where I sat, there were two explanations as to why. Either he didn't want me involved in family business because he didn't want his own toes stepped on, or he didn't trust me. Maybe both.

"Pickup?" I asked.

Henrik leaned onto the table. "A little gift left behind after our friend Holland fell from grace. Every week we distribute copies of the harbormaster's logs and there isn't a bastard in Bastian who doesn't want a copy."

Holland. I knew that name. She was the most powerful merchant in the Unnamed Sea before she was stripped of her ring and ousted from the guild for trading fake gems. News of the scandal had made its way to Nimsmire and people still talked about it.

"She used to control the distribution of the manifest. Now we do."

It was only one of many illegal parts of the family business and every port city had an enterprise just like it. Someone always had the harbormaster in their pocket, and they'd sell copies of the weekly manifest for coin. Somehow, Henrik had been lucky enough to seize hold of the trade when Holland lost her place of power. It was probably the reason Ezra knew what was in that ship's inventory.

"You'll pick up payment and deliver the manifest, that's all," Henrik said. "She can handle it," he added, glancing at Ezra.

Something unspoken passed between them, but beside me, Murrow was silent.

"Bryn?" Henrik looked to me. "What do you say?"

Ezra's gaze left a burning trail on my skin as it raked over me. I'd dealt with men like him my entire life. He wasn't going to accept me unless I played their game, and I couldn't do what I'd come to do if he was against me. "I can do it," I said.

Henrik's smile lifted the corners of his mouth, making the wrinkles around his eyes come to life. "Of course you can."

Ezra let out a deep, controlled breath as his eyes dropped down and I was sure he was going to argue. But just when I expected him to open his mouth, he stood, straightening his vest and buttoning his dark gray jacket.

He pushed out of the room a moment later and Henrik and Murrow said nothing, finishing their breakfast in silence. Once Henrik's cup was empty, he, too, was standing. "Do put on something a little more presentable, Bryn. Yes?"

My eyes flickered up. "What?"

"The watchmaker," he said. "First impressions are important."

My lips parted with an unspoken argument, but I snapped them shut before I could utter a word.

Temper, Bryn.

My great-aunt's perpetual rebuke was so loud in my head that it was as if she were standing in the room.

I gritted my teeth, glancing down at my frock. I may have escaped Sariah's narrow attention, but apparently being out from under her watch wasn't going to afford me the luxury of choosing my own clothes.

Murrow slid back in his seat as soon as Henrik was gone, relaxing.

"He doesn't like me," I said, shooting an irritated look to Ezra's empty chair.

Murrow half laughed, crossing his arms over his chest. "I wouldn't take it personally. Ezra doesn't like anyone." There was an ease about Murrow that I found calming, but I wondered what lay beneath it. He was all charm and quick-witted tongue, but he was the first to straighten under our uncle's gaze.

"Best to listen to Henrik, though. He likes for things to run on a strict schedule and he won't tolerate disorder."

"I didn't know about breakfast," I muttered.

"If I were you, I'd start assuming there are rules where maybe there weren't any before. Starting with those boots."

I scowled at him. "What's wrong with my boots?"

"They've got mud on them."

I lifted my skirt slightly to get a look at them. A stripe of dirt was dried along the sole from the walk through the city the day before.

"Put them outside your room at night. They'll be cleaned and waiting for you in the morning."

I dropped my skirt and tucked my foot under the table, a little embarrassed. "Anything else I should know?"

"Yeah," he answered. "You need to start talking."

"Talking?"

"Speak up or they won't respect you. Being so quiet is going to make them wonder what you're thinking. And you *don't* want that." He looked down at me, the humor gone now. It was a real warning. But I didn't like the feeling it gave me, as if I was being watched more carefully than I'd realized.

"Thank you," I said, setting the silver back down and abandoning the cheese. My stomach was in knots.

"You're welcome." He tossed his napkin on his plate and stood with a sigh. "Now, let's go."

"Where?"

He smiled, giving me a wink. "To get you a watch."

"All right. Just let me get my coin."

Murrow laughed. "You're a Roth, Bryn. We have everything you need."

FIVE

There were things about the world of the guilds that were true everywhere. Hallmarks of the way they lived.

The grimy streets of Lower Vale bled away as I followed Murrow up the hill, toward the Merchant's District. I wouldn't have needed a guide to find it. As soon as we reached the freshly painted buildings with new roof shingles, we were among the city's deepest pockets.

This was a world I knew. And as we passed the decorated shop windows and I caught my reflection in them, I belonged in the picture I saw. Sariah had made it her intention to bring me up a proper young lady who would charm the likes of the guilds and build a bridge between the Roths and the merchants that had long been their enemies. One that would reflect well on her and the family. But now that I'd met the Roths, I also wondered if it was her attempt at some kind of redemption. Maybe she wanted to re-create them in a new image and erase the more unseemly deeds they were known for.

Murrow kept a quick pace as we walked, his eyes cutting up to the windows overhead every few steps. I recognized the habit. Sariah always did that, as if she thought that at any moment someone would come for her out of the shadows. It was a practice I'd unconsciously picked up, too, and it was rare that I didn't feel as if there were eyes on me.

In this case, I wasn't imagining it. Everyone we passed on the street was looking at us, some even taking second glances. I'd changed my frock as Henrik instructed, and I'd pulled up my hair, but in this part of the city, it was probably unusual to see unfamiliar faces. Murrow wasn't a stranger here though, and I was sure that there were many among the guilds who didn't like the idea of a Roth in the Merchant's District. Their business with my family was like a game of Three Widows— the merchants liked to keep both in the shadows.

We passed shop after shop, their beveled glass windows filled with stands of freshly baked bread or shelves of wares and hand-stitched boots. The Merchant's District was exactly what it sounded like, the corner of the city where anyone with a merchant's ring lived and worked. Among them, the most elite were the masters of the guilds that made up the members of the Trade Council. There wasn't any power in the Unnamed Sea to be had that they didn't hold. Even the traders that braved the storms of the open water were at their mercy to secure permits to trade. But there was still leverage to be acquired in Bastian without a seat at the merchant's table. The Roths were proof of that. Now, I needed to find my own.

Establishing a stake in the family was the best way of securing my place among them. I'd learned a lot from Sariah and the multifaceted schemes she ran on behalf of the Roths in Nimsmire. If I played my cards right, I could do the same here in Bastian.

"What is it you do for the family?" I asked, trying not to sound too inquisitive.

Murrow kept his pace, eyes on the street ahead. "I handle Henrik's relationships with the crews that come in on their regular routes. Navigators vying for a position as a helmsman, strykers with need of a little extra coin . . . whoever's willing to talk."

His trade was information, and I could see why he would be good at it. Murrow was as amiable as he was handsome.

Of all the things I'd heard discussed at dinner, nothing sounded out of the ordinary. They were all the pieces of a well-thought-out plan and they'd worked for three generations. But if I was going to impress Henrik, I needed an idea. A good one.

"Already scheming?" Murrow arched an eyebrow at me.

The corner of my mouth lifted. "Maybe."

"Good," he answered. "Eden was like that. Smart."

His mention of my mother caught me off guard. I hadn't heard anyone speak about her yet. "Sariah said the tea house Eden was going to open was here in the Merchant's District."

"Still is."

My brow furrowed. "What?"

"It's still there. Been boarded up for years."

"But why?"

Murrow shrugged. "Don't ask me. My father has tried

more than once to get Henrik to sell it, but he won't. It's just rotting at the end of Fig Alley."

I watched his face, trying to uncover whatever he wasn't saying. Sariah had told me about the tea house, but I'd assumed that when it didn't open, it was sold. It wasn't like the Roths to hold onto things that weren't producing coin.

Murrow led me up a set of wide steps, to a stained wooden door that was carved with a wreath of laurels. The shop front was immaculate, with a sign that hung from a golden chain and a window without a single smudge. Behind it, I could see a row of glass cases and a marble floor as white as moonlight.

"Choose the most expensive one," Murrow said, keeping his voice low.

"What?"

But he was already pulling the door open and moving aside for me to enter. I hesitated, the scent of balsam meeting me in a gust of warm air. Murrow jerked his chin, signaling for me to step inside, and I bit my tongue, obeying. Every time one of them opened their mouths, it was only to offer half-speak and riddles. I was tiring of trying to keep up, and it had only been a day.

Inside, stone walls encircled a small room where glass cases were lined up with a single aisle for customers to walk and browse. Behind one of them, a widely statured man looked up from his stool. His thick, gray beard covered his mouth beneath the gold-rimmed spectacles atop his round nose.

"Welcome." He stood, setting down the small tool in his hand before he straightened his burgundy vest. "How may I help you?"

His nice suit and the sparkling watch chain that hung from his pocket told me he wasn't an apprentice. He was the merchant of this shop.

Murrow's eyes skimmed the cases. Inside, gold and silver watches were set onto small, velvet cushions with an array of chains and faces to choose from. I recognized the maker's mark on the piece the man was working on. These watches were sold in Nimsmire, a favorite among the merchants' circle there.

The watchmaker's eyes squinted as he looked Murrow over. "I know you, don't I?"

"Murrow Roth." Murrow extended a hand a little too forcefully, his voice louder than necessary for the intimate size of the shop.

The man took it, shaking dutifully. "Ah. Henrik's nephew." There was the faintest trace of suspicion in his words. "I'm Simon."

The name was familiar, but I couldn't place it until I remembered Henrik saying it the night before at dinner. This was the man whom Henrik wanted an invitation from. To what, I had no idea, but I understood now why he'd wanted me to change my frock.

Simon took off his gloves and set them on the counter, revealing the merchant's ring on his finger. It was set with a polished tiger's-eye stone, signifying his membership to the gem guild of the Unnamed Sea. It was a ring that many craftsmen would kill for.

When he finally looked at me, he smiled. "And you are?"

"I'm Bryn." I gave him a respectful nod and Simon looked

pleased. I knew how to make an impression, as Henrik had put it. If this was a test from my uncle, I was going to pass it.

"A friend of yours?" He asked the question to Murrow, but his eyes were on me.

I answered before Murrow could. "My cousin," I said, pulling the reins of the conversation back into my own hands. "Bryn *Roth*." I let the name hang in the air between us.

Simon's eyebrows raised at that. It was exactly the kind of reaction Sariah would have loved. Anyone who spent a handful of minutes with my family would be able to see that they weren't refined, but they were also too elegant to seamlessly fit in Lower Vale. They were a strange breed of something in between. Now that I was in Bastian, it would be my job to give the Roths a seat at the table in the Merchant's District. That job began now. With the watchmaker.

"I see. I didn't know Henrik had a niece," Simon mused.

"I've just returned to Bastian from Nimsmire," I said.

His smile widened knowingly. "Ah, Sariah."

"You know my great-aunt?"

"Of course." He laughed. "There aren't many in this city who don't, even if it's been a long time since she made her escape."

My eyes narrowed at his words. After her son died at sea, Sariah convinced her brother, Felix, to let her set up her own stake as a fail-safe for the Roths' business in Nimsmire at a time when they had a lot of enemies in Bastian. It wasn't until after he died that she actually made the preparations for the move, and at Henrik's urging. According to Sariah,

Henrik didn't want her looking over his shoulder when he took charge of the family. I wasn't part of the deal until my parents died and Henrik was left with a four-year-old orphan girl to raise.

"I've heard she's made quite a place for herself up there in Nimsmire," Simon said.

"She has." It was true. Sariah was highly respected, and she had little competition because she'd never aspired to join the guild. She was an expert at mutually beneficial enterprise.

"I knew your mother, too." The tone of his voice changed, making me look up. But as soon as I met his eyes, Simon set both hands on the case before him. He was careful to only touch the bronze frame and keep his fingers from the glass. "And what exactly are we looking for today?"

"My uncle says I need a watch and that there isn't a finer piece in this city than the ones made in your workshop," I answered.

Beside me, a smile twitched on Murrow's lips.

"Well, he's correct. You've come to the right place." He moved around the cases, stopping before the one filled with silver watches. Murrow had backed off, letting me take the lead, but I could acutely feel his attention on me. *The most expensive one*, he'd said.

They were exquisite pieces, but gold was much more valuable than the silver. Simon was either being polite or he was being presumptuous, assuming the Roths wouldn't have the coin for a finer watch.

I didn't follow him, staying put to study the items inside

the case of gold pieces carefully. I was looking for the one with the most intricate clasp and chain. The truth was, I didn't know anything about watches. They were usually carried by men and Sariah had never given me one. But I knew gems, and there was only one in the case set with the rarest shade of spinel—a pale purple hue.

"I'd like to see that one, please." I set a finger on the glass, where it sat in the very center.

Simon looked at me approvingly as he took a key from his pocket and opened the case. He pulled out the one I had pointed to and placed it before me. "A very nice watch. The face is a polished mother-of-pearl from the reefs of Yuri's Constellation. I personally chose the specimen from the trader's haul."

I picked it up, opening the watch with a click. The case sprung open and inside, the delicate hands ticked away over the dial. It was so beautiful, it seemed impossible that human hands had made it.

"It's lovely," I said, turning it so the light moved over the pearl surface like rippling water. The patterns were unique, the colors vibrant. A watch like this belonged in the pocket of a guild master. "I'll take it."

Simon took the spectacles from his nose. "And the chain?"

"I'd like you to choose." I smiled. "No one knows better than the maker."

He nodded. "And shall I engrave it for you?"

"Yes." I set the watch back into his hands. "Please."

He replaced his spectacles and pushed them up a little,

taking a piece of parchment from the desk behind him.
"Bryn, you said?"

"That's right."

I watched him write my initials, *B.R.* There were times
when I had wished I could shed the Roth name like a skin.
But through the years, I'd grown to believe, or hope, it was
what gave me an anchor in the shifting seas. That maybe it
was the only thing keeping me from sinking into the life that
the girls in Nimsmire were cursed to live. While they were
marrying to give their families advantage, I would be building a destiny of my own making.

When he was finished, Simon wrapped a square of black
satin around the watch and set it into a wooden box. "That'll
be three hundred and forty coppers. Fifty now. The rest delivered is fine."

Murrow gave him a nod. "I'll have it sent over this afternoon." He reached into his jacket, producing a leather purse.
He counted out fifty coppers with quick fingers before he
closed it again and slid the purse across the glass.

Simon picked it up, not bothering to check the weight.

"Don't want to count it?" Murrow smirked.

"I know where to find you if it's short." There was a flash
in his eyes that hadn't been there before. A trace of something rough-edged. It reminded me of Henrik. "Should be
done in a couple of days."

"Thank you," I said as Murrow tipped his hat and opened
the door. The sunlight rushed back in, gleaming on the cases
and reflecting off the rims of Simon's spectacles.

I came down the steps, waiting for Murrow on the street. He was already grinning as he took off up the walk, not waiting for me. "You're good at this." His voice trailed back to meet me.

"Good at what?"

Murrow shot a glance in my direction. "The game."

SIX

Henrik's instructions had been simple enough.

Pier fourteen. Ask for Arthur. Tell him you're there to pick up.

It was as much an excuse to leave the house alone as it was a way to show Ezra that I would fight for my place among the Roths. I had no interest in taking his job, but I wasn't going to be pushed out, either. I knew how to stand my ground and that was exactly what I was going to do.

I walked the street that ran along the harbor, eyeing the numbers on the crowded buildings. Piers lined the water beyond the merchant's house before scaling the steep hill in the distance. In Nimsmire, there had been only two rows of piers, but here, there were so many that they weren't even set into rows. They twisted around each other along haphazard streets, some of which seemed to dead-end or disappear completely.

The walks were filled with people coming and going from the long string of shops as they closed their doors for the day, carrying everything from baskets of apples to crates of iron remnants. The city would go to sleep until dawn, when the tradespeople would begin all over again, hauling their carts back down to the market or docks.

When I reached the largest pier on the water, I stopped before the grand double doors. They were still painted with the emblem of Holland, the gem merchant who'd been stripped of her ring, but the windows were black, the work that once went on between its walls ceased. Now, it stood at the entrance to the piers like a hollow cask.

The other buildings followed the shore. I studied their hand-painted signs with letters scratched and faded from the sea winds, making my way farther from the city's center. The nearly illegible numbers jumped from three to seven to nine, and then up to fifteen, with seemingly no order to them. There wasn't a single pier I could see with the number fourteen.

I grumbled a curse. If I couldn't even find a pier on my own, there was little chance Henrik would trust me with anything else. And I wasn't going to give Ezra more reason to argue with him about giving me the next job. The only way I was going to earn a stake in the family was by doing what I was told and doing it well.

I stood in the middle of the street, turning in a circle when a woman came around the corner with a long loaf of bread tucked beneath her arm. Her scrutinizing attention found my frock as she passed. I'd changed back into the simple purple one I'd worn that morning, but it was still too nice to be worn beyond the harbor and it was drawing attention.

"Excuse me." I stepped forward and the woman instantly

moved back, nearly hitting me with the bread. "Sorry." I cleared my throat. "I'm looking for pier fourteen."

Her mouth went crooked with a frown. "Up there." She nudged a shoulder toward the top of the next hill and kept walking.

I looked down at the piece of torn parchment in my hand, sighing. That couldn't be right. If it was a pier, it should have been on the water, but the building at the top of the hill was in the opposite direction. Its chimney was blackened at the mouth, the roof shingles crumbling, and there were no windows to speak of.

I wove in and out of the people flooding down toward the street, turning to press myself against the nearest building when a caravan of carts piled with freshly shorn wool came barreling through. One of the wheels caught a groove in the cobblestones and I jumped to the side as a spray of mud splashed my skirts. I groaned, shaking them out and kicking the water from my boots.

The street narrowed into an alley and soon I found myself alone, the sun going down at my back. The streetlamps were still unlit, but the shop windows down the hill were filled with candlelight as the apprentices closed up.

A sound like a heartbeat echoed between the brick walls and I stopped, turning toward the water. It was the feeling I always had—like I was being watched. But the street was empty except for two women making their way down the hill. I waited another moment before I started again, keeping my steps quiet so I could listen more carefully. I didn't know if it was the dimming light or the darkened windows overhead, but a chill crept up my spine and I was suddenly aware of just how bare the streets were. I was alone in a city I didn't know, night falling by the minute. In another hour, it would be dark.

I swallowed hard, picking up my pace. Murrow hadn't offered to come with me, and I hadn't had the courage to ask him. Certainly not in front of Ezra. The last thing I needed was for any of the Roths to think I needed taking care of.

The sign hung from the northeast corner of the warehouse, the numbers one and four crudely etched into the metal with what looked like the tip of a blade. I'd never have seen it from the street, but I was beginning to realize that the buildings sprawled over the hill were probably all called piers, no matter their distance from the water below.

I tucked the parchment into the pocket of my skirt and followed the uneven cobblestones around the side of the building until I found a door. It was lined with iron rivets, no handle in sight. The cold iron stung my knuckles as I knocked, and I shook out my hand, watching the narrow alley behind me. There was no one, but I still had that feeling, as if someone's eyes were following me.

When there was no answer, I knocked harder, and without warning, the door flung open, almost slamming into me. A thin man wearing a worn woolen cap stared down at me with an irritated look that turned inquisitive as his eyes adjusted. "Yes?"

My gaze went past him, into the dark warehouse, where there were rows of long tables lit with lanterns. From the acrid smell coming out, I guessed it was some kind of precious-metal workshop. Palladium, maybe. "I'm looking for Arthur."

The man almost laughed, his hand slipping from the edge of the door. "Arthur?"

"That's right," I said, impatient. At the end of the alley, the streetlamps began flickering to life one by one.

He stared at me before he let the door close, leaving me standing out on the street. "Arthur!"

His voice echoed behind the walls and I stuck my cold hands into the pockets of my skirts, waiting. A workshop like this one would supply merchants like the watchmaker, refining metals before they were melted down for jewelry and other items. But I wasn't here for silver or gold or palladium.

I pulled the small, folded envelope Henrik had given me from my pocket, turning it over. There was no inscription, and it wasn't sealed. Inside there would be lists of ships that came and went from the harbor the week before and what was in their cargo holds. There were only three types of people who bought that kind of information: traders who wanted to know what was moving at each port, merchants who wanted to keep an eye on their competition, and people like the Roths, who were looking to take what wasn't theirs. Arthur was one of probably dozens in Bastian paying the Roths for copies of the logs.

When the door opened again, a large man with a head of curling black hair appeared. He grimaced when he saw me, leaning on the doorframe with one shoulder. "Well, what is it?"

"Are you Arthur?"

His eyes swept the street behind me, as if he expected someone else to be there. "I am."

I lifted the folded parchment into the air. "I'm here for pickup."

I recited the words just as Henrik had told me to, but before they'd even finished leaving my mouth, Arthur's expression shifted from annoyed to uneasy.

"What is this?" he growled.

"I'm . . ." My eyes went to the tables inside. "I'm here for payment. For Henrik Roth."

He stared at me, as if deciding something. And before I realized he was moving, he'd pushed out into the street, nearly stepping on me. His gaze drifted from one corner of the alley to the next before he snatched up my arm by the wrist, yanking me forward. The log slipped from my fingers, landing in a puddle at my feet.

"What are you—" I tried to pull away, but his hand clamped down harder until pain was shooting up into my elbow. He shoved up the sleeve of my frock, tearing the tiny pearl button from where it was sewn.

"This some kind of joke?" He let me go and I stumbled backward, almost falling into the street. "A stunt by the harbor watch?" He turned toward the door, not waiting for an answer. "Get the hell out of here."

I cradled my arm, watching the light on the street shrink as the door began to shut. But I wasn't returning to my uncle empty-handed. Before I thought better of it, I caught the edge of door with one hand. "Wait."

He whirled on me, his hand flying through the air so fast

that I hardly saw it coming before it struck me across the face. My head whipped to the side and I hit the brick wall with my shoulder, gasping.

The explosion of pain in my mouth made me pinch my eyes closed and the taste of iron lit on my tongue. I tried to draw a shallow breath, and two footsteps sounded behind me, followed by the heavy door of the pier slamming shut.

Tears welled in my eyes as I looked up. I was alone in the alley. The steady, warm drip of blood streamed from my chin and I swallowed down the aching cry in my throat. My hands shook as I wiped at my mouth and when I looked down at the sleeve of my dress, the purple linen was stained almost black. The button at my wrist was gone where the man had torn my sleeve, a bright, red scratch trailing where his fingernail had scraped me.

The smooth, pale skin of my forearm was milk white in the darkness and a sinking, uneasy feeling settled in my gut when I realized what he'd been looking for. He was looking for the mark of the Roths.

SEVEN

I'd never been struck in my life. Not by anyone.

I stood before Henrik's desk in his empty study, my eyes locked on the portrait that hung on the wall. The four Roth siblings looked down at me from the gilded frame, their mouths set in straight lines and their chins lifted. They looked as if they each belonged there side by side with the other members of the family. I wondered how long that had taken, *what* it had taken, to be true.

Murrow came through the door and handed me a damp, folded cloth that smelled of pungent vinegar. I'd heard him arguing with Sylvie in the kitchen, who was demanding to know who was bleeding.

I pressed the linen to my swollen lip, wincing. I could still taste blood despite the shot of rye Murrow had given me when I came through the door. It was as if he'd been waiting for me, sitting there at the table in the dining room with the bottle and a single glass.

We could hear his footsteps before the door of the workshop opened and Henrik appeared, his apron still tied around his middle. There wasn't even the slightest flinch in his eyes as he looked at me.

"Bryn. You're back," he said, simply. As if my cut-up face was the most normal thing in the world. He patiently tugged at the strings of his apron and pulled it over his head, hanging it on the wall. "And? How did it go?"

The cloth fell from my mouth and I stared at the pink stain there before I looked from him to Murrow, stunned. I waited for some clue as to what I was supposed to say, but Murrow kept his attention on the fire flickering in the hearth.

"Bryn?" Henrik leaned into the desk with both hands. His eager eyes were on mine.

"I did what you said." The cut in my lip pulled painfully as I spoke. "I asked for the payment and he told me to leave."

"Yes?" Henrik pressed.

"When I insisted, the man . . . Arthur"—I swallowed—"he hit me when he saw I had no mark."

Henrik straightened and crossed his arms over his chest, his bottom lip protruding in thought. "I see."

"I didn't get the payment," I said, dropping the cloth to the desk and bracing myself for his disappointment. This was exactly what I didn't want to happen. There was no way for me to earn my stake in the family if Henrik didn't trust me, and I'd botched one of the first tasks he'd given me.

The wrinkle cast across Henrik's forehead deepened, as if he was confused. "Oh, don't worry about that." He waved a dismissive hand in the air.

I tried to read him. He didn't look angry. He didn't even look surprised. If I didn't know better, I would have said there was a sparkle in his eye. A glimmer of dancing light. My head was aching and my jaw throbbing, but more unsettling than the memory of the man in the alley or the pain in my mouth was the expression on my uncle's face. He looked almost . . . *pleased*.

Again, my gaze trailed to Murrow. This time, he managed a quick glance in my direction, but still, he said nothing. His eyes went past me and I looked over my shoulder to see Ezra standing silent in the corner of the study. He was half-wrapped in shadow, his coal-colored suit making him look like he was folded into the darkness.

I swallowed hard, a sudden chill creeping over my skin. I hadn't even heard him come in.

His jacket was buttoned, one foot crossed over the other as he watched us. Black eyes flitted over me, to Henrik, but he didn't speak.

"Would you like me to have Sylvie look at that for you?" Henrik said, finally acknowledging my face.

I blinked, turning back to him. His attention dropped to my lip for a fleeting moment, but he seemed wholly uninterested despite the offer.

"No," I said, too quickly. Too sharply. There was some scheme at play here that I didn't understand. It was evident in how the three of them looked at each other. But I couldn't tell which side of it I was on.

"Thank you, Bryn," Henrik said, sincerely. "You've been very helpful."

I stared at him, trying to make sense of the hollow words, pulling them apart and putting them back together in different arrangements. I wasn't sure what I'd expected when I walked into the house with blood on my skirts, but it wasn't this.

"*Helpful?*" I repeated. Beside me, Murrow shifted on his feet. "The man *hit* me."

Temper, Bryn. Sariah's warning echoed in my mind again. My hands fisted at my sides and I swallowed down the curse on my tongue.

"Yes, that really is unfortunate." Henrik tsked. "I do wish that hadn't needed to happen."

I didn't miss the way he said it. Not *I wish that hadn't happened.* He'd said, *I wish that hadn't* needed *to happen.*

The number of questions I had was growing by the minute, but there were no answers in Henrik's icy gaze as he surveyed me.

"Murrow, you've got work to do, I think," he said, lifting a finger to the door behind him.

Murrow answered with a silent nod, turning on his heel and dismissing himself. His footsteps trailed down the hallway until the door to the street opened and closed. It was well after dark, so I didn't know where he could be going. The only places open at this hour were the haunts of trading crews docked for the night.

"You best get up to bed. Sleep will do you some good." Henrik's attempt at gentleness fell short. It was missing any semblance of concern or warmth. He was ordering me to my room again.

Maybe he *was* disappointed in me. Or maybe he was thinking he'd made a mistake by asking me to go to the pier in the first place. Either way, I'd failed his test and I didn't want to know what I'd have to do to make up for it.

I stared at him for another moment before I finally snatched the bloody cloth up from the desk. I flung the door to the study open with the burn of Ezra's gaze following me, but my uncle's voice made me stop short.

"And Bryn?" Henrik's voice cut into the silence.

I turned, clenching my teeth painfully to keep from speaking.

My uncle's gaze dropped to my feet. "Please do something about those boots," he said, each word like the swing of a hammer.

I gaped at him, no longer needing to swallow down the curse that sat on the tip of my tongue. I was completely speechless.

I'd been taught to deal with men. How to charm them. How to persuade them. I'd been doing it for my great-aunt for years. But *this* man was something entirely different. He was so tangled in knots, I realized, that there may be no unraveling him.

He gave me a nod, as if allowing me to go, and I stepped out into the dark hallway, forcing one foot in front of the other until I reached the stairs. I paused midstride halfway up when I heard his voice again, going still. My hand clutched the railing and I slowed my breath, leaning into the wall as I listened. But the sound was muffled, distorted by the wind rattling the windows upstairs.

I took a careful step backward, and another, until I was at

the bottom of the stairwell. Sylvie was still shuffling around in the kitchen and the glow from Henrik's office bled out into the hallway. I could see his shadow rippling over the worn, uneven floorboards.

". . . by morning. Should do the trick." Henrik was speaking to Ezra now.

I took another step, my eyes searching the darkness as I listened. The sound of a drawer sliding open and shut in his desk, the tap of his pipe as he emptied the chamber.

"How'd she do?" he rasped.

"Fine," Ezra answered.

"Fine?" Henrik was growing impatient again. Annoyed, even.

"She did fine," Ezra said. "It happened just like she said."

His deep voice was like a hot iron as the words sank in. He said it as if he was reporting what he'd seen. As if he'd been there.

Frost filled my veins, my heart beating so loud in my chest that it was difficult to hear over the heavy thrum. That presence I'd felt in the alley had been real. Someone *had* been watching. Ezra.

"Arthur checked her for the mark and when he didn't see it, he figured it was a trap. Said something about the harbor watch, and when she tried to stop him, he struck her." The words went on, making the walls of the stairwell feel as if they were closing in.

He had been there. Ezra had been there, watching. And he'd done *nothing*. Even more unsettling was that Henrik knew. It almost sounded like it had been planned.

"I want you working on the collection night and day. I want it done in time for the exhibition."

The exhibition.

Slowly, the thoughts came together. The exhibition was the last step in the process of securing a merchant's ring. There were only a certain number of rings in each guild and they only became available when a merchant died or was denounced. It was a rare opportunity, with a strict set of rules. Anyone vying for an available ring first had to secure a patron—an existing merchant who put you forth as a candidate. Then, the candidates submitted a collection to the guild, who would vote on who received the ring.

Henrik had a merchant's ring to trade in the Narrows. Now he wanted one for the Unnamed Sea. But what did that have to do with a precious-metal smith on the other side of the harbor? What did it have to do with me?

"I told you, didn't I?" Henrik said, a sudden, arrogant lightness in his tone.

There was a long pause. "You did."

The frost turned to sharp, brittle ice and the sight of the firelight wavered as my eyes filled with furious tears. Henrik had known exactly what he was doing when he sent me to the pier. He'd sent me to Arthur for exactly this purpose. But why?

A sick feeling twisted inside of me and I took the wooden steps slowly, careful not to make a sound. I drifted toward my room, my whole body cold, and after I closed the door and lit the candle, I sank onto my bed with my heart in my throat.

My mother and father were stealing six crates of gemstones from a pier on the night they died. It was a carefully planned job gone horribly wrong when the man Henrik paid off to miss his shift at the harbor watch was replaced by another.

My uncle had sent my parents to their deaths for gemstones and tonight, he'd sent me into harm's way, too. It occurred to me just how close to death I may have come. If Arthur thought I was with the watch, he could have killed me. Maybe Ezra would have watched as he dumped me into the dark water to be devoured by the sea's creatures.

I swallowed down the nausea in my belly as I unlaced my boots with numb fingers and pulled them off. They toppled to the floor, the candlelight moving over the muddy leather. A tear slipped down my sore cheek as I got back to my feet and picked them up, opening the door. I set the boots into the dark hallway and then closed it, staring at the wood.

Sariah had tried to tell me, many times. But the words were only beginning to make sense. There was family, and there was business. And there was more to the Roths than the name.

EIGHT

The boots practically looked new. I stood in the open doorway in my nightdress, staring at them on the wooden floor. They'd been lined up perfectly side by side and were fit with new laces, the nutmeg-stained leather glowing rich in the morning light.

I'd always taken Sariah's preoccupation with presentation as vanity. Eccentricity, even. But now, it was beginning to make sense. *Tidy and timely.* She'd grown up in this dark, damp house with the same rules as the other Roths and I was less and less curious what the consequences for breaking those rules were.

Beside the boots, my frock was neatly folded on a short stool. I bent low to pick it up, letting the violet fabric unroll before me. The blood had been scrubbed clean and the button at the wrist replaced with another that was almost identical. Everything was as it should be. As if the previous night had never happened.

The door beside mine suddenly swung open, filling the hallway with bright light, and I jumped, clutching the frock to me. Ezra came out of his room and shut the door heavily behind him, barely glancing in my direction as he made his way to the stairs. There was a coldness to him that filled the air every time he entered a room, and it made me shiver beneath my nightdress.

I didn't know what kind of hard-heartedness it took to stand in the shadows and watch someone be slapped across the face. More infuriating was the knowledge that he'd probably watched me cry in that alley, wiping the blood from my chin.

I swallowed down the thought and picked up my boots by the laces. When my door shut, I let out the breath I was holding. Maybe Ezra thought his problem had been dealt with, his point proven. He'd made it clear that he didn't want the long-lost niece from Nimsmire here and that his part in the family business was his alone. Maybe he and Henrik had schemed together on whatever plot they'd been discussing in the study last night. But Ezra didn't know me, and neither did Henrik. I'd spent years dressed in petticoats with combs in my hair, but I was still a Roth. And if I was going to avoid another incident like the one at the pier, I needed to act like it.

I tossed the frock on the bed and went to the mirror, inspecting the bruise at the corner of my mouth. My face looked much worse this morning. Even though I'd told Henrik I didn't want Sylvie's help, he'd still sent her to my room, and she'd done her best to clean it by candlelight. She'd also ordered me to use a compress every hour that she'd had delivered to my room throughout the night. Clearly, she'd seen her fair share of cuts and bruises in this house. I didn't doubt that it came with the territory. And if he troubled himself with the upkeep of my boots, I could only imagine what Henrik would think about my looking like this. There was a part of me that relished the idea.

I got dressed quickly, checking myself in the mirror more than once to be sure nothing was out of place. This time when I went downstairs to the busy breakfast room, I wasn't late.

Casimir, Murrow, and Ezra were waiting beside their places at the table. When I came into the room, Casimir stared at my cheek, studying the bruise.

"That'll smart for a few days," Murrow jabbed. That seemed to be his way—making light of heavy things.

But I wasn't laughing. "Yes, it will." I enunciated the words, speaking more loudly than was necessary as I set my gaze on Ezra. I waited until his eyes lifted.

The corners of his mouth turned down just slightly, giving him away. He knew that I knew. I may not have known who my allies were in this house, but I'd definitely marked an enemy. And I wanted him to know it.

Murrow's fingers tapped the back of his chair impatiently as Sylvie set out a silver tray of cheese and two pots of tea. When he took the watch from his pocket to check the time, the hand moved to seven. The very same moment, Henrik's footsteps sounded from the hall and he appeared, his own watch in hand. He snapped it closed as he took his seat and the rest of us followed, pulling out our chairs.

"Any messages?" He glanced at Casimir, reaching for the tea.

Casimir answered with a shake of his head. "Not yet."

"It'll come," Henrik said, almost to himself.

I was beginning to recognize when there was something at play, and this was one of those times. Henrik had asked the same question at dinner two nights before and again at breakfast yesterday.

"What do you have on this business with the *Serpent*?"

Casimir tore the piece of bread in his hands. "Looks like both Violet Blake and Simon are vying for the contract. Won't be pretty by the time all is said and done."

"Violet Blake," Henrik echoed, the wheels turning behind his eyes.

That one was easier to decipher. Simon was the watchmaker, and the *Serpent* was the ship they'd spoken about at family dinner. The contract was likely an agreement for trade. If Simon was bidding on it, then Violet Blake was his competition, another gem merchant in the guild.

"Wouldn't want to be caught between those two," Casimir added. "Violet Blake is playing with fire. No one crosses Simon and lives to tell the tale.

I took a bite, listening. The Simon that Casimir described didn't sound like the Simon I'd met. But I knew enough about the guilds to know that there was plenty of dirty business to drown every single merchant in.

"I have a feeling Simon has underestimated Violet. There's a snake beneath all that pretty silk and lace," Henrik mused. "Either way, Simon and Violet at each other's throats will only help us. I couldn't have planned it better myself."

Ezra set his elbows onto the table as he sipped from his cup, barely touching the food on his plate. He was quiet as usual, giving one-word answers to Henrik's inquiries, and the set of his brow made him look indignant. But this morning, his gaze drifted to me more than usual.

Henrik went over the day's agenda, checking things from his book as he went from Casimir to Murrow to Ezra. Not a word was spoken about the night before and I was glad. It had been humiliating enough to stand there in the study with blood on my frock, and Henrik had made it clear that it was the least of his concerns.

When they were finished, they dismissed themselves one by one, setting out to the day's tasks, and finally Henrik turned to me. "You're with me today, Bryn."

I folded my napkin without question and followed him out of the breakfast room, happy to be released from my unfinished food. The hot tea hurt my lip and chewing woke the furious ache in my jaw. I'd lost my appetite anyway.

I followed him past the kitchens to the black door at the end of the hallway that I had yet to see open. He pulled a key from inside his vest pocket and fit it into the lock, turning it with a click. The damp scent of wet stone came from inside and my eyes trailed over the long rectangular room. Three worktables were set into even rows before a forge that glowed in one corner and a furnace in the other. Dim blue light cast down from the grimy glass ceiling, the corner of the slanted panes darkened with moss and soot. A few of the panes were propped open to let the heat of the forge and furnace escape.

At the end of the table to the right, Ezra was slipping an apron over his head and tying it around his waist.

So, this was where he disappeared to during the day.

Henrik took another apron from a hook on the wall and put it on unceremoniously as I studied the details of the room. It was a workshop. There was only one other door that looked as if it led outside and the wall beside the forge was covered in hammers of all shapes and sizes, hung by their heads on rusted nails. They were one of the only things in the room that shined brightly, the iron polished and gleaming. Beneath them, a long shelf was filled with other tools—picks and files and hand saws.

"We all have a job, Bryn," Henrik began, weaving through the tables to the opposite corner.

I followed, watching Ezra from the corner of my eye. He kept his back to us as he stoked the coals in the forge, giving no indication that he'd even heard us come in.

"You'll earn your keep, like everyone else." Henrik pulled up a stool in front of a set of scales and motioned for me to sit.

The table was filled with gems. Obsidian, sapphires, tiger's-eyes, and emeralds glittered in small wooden trays. Another pile that looked like raw-cut rubies was sitting in one end of the scales.

I picked up one of the tiger's-eyes. It was tumbled smooth, revealing the black veins within the stone.

"Every day, after breakfast, you'll check the weights and

mark them down," Henrik continued, dropping a small book beside me. He opened it to the last recorded page, showing me where the date and labels should go.

"They're all fakes?" I asked.

"Not all of them. We use the real ones to create uniformity and to pass inspections. Some will be used in commissioned pieces, others will be sold to merchants. But all will fetch coin."

"How do you tell the difference?"

Henrik smirked. "You can't. That's the point. The only eyes that can spot these fakes are those of a gem sage. Luckily for us, there are few out there anymore." He took the tiger's-eye from my fingers, setting it down. "I trust Sariah taught you your gems?"

I nodded. She'd painstakingly taught me from the time I was little. I could tell you their names, the ways they were cleaned and cut, and I could identify the impurities and patterns of every single one. I wondered now if that had been part of her deal with Henrik, too.

"Good."

He set himself up beside me, taking me step-by-step through the process with a surprising amount of patience when I asked questions, or requested he show me something a second time. There was an ease to Henrik within the walls of the workshop that I hadn't seen before. He worked with steady, thoughtful movements, talking me through every aspect with care. It was evident that the work was important to him. He hadn't shown even half of that concern to me the night before, and that told me more about him than I'd been able to put together in the few days I'd spent in Bastian.

"Three times," he said. "Always three." His finger tapped the page, where each weight had been written in triplicate down the columns. "If a single stone goes missing, I will know. And if the weights are off, I will know that, too." His brows lifted, waiting for me to acknowledge what he'd said.

When I did, he got up, going to the opposite side of the table, where he had long, flat trays of glass sorted by color. Muted blues, dusty greens, and pale ambers were broken into pieces of every size and shape.

He set his focus on the glass and I watched him as I placed the tiger's-eye onto the scale. There was a delicate balance between Henrik's warmth and the brittle cold in him. They shifted so fast that I couldn't tell the difference between the two until I felt the pointed edge of his displeasure. He was like a knife that appeared deceivingly dull but was sharp enough to cut through bone.

I set another stone into the tray, getting to work. I didn't want to find myself beneath that blade.

NINE

By the time I finished the weights, Henrik had another tray waiting for me. They were a couple dozen red beryl fakes that were cut into various sizes and more than convincing.

I understood the basic process after watching him for only a couple of hours. He carefully chose the glass remnants from his extensive collection, mixing the colors with precision to recast the shattered pieces. They went into the furnace, where they were reheated, and when they first came out, they appeared to be no more than large, glowing droplets of liquid. But once they began to cool, he meticulously formed them and worked at their shapes with fine-edged tools to create convincing rough cuts. It looked as if they were straight from a gem merchant's turnover.

It was incredible, really, a series of very specific steps that produced very specific results. It was the kind of process that took generations to perfect and I guessed that he'd spent his childhood in this very workshop at my grand-father Felix's side, learning it.

What I couldn't figure out was how he managed to get the weights right. Each fake looked like it was made with the same few ingredients, but the weights were all different. Each tray he handed me was right where it should be for whichever stone the glass was impersonating. It was a mind-boggling feat, and one I hadn't been able to decode in my quick glances between recording the numbers.

I picked up one of the red beryls and held it up to the light coming from the furnace, turning it slightly. There was no apparent distinction between the glass and the real thing and some poor bastard in Ceros would pay a purse full of coppers for it.

I set it into the tray, my eyes drifting to Henrik, who was taking a large jar from the shelf. It was filled with what looked like a black powder. I squinted, watching him remove the lid until my eyes refocused on what lay beyond the table. Across the room, Ezra was polishing the head of a pointed hammer with a clean rag. But his gaze was on me.

I froze, making the scales swing on the table and his attention cut quickly to Henrik, who was scooping the black powder from the jar. In the next instant, I could have sworn that Ezra gave me the slightest shake of his head.

My eyes instinctively dropped before I glanced over my shoulder. Henrik had a long pick clutched in his teeth, his brow furrowed anxiously as he searched the box of tools on his workbench for whatever he was looking for. When I looked to Ezra, he had his back turned again.

I didn't know if I'd imagined it or if my eyes were playing tricks on me in the low light of the workshop. But it appeared as if Ezra was giving me a warning. And not one laced with a threat.

A rattling knock sounded at the workshop's entrance, making me jump, and Ezra dropped what he was doing, hanging the hammer on the wall. I watched as he walked toward the door, cracking it only a few inches until he saw who it was.

"Henrik," he called out, letting the door open wider.

Murrow stood in the hallway, waving the folded parchment in his hand. There was a devious smirk on his lips. "It's here."

I turned on my stool to see the same wide, wicked grin spread across Henrik's face. "All right"—he dropped the pick on the table with a loud ping—"get everyone in the study."

"I've already sent for Noel," Murrow said. He was beaming.

Henrik abandoned the jar of black powder and untied his apron with quick fingers. Across the workshop, Ezra did the same before disappearing through the door.

"Well?" Henrik said, staring at me. "Come on."

Surprised, I slid from the stool and followed him. There were voices coming from the study, where the fire was lit, and Henrik immediately took to his pipe, sitting before the closed envelope on his desk. Beside it, there was a small package wrapped in brown paper. Henrik's name and the address of the house was penned in a delicate script across its front.

Casimir sat in one of the armchairs with Murrow stationed behind him, and Ezra was leaning into the corner, which I was beginning to think was his usual spot. I wasn't sure where my place was, but I was sure that in Henrik's mind, there was one. Unspoken expectations were drawn beneath everything in this family.

When no one directed me, I went to stand next to Murrow, the only place in the house I seemed to be the slightest bit comfortable. He continued to grin, as if there was a delicious secret in the room, but still, no one spoke. Henrik puffed on his pipe silently until we heard Noel come into the house.

It had taken him only minutes to arrive, and Tru was on his heels, stopping at the study door before his father closed it. It wasn't until Noel was sitting in the other chair that Henrik finally looked up from the message. He cleared his throat before he picked it up, and that mischievous smile returned as he tore his silver letter opener through the wax seal.

Everyone waited as his gaze skipped over the contents and when he looked up, there was a bright twinkle in his eye. "Five days."

Casimir clapped his hands together with a loud pop, making me wince. When I searched the faces of everyone in the room, they all looked delighted. More than delighted. But Ezra still stood in the corner, looking grim. He was the only one who wasn't celebrating.

"Is it enough time?" Noel asked. He was on the verge of an uncharacteristic smile himself.

Henrik dismissed the question with a wave of his hand. "Of course it is."

"But—" Noel started, and Henrik cut him off.

"Don't worry. Bryn will be ready."

"Ready for what?" I said it without thinking. My hand gripped tight to the back of Casimir's chair and Murrow stiffened beside me.

Silence fell over the study and Henrik set down the letter, sticking the pipe back into his mouth and folding his hands in front of him. "You didn't think you were only here to work the scales, did you?" He laughed. "No, we've got more important plans for you, my dear. We've been officially invited to a dinner at a very influential merchant's house. And in a matter of days, we'll have his patronage to the guild."

Understanding sunk in slowly. I was right. Henrik was after Holland's merchant's ring.

He picked up the small, wrapped package. "It came with this." He held it out to me.

I stepped forward, taking it from him, and everyone watched, waiting. I swallowed, prying up the corner of the wrapping until the small box inside was sitting in my hand. When I lifted the latch, the light gleamed on the smooth gold surface.

It was the watch, the face engraved with my initials. *B.R.*

"The watchmaker," I said, almost to myself. Henrik was courting the patronage of Simon.

"Well done." Henrik's approval dripped from the words. "Murrow said you charmed him."

I didn't know if it was the heat of the fire or the narrowed eyes of my uncles on me, but I was sweating. "What do you mean I'll be ready?"

Henrik leaned forward. "Most of the members of the guild inherited their rings from aging family members or had powerful connections. Simon, however, is the only member of the guild who rose up the ranks from the bottom. The very bottom."

That was why Henrik believed he could win his patronage. He thought they were the same.

"But he's not going to take us on as our patron unless he believes we won't make a fool of him. This dinner will set into motion everything we've been working for. If we are granted Simon's patronage, we will have that ring. And once we have license to trade in Bastian, everything will change for us." His eyes flicked to the portrait of the Roth siblings on the wall. So quickly, I wasn't sure I'd even seen it. He was antsy, nearly coming apart beneath his skin. It was unnerving to watch. "We'll be counting on you, Bryn."

"For what?"

He set the letter down gingerly before him. "I don't know if you've noticed, but we aren't particularly well versed in this kind of company. You, however, are a proper young lady with proper manners, and I have a feeling that you'll smooth out our rough edges in no time."

"I . . ." I didn't know what to say. "I don't think I understand."

"I'd like you to prepare us for the dinner. No detail should go overlooked. No expense spared. We will have one night to convince Simon to give us the patronage and we can't waste it. You and I will need garments for dinner. Ezra, too."

I glanced at the silversmith, who was still standing wordlessly in the corner. He didn't look surprised by Henrik's plan, but I was. Why would Henrik take his silversmith to a dinner with a guild member? It didn't make any sense.

"I also want every member of this family outfitted for the exhibition. Can you do that?"

I met his eyes, searching them. There was a desperation in the request. He needed me, and that was an advantageous position. After what happened at the pier, I needed it. "Yes," I answered.

"Good." He let out a heavy breath. "Worth a little blood on your frock, eh?"

I went still. The slow, sickening realization of what had transpired was only beginning to come together in my mind, the facts still in pieces. It was obvious that Murrow taking me to the watchmaker wasn't just about me getting a watch. They were dangling me in front of Simon like a carrot. But the blood on the frock . . . I reached up, absently touching the cut on my lip. Sending me to Arthur's wasn't about giving me a job. That, too, had something to do with the invitation in Henrik's hand.

As if he'd read my mind, he stood, dropping it on the desk. "I've been working to secure this patronage for months, but word had it that Simon was considering offering himself as patron to Arthur. As soon as the story about him laying his hands on a young woman, especially one as pretty and proper as you, started circulating last night, I knew Simon would be forced to cut ties. It doesn't matter what kind of slum he came from, he wouldn't want to be tied to someone wrapped in rumors." Henrik was absolutely gleeful. "Now, it's time to get to work," he said, throwing his acute attention on the others. "You all know what needs doing. And we have five days to do it."

Casimir, Noel, Ezra, and Murrow answered with nods and grunts, but my stomach was twisting on itself, nausea climbing up my throat.

He'd *used* me.

I knew when I came to Bastian that Henrik would have plans for me, as he called it. Sariah had made sure I understood that much. But he'd willingly sent me to that pier knowing I'd be hurt. And he'd done it for his own gain.

My eyes trailed up to the portrait on the wall, to where my mother looked down at me. The pendulum swing of my uncle's wrath and affection was a dangerous, shifting wind. In only a few days, I'd seen it firsthand, and I knew there were much darker deeds in this family than the ones I'd witnessed. This was only the beginning.

TEN

It was going to take more than fine garments to impress the watchmaker, but a visit to the couturier was a start.

The nimble-fingered work of a talented seamstress was more than enough for the usual commissions of frocks and jackets, but Sariah had taught me that if you wanted garments cut for the likes of a guild member, a seamstress wouldn't do.

Sariah's wardrobe had been the envy of Nimsmire, every stitch and seam perfect, every bead exquisite. While the other women went to a seamstress, she went to the couturier—the skilled tradesmen that crafted the finest suits and boots.

There was only one in the Merchant's District, and I'd sent a message ahead to reserve the shop for the entire afternoon. I would need his full attention if I was going to outfit the whole family and I needed first pick of the fabrics that had arrived on the ships that morning. With a little charm, I'd have my pick of trimmings, too. Buttons made of animal horn or polished onyx, thread that glistened with the shimmer of gold.

My freshly shined boots clipped at a quick pace as I followed the street curving through the Merchant's District. I'd put on one of my nicest frocks and pinned my hair back with emerald-studded combs. I had to look the part if I was going to get the couturier to take me seriously.

Nearly everyone in this part of the city was cleaned of the grime of the sea and docks, the red, windblown faces replaced with smooth ones. Traders didn't come this far from the taverns down by the water. They rarely had need to.

The family had been in a flurry since the invitation had come, with Ezra getting straight to work on the pieces they would present to the guild in the exhibition. There would be no fake gems or sleights of hand. These would be the creations of a master silversmith, the best curated work to convince the guild of Henrik's worthiness of the merchant's ring. My uncle had placed an enormous amount of trust in Ezra and that was more than a little puzzling. For someone not even related by blood, he held the family's fate in his scarred hands.

If Henrik got the merchant's ring, everything would change. With enough time, coin, and recognition, the sullied reputation of the Roths would fade into obscurity. Henrik would be allowed to trade as a merchant, building his own inventory outside of Ceros. It was something my great-grandfather Sawyer and my grandfather Felix had only ever dreamed of. But with the winds changing in the Unnamed Sea with the fall of Holland and the Narrows rising in influence, there was new power to be found. If Henrik had his way, he'd be climbing the ranks of Bastian by the next winter.

Copper jingled in my skirt pockets as I walked, and my

hand curled around the smooth case of my watch. It felt like an anchor, seeing my initials engraved into the gold. As if that single thing gave me claim to what I was about to do. In the next several days, it would be up to me to refine the Roths into some semblance of acceptable company.

The wealthy were as much concerned with association as they were coin, because they were intrinsically tied together. Until now, the Roths had relied on their brutality to get what they wanted. But breaking noses and bribing apprentices wasn't going to help them edge into this corner of society.

A tall building appeared ahead, its smooth white face standing out from the others. Two large lanterns were lit on either side of the double doors, with dancing flames despite the early hour.

The commission. I stopped, staring up at the seal of Bastian carved into the stone wall. The commission was the meeting house for the guild when it was in session. In a few weeks, it would house the exhibition, where the members would vote on the recipient of the merchant's ring. When the Roths walked through those doors, they would turn every head. I would make sure of it. My reward would be Henrik's trust. And the more trust I had, the closer I got to my own stake. My own power and safety.

I pulled the folded parchment from my pocket, glancing at the crude map Murrow had drawn for me of the Merchant's District. I would need to memorize these streets and the shops, along with the names of their proprietors, in the coming weeks. Every detail mattered and there was no telling when I'd need the fragments of information at my disposal. It was all part of the task Henrik had given me and while there were some things that were true everywhere in the Unnamed Sea, the guilds in Bastian would have their own little secrets.

I paused when my eyes followed a small side street labeled with Murrow's messy handwriting as Fig Alley.

It's just rotting at the end of Fig Alley.

That's what he'd said when we'd gone to the watchmaker's shop.

I watched the busy district around me, searching the blue placards on the corners of the buildings until I found the one that read Fig Alley. I walked toward the break in the street, where the pavers ended and a narrow path opened up between the shops. It was lined with shorter streetlamps on either side, where a few windows were scattered along the brick walls. But the storefronts didn't come this far. It looked to be more of a shortcut that led to the other end of the Merchant's District than an actual path. It wasn't until the curve in the alley took me out of sight from the main thoroughfare that I saw it.

A single wood-framed building was set between two brick walls with a boarded-up door. The glass of the tall windows was hazy with the salt in the air, but the sign that hung above them was still legible.

Eden's Tea House

I stopped, the soles of my boots sinking into the soft earth. It was run-down and forgotten, much like some of the storefronts I'd seen in Lower Vale, but my mother's tea house was still here, tucked back into the shadows of the Merchant's District.

I walked toward it slowly, cupping my hands around my eyes to peer through the glass. It looked as if it hadn't been touched since my mother died. Inside, I could see tables and chairs and wood-carved booths along the wall. Above them, dingy chandeliers hung from the ceiling.

Rotting was the right word. The fabric covering the chairs was eaten through by moths in some places, the large mirror behind the bar losing its silver backing. It was like the inside of a sunken ship, left to decay in the dark.

"So very unfortunate." The sound of a voice made me jolt and I looked up to see the reflection of a woman in the window behind me.

I pressed a hand to my chest, turning to face her. "I'm sorry?"

The woman stood only a few feet away, her hands gently clasped together on top of her full silk skirts. Delicate black feathers edged the collar and cuffs of her brilliant red frock, the same hue painted onto her curved lips. She watched me like a cat, her fixed stare meeting mine.

"I always thought it was such a shame this place never opened," she said, her eyes lifting to the sign over the windows. "Tried to buy it myself a time or two, but the owner wouldn't hear of it."

She stepped past me, the toe of a glossy black boot peeking out from beneath her skirt as she peered into the window. Her glistening black hair was braided up at the crown of her head, beneath a semicircle of what looked like sapphires.

They sparkled, catching the sunlight like the quick flashes of a lighthouse.

"I don't believe I've seen you before." Her green eyes brightened as she studied me.

Whoever she was, this woman was clearly affluent. And I wasn't going to give more away than necessary before I knew just how important she was.

"I've only just arrived from Nimsmire. I'm Bryn," I said, reaching out a hand and taking care not to mention the name Roth.

The woman glided toward me, a rueful smile stretching across her red lips. "It's lovely to meet you, Bryn." She put her hand into mine and squeezed, her eyes falling to my mouth. "Looks like you met some trouble there."

I reached up, remembering the cut and bruise that still stained my skin. But she didn't stare, her attention returning to the window behind us just as the clap of boots came down the alley. When I heard voices, I turned to see two men coming around the bend in the path. They didn't even notice us as they sauntered by, lost in what sounded like the beginnings of an argument.

"I . . ." The word dissolved on my tongue when I turned back around.

The woman who'd been there only a moment ago was gone, her bloodred frock already turning the corner ahead.

The sound of her footsteps faded, leaving me in the silence of the empty alley. I hadn't even gotten her name.

I smoothed my hands over my blue skirts, looking up to the sign that hung over the tea house. The woman was right. It was a waste, just sitting here in a back alley of the Merchant's District. A perfectly good enterprise if Henrik had ever bothered to open it.

A thought like a single flame ignited behind my eyes as I stared at it, the paintbrush of my imagination coloring the tea house to life. Glowing candles on the crystal chandeliers. Velvet curtains draped behind the windows. The soft clink of teacups and the high-pitched jingle of a bell on the door.

Maybe . . . my mind whirled.

Maybe I didn't need to carve out my own stake in the family after all. Maybe I could take the one my mother had left behind.

Until I had earned a place for myself among them, I would be an outsider to the Roths. Sariah had taught me from a young age that being indispensable was the best protection. That's why Henrik had sent me to Arthur's and hooked me on a line like a lure to Simon. He hadn't truly *needed* me yet.

Perhaps it was Henrik's own superstition that had kept the doors of the tea house closed. Maybe in his mind, this place was some kind of monument to his sister. Or maybe, this gem rotting in the belly of Bastian had just been waiting for me.

ELEVEN

This was something I knew how to do.

I stood before the long table in the couturier's shop as he laid out the bolts of fabric. He worked with quick hands, lining everything up side by side, and unrolling a flap of every tweed, wool, and silk taffeta in a cascade of colors to be inspected.

A fresh pot of tea sat on the counter behind him, steam pouring from its spout, and a half-moon of cakes from the baker was arranged on a porcelain plate. This was going to take all afternoon and the couturier had prepared, making sure to have everything ready with his stock at hand.

Tru had been the first to arrive, and when he got too close to the table of fabrics with his teacup, the man nearly bored a hole into him with his glowering. Couturiers were fiercely protective of their supplies and you never so much as lit a candle near their fabrics. Even the cuts of leather for boots were under lock and key in the glass cases along the wall. There was no telling what the items in this shop added up to in coin.

"All right, what will it be?"

I walked down the table, studying the cloths and feeling their corners. "This one." I set a hand on a dark blue tweed. This would be for Henrik. He needed something to brighten and balance that dark gloom in his eyes. "And this one." The emerald color was next—a perfect hue for Murrow. Dressed in green, his light brown hair would look like a rich auburn, and there would be more than one young lady at the exhibition who would be looking at him.

But Ezra . . . My hand flitted from bolt to bolt as I conjured the image of him to mind. He was fair and stark, with a pale smooth complexion and raven hair, his narrowed gaze intent. These colors wouldn't do for him. They'd only look like a costume.

No, his would be the obsidian. A deep, inky black.

I unfolded the edge of the wool, holding it in my open hand, and a feeling like embers under my skin made me shiver as I pictured it. The way his gray eyes would smolder in this color.

I blinked the image away, dropping the cloth and curling my fingers into a fist, as if it had bitten me.

"Next?" The couturier waited, the knife clutched in his hand.

I chose fabric after fabric, piecing them together until I had every Roth dressed up like a set of chess pieces in my mind. Together, they would be magnificent.

Henrik was taking Ezra and me to the dinner at the watchmaker's house, but he wanted formal garments for everyone in the family. The first of many engagements, he'd called it. The Roths knew how to present themselves, their clothes and boots and watches pristine even when there was no company. But dressing for polite society was another thing altogether. It didn't matter how white their shirts were, my uncles and cousins and Ezra had the manners of wolves and the guild would spot it a mile away. If Henrik wanted to be accepted by them, he would have to learn to be civilized. That was going to take some time, so we'd start where we could—the garments.

The couturier started cutting right away, sliding the blade of his cloth knife down the stitching in clean edges and setting aside the bolts we weren't using.

"All dinner clothes?" He pulled a strand of thread with his teeth, biting the length so he could use it to measure.

"That's right." I went to the window, watching the street. Murrow and Ezra were late. "Where are they?" I murmured to myself.

"They'll be here," Tru said, dropping a third cube of sugar into his cup.

I pulled out my watch, checking the time.

"Boots?" the couturier asked, still cutting into the fabric.

"Everything," I answered. "Silk cravats. I want the jackets lined with silk as well."

He nodded approvingly. This wasn't my first time around a man's proper suit and Henrik had said to spare no expense, so I wouldn't.

"And for you, miss?" His eyes looked me over from head to toe.

I reached out to touch the fawn-brown bolt of cloth beside me. I'd gone to the couturier's shop in Nimsmire every time my great-aunt went, and I'd always secretly fantasized about pulling on the tailored fabrics reserved for the men's suits and tugging my hair from its braids. I'd never liked the silly frocks that Sariah had made for me or the heavy jewels she insisted I wear. I was a bird wearing the wrong feathers, and if I had my way, I'd be donning a jacket instead of skirts. But Sariah would have sooner seen me walk the street naked than see me in a pair of trousers. In a shop filled with the finest tweeds and wools in the Unnamed Sea, I had to choose something fit for a lady.

I sighed. If it was image Henrik wanted, I needed a gown that was sophisticated. Not so highbrow that I put anyone off, but impressive enough to draw attention and make an impression. I stood before the other bolts of cloth, thinking. The organza would be too frilly, the satin too sultry. Silk was the common choice, but I needed to be memorable. That's what they'd want from me. And I was good at giving people what they wanted. It was only a matter of presentation.

"This one," I said, letting my eyes fall to a bolt of chiffon. It was a shade of warm silver, on the verge of pale gold. I picked it up, cradling the fabric in my arms.

The tailor gave another approving nod, lifting a piece to hold against my skin. "A good choice." His eyes went to the door behind me and the bell jingled as it opened.

Ezra came up the steps with the sun at his back, his cap pulled low over his eyes and his open watch in his hand.

"There you are," I said, glaring at him.

He ignored the implication that he was late. Instead, he went straight to the pot of tea beside Tru and poured himself a cup without bothering to remove his jacket.

"He needs to fit you." I handed the bolt of chiffon to the couturier and he set it down with the others I'd chosen.

Ezra answered with a sigh, unbuttoning his jacket with rough fingers. "This needs to be quick."

I'd taken him away from his work and from what I'd seen, the workshop was the only place that Ezra was relaxed. Standing in front of that forge with the wall of tools behind him was the only time I'd seen that scowl off his face.

"It'll take as long as it takes," I said flatly.

He shot me a cold look before he dropped his jacket to the chair Tru was sitting in, burying him in it. Then he shrugged out of his vest. Beneath it, the seams of his white shirt were cut around him with an expert hand. It fit his form perfectly, hugging the shape of him.

"Here." The couturier directed him to stand before the large, wood-framed mirror and he reluctantly obeyed, turning his back to the table.

The couturier stilled when he spotted the knife at the back of Ezra's belt, his mouth flattening into a straight line. Ezra ignored him, pulling the suspenders down his arms and letting them hang from his waist. I watched as the man took the measure and drew it across his broad shoulders. He easily stood within the width of Ezra's frame and Ezra was an entire head taller than his height.

Ezra stood perfectly still, his silver-striped hands hanging at his sides. The scars were like shimmering bands that disappeared beneath the cuffs of his shirt.

"Lapels?" The couturier looked to me.

"Notch," I answered.

"Brass buttons?"

I met his eyes in the mirror, tilting my head to the side. "Would you give a merchant brass buttons?" I asked.

"No, miss."

"Horn. Or cowry shell," I said, an edge in my voice.

He nodded sheepishly. The couturier wasn't stupid. He knew who we were. And I wasn't going to let him cheat us because he thought we didn't know the difference between pauper buttons and sophisticated ones.

Ezra waited impatiently as he wrote down the measurements, lifting his arms when instructed to and turning on command. When the couturier reached for the tail of his shirt, he bristled. "I can untuck my own shirt," he muttered, pulling it from where it was stuffed into the waist of his pants.

A slice of smooth, pale skin appeared when he lifted it and the couturier took the measure around Ezra's hips. He was the kind of creature that was as beautiful to look at as he was unnerving. But there was almost an unawareness about him, as if he didn't really know how much his silent presence seemed to fill every room he entered. With better breeding, he would have been the prize of any family in Nimsmire.

When I looked into the mirror, Ezra was watching me. He'd caught me staring. I blinked, looking away to hide the burn in my cheeks.

The bell jingled and Murrow came barreling into the shop, his face flushed as if he'd run half the distance.

"What happened to tidy and timely?" I glowered at him.

"Sorry," Murrow said, winking at me. "Had business in North End."

The humor left his eyes as he reached into his jacket. When his hand reemerged, he had Henrik's leather-bound ledger. He cleared his throat. "Ezra."

"What?" He didn't bother turning around, letting the tailor finish with the measurements around his chest.

Murrow's eyes shifted to me. He almost looked nervous. "I've just done the count."

Ezra dropped his arms, finally turning. "And?"

"It's off," Murrow said, heavily.

Ezra's gaze sharpened. "Whose is off?"

Murrow's attention cut to Tru, who was watching with wide eyes from the armchair. "Tru's."

Ezra's jaw clenched and Tru shrank beneath his stare, his shoulders hunching.

"Get out," Ezra said.

The couturier obeyed immediately, setting down his quill and dismissing himself through the door that led to the back room. As soon as he was gone, Ezra stepped off the platform, stopping in front of Tru. The boy was already on his feet.

Ezra folded his arms over his chest. "Why is the count off, Tru?"

Tru cleared his throat, his hands finding his pockets.

"Did you check it three times?" Ezra stared at him.

Tru swallowed. "No."

Murrow and Ezra met eyes across the table. In the back room, I could hear the couturier opening drawers and closing them.

"Why not?" Ezra's voice deepened.

"I forgot," Tru answered.

"You forgot."

"He made a mistake." I looked between them, confused. "Can this wait?"

"No, it can't." Ezra looked at me as if I'd said something incomprehensible. "Come here," he said, gesturing to the floor in front of him.

Tru hesitated and the hair on the back of my neck rose, the eerie stillness in the room making me nervous. The calm on Ezra's face didn't match the tension in the air. There was a cavern between the two and I felt as if we were all about to fall into it.

Tru came to stand in front of him, taking a deep breath, and after a moment, he looked up. His hands fell from his pockets and I realized too late that he was waiting. Bracing himself.

I took a small step forward. "What are you—"

Ezra's hand lifted into the air and he brought it down so quickly that the scream was trapped in my throat. His hand flew across Tru's face, whipping it to the side, and I lunged forward as he toppled backward, hitting the chair.

"What are you doing?" I cried, my voice breaking as I came around the table.

I took Tru's hot face into my hands, turning it toward the

light coming through the window. His eyes were filled with tears, a stripe of blood lining his bottom lip. He reached up, wiping it away with the back of his hand, but the redness was already blooming deep under the skin where Ezra's hand had struck. The whole side of his face would be bruised.

Heat boiled in my veins and I let him go, turning toward Ezra. I shoved hard into his chest with both hands, and he looked so surprised that I thought he was going to stumble straight into the mirror behind him. His eyes widened as he looked down at me, and for the first time since I'd come to Bastian, I could see beneath the stone mask he wore.

"Bryn." Murrow's voice sounded behind me, but I could hardly hear it. My fiery gaze was fixed on Ezra.

"You touch him again, and I'll put that mark on *your* face." I spoke the words through gritted teeth.

Ezra looked stunned, taking a second to compose himself. He ran one hand through his mussed hair, and he stared at me, his eyes jumping back and forth on mine.

But the mask returned as his breath slowed, and the familiar emptiness that usually filled his eyes turned them even darker.

"We done?" he said, his tone hollow.

Ezra was speaking to the couturier, who was now standing in the doorway behind us with wide eyes.

"Yes," he answered unevenly.

Ezra took a step toward me, until he was standing so close that I could smell the scent of cloves and the blackest of tea leaves coming off of him. There was a small spatter of blood on his white shirt. Tru's blood.

When his hand moved nearer, I stopped breathing. My lungs twisted behind my ribs, my pulse racing as he reached around me to the chair and took his vest and jacket from its back. His eyes didn't leave mine as he slipped them back on.

"Give it to me," he said, holding out a hand to Murrow.

Murrow set Henrik's book into it and Ezra finally stepped past me. "Let's go."

Tru was already moving toward the door, following on Ezra's heels as he went down the steps to the street.

I let out the breath I was holding, angry tears pricking my eyes.

Murrow watched out the window as Ezra disappeared. "Don't think I've ever seen that before," he said.

"What?" I snapped.

He gave me a bewildered look. "You might be the only soul in Bastian to be left standing after putting hands on that scary bastard."

TWELVE

Dear Sariah,

I stared at the parchment until my great-aunt's name looked strange and unfamiliar. I'd tried to write the letter over the last two days, but I didn't know what to say.

There had been no messages from Nimsmire and there wouldn't be for some time, I guessed. That had never been Sariah's way. She'd said all she needed to when she said goodbye. Whatever else she'd wanted to part with was written in the letter in my drawer, but I still hadn't opened it. I didn't know if I ever would.

The days since I'd arrived in Bastian were no more than echoes of the stories she'd always told me. Still, I'd underestimated the brutality and coldness of my uncles. This house was like shifting ground beneath my feet.

Nimsmire hadn't really ever felt like home, but I found myself longing for the routine and quiet of that big empty estate and the few words my great-aunt spoke. Looking back, I'd spent so much time waiting to leave that I'd never really settled there. I'd never made friends, and aside from a few stolen kisses in the darkened corners of parlors at elaborate dinners, I'd never given my heart away, either.

My life before Bastian had always felt like a very long stop on my way back to the Roths. And now that I had reached my destination, I was only more sure that maybe I didn't belong anywhere.

Someone rapped on my bedroom door and I startled, dropping the quill. It rolled across the slanted table as I stood and shuffled my papers to cover the unwritten letter. There was nothing there to hide, I realized, but everything in this house felt like a secret.

I made my way across the floor and opened the door to find Henrik. He stood in the hallway with a small wooden chest in his hands, Ezra's brooding shadow lurking behind him. I frowned.

"May we come in?" Henrik asked.

His tone was impatient but not in the usual way. He was excited, and if anything, that instantly put me on edge. I stepped back, letting them cross the threshold, and Ezra's eyes fell briefly to my bare feet as he passed, going to the window. He looked even more irritated than normal, and I wondered if Henrik had heard about what happened at the couturier that afternoon. I hadn't seen Ezra since I'd screamed at and shoved him. The thought made my blood boil all over again. From the look on his face, he was thinking the same thing.

"There's something I need you to do," Henrik began, setting the chest down onto my little desk.

I stood against the wall opposite Ezra, leaving as much space between us as possible. I didn't like him being in my room. Looking at my things. I didn't like feeling like he'd invaded the only private space I had in this house.

"Have you ever picked a lock?"

I blinked, looking up at Henrik. "What? No."

He let out an irritated sigh. "I thought that might be the case." He looked genuinely let down by the revelation.

"Why would I need to know how to pick a lock?" I was afraid of the answer, I realized.

Henrik tapped the top of the wooden box. "At some point during the dinner at the watchmaker's, I need you to find a way into the study. There is a desk with a drawer that has a lock similar to this one, and I need you to open it."

I stared at him, my mouth dropping open. He couldn't be serious. "You want me to *steal* something?"

"No." He nearly laughed. "If Simon knows anything is missing after a dinner we attended, he will know exactly who took it. I just need you to find out what's inside. There should be a ledger or trade records of some kind."

"I can't do that," I huffed. "What if I'm caught?"

Henrik looked confused. "Bryn, this is what I need from you." He said it so simply. As if that was the only answer required of him. And it was. There wasn't anyone in this family who denied the man anything.

"But . . . I thought you're trying to get his patronage."

"I am," he said. "I also like to be prepared. If he decides to be less than agreeable, I will need leverage. Simon may have been able to fool the guild, but I happen to know his business isn't as clean as they believe it is. I need something I can use if things don't go my way."

My heartbeat ticked up, my hands clenched behind my back. "I wouldn't even know what to look for."

"A name," he said. "It's only a name."

I let out a heavy breath, looking to Ezra. But he was the last one who'd take my side. "What name?" I murmured.

Henrik smiled. "Holland."

"The gem merchant?"

"*Former* gem merchant," he amended. "Simon is still doing business with her. I just need to be able to prove it. If you find her name listed in the ledger, that will be enough."

If the guild found out that Simon was still working with Holland, it would cost him his ring. Henrik wanted leverage to hold that possibility over his head, but I was the last person in this family qualified to pick a lock in a dark study during that dinner.

"You said you needed me to get the family ready. Garments. Decorum. That sort of thing."

"I didn't realize that was all you were capable of." Henrik paused, assessing me. "Are you saying you *can't* do it?"

The words stung. Fiercely. I'd backed myself into a corner, revealing the chasm between the pampered, frilly girl Sariah had raised and the Roth blood in my veins. I'd been so eager to make them see me as more than the doll I'd been dressed up to be and here I was, acting delicate. Across the room, Ezra surveyed me as if he could hear every single thought as it skipped through my mind.

I swallowed. There were no *ladies* and *gentlemen* in this family. There were only Roths. And that's exactly what I'd wanted to find when I stepped off the *Jasper*.

"I can do it," I said, meaning the words.

Every task was an opportunity. And each one brought my stake in the family closer. If he wanted me to pick a lock, I'd do it. If he wanted me to scale the rooftops of the Merchant's District in a rainstorm, I'd do it.

"Good," he said. "Ezra will give you the basics. I'm sure you can handle it."

My eyes cut to Ezra, who stood silent against the window. Henrik looked between us before turning on his heel. He ducked out, shutting the door.

We stood staring at each other and the walls of my room felt suddenly closer, the air warmer. Ezra was impossibly still, unblinking.

"Isn't there someone else who can do this?" I asked.

"You want to ask Henrik? Be my guest." Ezra pulled the stool from the corner and set it roughly beside the table. When he sat, I hesitated, my eyes trailing around the room before I took the chair beside him.

"It's called a key pin lock and they all pretty much operate the same way." He got right to work, sliding the box toward us.

I gritted my teeth, giving him an icy stare. He was going to act like nothing had happened. Like changing into a clean shirt would erase what he'd done to Tru. I'd been ready to tear his head off only hours ago and I was still furious. I wasn't going to pretend like I wasn't.

"Inside, there are five key pins, each set to different heights," he continued. "You'll have to manipulate them all into position in order to get the lock to turn."

He looked at me, waiting. When I said nothing, he let out a breath. "Look, can we just get this over with?"

I could see that he didn't want to be here any more than I wanted him to be. And he was right. The sooner we did what Henrik asked, the sooner he could get out of my room and leave me alone.

I sat up straighter, turning my attention to the lock. "How am I supposed to get them into position if I can't see them?"

Ezra shifted on the stool and when his hand moved toward me, I flinched, drawing back. He ignored my reaction, his fingers drifting past my face until they were slipping into my hair behind my ear.

I froze as he found the two hairpins there and gently pulled them free. The waving strand that had been pinned away from my face fell onto my shoulder and Ezra looked at it before holding the pins between us.

I struggled to draw a breath into my tight chest. "Hairpins."

"They're as good as anything else," he answered, setting one of them down.

I could still feel his touch, the trail of it burning on my skin. But he had turned his attention back to the chest.

"You'll need extra in your hair just in case. The first, you'll bend like this." He shaped the metal into a point. "You're left-handed, so the other, you'll use in that hand."

"How do you know I'm left-handed?" I studied him, suspicious.

"I have eyes." He fit the bent one inside the lock's opening
before sliding the straight pin in beneath it. "Like this." Once
he'd shown me, he pulled them back out to let me try.

I took the pins from his fingers, taking care not to touch
him, and slid the chest closer to me. I mimicked what he'd
done, putting the folded pin in first, then the straight one.

"Use the top one to feel where the pins are. They'll slide
up easily until you reach the key pin."

I pressed the tip of the pin up from back to front, finding
the openings in the metal. "What does the key pin feel like?"

"It will be more resistant than the others. More rigid." He
was slipping into the ease of work, his rough edges and the
tension in his voice softening. "When you find it, use the pin
to gently push it up until it clicks into place. You'll hear it."

I trained my eyes on the edge of the table, trying to feel
my way through until I reached a pin that was heavier than
the others. It took a few tries, but I finally wedged the pin up
enough to lift it and heard a soft click.

"Good. That's the easy one. Now do the same thing, looking for the next one."

I lowered the pin and moved it forward, but the metal
wall inside was smooth. "I don't feel it."

Ezra drifted closer to me and I inhaled the smell of cloves
coming off of him. His jacket. His hair. The scent followed
him wherever he went. I could taste it on my tongue.

I immediately leaned back, putting more air between us.

He reached up, positioning his hand against mine and

the tips of his fingers slid over my knuckles until he was directing my movements. The warmth of his skin made my stomach feel like it was full of stones.

"There." He tilted the pin upward at an angle until the tip found the next groove.

But when he let me go and I tried lifting, it snapped back down, bringing the other pin with it. "Damn it." I groaned.

"It's going to take practice. Try again."

"I *am* trying." I shot him a pointed look.

He tossed the second pin onto the stack of parchments, setting his elbows onto the desk. "If you have something to say, then say it."

Heat crept up from the neck of my frock as his eyes ran over my face. "Fine. You shouldn't have hit him. He's a child."

Ezra scoffed. "He's hardly a child. He's ten years old."

"Exactly."

"I don't know what you were doing at that age, but I wasn't being served tea with sugar and playing with toys," he said, flatly.

I narrowed my eyes. He was implying that being raised in Nimsmire had made me soft. Fragile. That I couldn't possibly understand the way they did things. It all came down to the same point: I wasn't one of them. "Child or not, you don't just hit someone when they don't do what you tell them to."

He shook his head, muttering something under his breath that I couldn't understand.

"What?"

"You have no idea what you're talking about," he snapped.

"Neither do you. I know you think I'm ridiculous. That

I don't deserve to be here. You look at me and you see a girl raised in Nimsmire with sugar in her tea." My voice rose, repeating his own words back to him. "You think I can't do this."

But Ezra didn't look angry, which made me feel even more foolish. He leveled his gaze at me, speaking evenly. "I don't think that."

"Then what?" I snapped.

He said nothing for a moment, eyes running over my face and making me want to shove away from my stool. He leaned in closer, meeting my eyes. "I see a girl hiding beneath silk skirts." He breathed. "Makes me wonder what you're afraid they'll see."

I swallowed against the pain in my throat. I'd thought more than once that I'd known a hundred men like him, but I was beginning to wonder if I was wrong. There was an unsettling feeling inside of me when Ezra looked at me. As if he could see much more than I wanted him to.

And I wasn't only angry that he'd hit Tru. I was angry that he'd watched Arthur hit *me*.

"I know you were there in the alley," I whispered. "When I went to the pier."

The set of his mouth faltered, and I watched as his lips pressed together for just a moment. "I wasn't even supposed to be there," he muttered.

"What?"

"Look," Ezra said suddenly. "I'm only going to say this once." He kept his voice low, as if he was being careful not to be overheard. "Family means something different to these people, Bryn."

I bit down on my bottom lip painfully. He had never said my name. I was sure he hadn't, because I'd never felt that bloom in my chest before. He was horrible and callous and cruel. But there was something else about Ezra that felt like a sinking stone in water. One that never hit bottom.

"Now . . ." He returned his gaze to the lock and he picked up the pin, holding it out to me. "Again."

THIRTEEN

The couturier had worked through the night, appearing at the door after breakfast with an enormous armload of unfinished jackets and trousers. His hair was spilling from his hat, his eyes darkened with sleeplessness, but as soon as I let him into the library, he got to work.

The raw stitching along the hems of the garments was only a placeholder for the detailed handwork he would do once the fit had been checked. A couturier never relied solely on measurements. Until he saw the fabric draped over the body, he wouldn't finalize a single seam.

I didn't miss the way his eyes traveled over the room as he got his things organized. He was probably used to working in the most decadent homes of the guild, but coin was coin. He was a fool if he let pride get in the way of a full purse, and I wondered now if whispered rumors had already begun in the Merchant's District about Henrik. If Simon had managed to keep his invitation a secret, it wouldn't stay that way for long.

"I'll take the boy first," he said, finding the smallest jacket in the stack. Tru's jacket.

I leaned out of the study, calling his name, and my voice echoed up the stairwell. It was followed by the sound of footsteps and soon Tru was coming through the door.

I'd tried not to stare at him when he arrived after breakfast to help Henrik in the workshop, but one of his eyes was blackened, his cheek swollen. From the way he chewed on only one side when Sylvie gave him a biscuit, I guessed the inside of his mouth had a nasty cut as well. But he didn't complain, and I didn't want to embarrass him by calling attention to it. The couturier, on the other hand, inspected Tru's face with sharp eyes as the boy unbuttoned his jacket. Whatever he was thinking, he bit his tongue.

Tru stood before the window and held his arms out to either side so the couturier could slide on what would become his new waistcoat. Even with the seams unfinished, his work was flawless. The fit hugged all the right places despite Tru's small stature, making him look older than his ten years. The dinner jacket was next, and Tru seemed confused by its length, instinctively pushing the tails away from his legs.

"These look funny," he straightened the collar beneath his chin.

"Well, *you* don't look funny." I smirked. "You look handsome." I pushed his hands out of the way, doing the buttons up myself before he could smudge the white fabric of the shirt. In the light, his eye didn't appear quite as dark as it had in the workshop, but it still looked like it hurt. I waited for the couturier to go back to the study before I finally spoke in a low voice. "You shouldn't let them treat you like that, you know."

Tru gave me a puzzled look, shaking out one of his sleeves to measure the cuff's length. "Like what?"

"What happened yesterday. With Ezra." I tipped my chin toward the open doorway where I could hear Ezra's hammer echoing through the house. I'd heard him leave the house after we finished with the lock and he hadn't returned until almost morning.

Tru still looked confused. "But I forgot to check the count."

I stared at him blankly before I sighed, turning him around to check the fit across the shoulders. They were insane. All of them. Even Tru wasn't angry about what Ezra had done. The words he'd spoken last night in my room came back to me, making me shiver. *Family means something different to these people.*

"What did your father say about your face?" I asked, a bite edging the words.

He shrugged. "To check the count next time."

I scoffed. "And your mother?"

That was the only question he didn't seem keen to answer. He stared straight ahead, out the window.

Though she'd been the only other woman in the house apart from Sylvie, she hadn't said one word to me in the few times I'd seen her. I'd sensed a tension between Anthelia and the others at the family dinner. There was a distance there, even if it was a polite one. Sariah had never met her or Tru and Jameson, so I wasn't sure if Anthelia had known my parents.

But she'd married into the Roths, which seemed like its own kind of insanity.

I turned him again. "I don't remember my parents, you know," I said, watching his face carefully. "I was about as big as Jameson when they died."

"I know," he said, softly.

"I'm sure you've heard more stories about them than I have. Maybe you could tell me about them."

"He doesn't like it when we talk about Aunt Eden," Tru whispered, his mouth twisting up on one side. He winced, as if the motion hurt.

My brow furrowed. "Henrik?"

He nodded.

I hadn't heard Henrik speak of my parents. Not once. I searched Tru's face for whatever he wasn't saying.

"Auster, either," he added.

"Auster." I studied him. "Sariah's grandson?"

Tru nodded, whispering, "He used to live in your room, but he ran away a long time ago. Climbed out the window and never came back."

That's who Murrow had been talking about when he said whoever lived in my room was gone. The few times Sariah had spoken about Auster, it had sounded like he was dead. But now that I thought about it, she'd never actually said that.

My mind went to the discolored spot on the papered wall of the study. Maybe his was the portrait that had been taken down.

I had a feeling if I pressed, Tru would tell me more, but I

wasn't going to get him into any more trouble with the others. I brushed off the shoulders of the jacket, giving him one last look over.

"Am I done?" He perked up instantly.

I smiled at him. "You're done."

He slipped out of the waistcoat and out of the room before I heard the door to the workshop open and close again. Murrow was already waiting outside of the study, reading over a stack of parchments silently. His hair was always just on the verge of unkempt and his pants a little too short, but he was very easy on the eyes. I could see all three of my uncles in him and I wondered if somewhere in there, he looked like my mother, too. But that was a face I didn't know well enough to recognize.

"You're next," I said, waving him inside.

He finished reading before he glanced up at me. "In a minute. I have to . . ."

"Now," I said, raising an eyebrow at him.

He groaned, setting the pages onto Henrik's desk before he came through the doors of the library. The couturier was already holding up the green jacket and Murrow begrudgingly got into place, sliding his arms inside. Once it was on, I straightened it, giving the couturier a nod. The green wool looked good on him.

"I still don't understand why we need new clothes," he muttered. "What difference is it going to make? Coin is coin. As long as we have enough, we'll be fine."

"It will make all the difference in the world," I answered. "These people don't need copper. Image is what matters to them. If you don't look the part, you don't belong. They'll never invite the Roths into the guild unless they believe you can act like one of them."

Murrow's jaw clenched. He didn't like that answer.

I studied him. "You don't want to join the guild?" I guessed.

"I don't know. Do you?"

The question caught me off guard. No one in this house had asked me what I thought about anything. But Murrow stared into my eyes, waiting, as if he really wanted to know. "I don't know," I admitted. "I guess I still don't understand enough about any of this to know what I think about Henrik getting a merchant's ring."

"But you know about the guilds. How they work."

I shrugged. "Sariah works closely with the guilds in Nimsmire, but she's not a merchant. Even they don't want to fully associate with a Roth."

"Simon did it, somehow."

"The watchmaker?"

"He used to run the same kind of trade in North End. Didn't come from a merchant family and somehow worked his way into the guild."

"You wouldn't know it by looking at him," I said.

"He may look like them, but he's still the same bastard he was in North End. Anyone who crosses him doesn't come out the other side of it. He's dumped more bodies into the water than our entire family combined."

My eyes widened at the admission, my hands stilling on the lapels of his jacket.

Murrow laughed. "Don't tell me you're too refined to speak of such things. It's no secret."

I glared at him, annoyed at the implication. "How did Henrik end up with the merchant's ring from Ceros, anyway?"

Murrow pulled the sleeves of his shirt down to check the length. He looked surprised when he saw that the cuffs fell perfectly against his wrists. "He got very lucky."

"How?"

Murrow paused, looking over his shoulder to be sure the couturier wasn't listening. "Someone needed something from him at a very opportune moment. I don't know if he'll find the same luck again."

"Then why are you going along with all of this?"

He almost laughed again. "If Henrik wants to know what I think, it would be the first time. That isn't how things work here. Ezra is the one he listens to."

I wanted to ask what he meant, but I was beginning to fear the edge of the boundaries in this house. If Tru got a black eye for not counting the coin correctly, what would asking too many questions get me? "Is that why you stood by yesterday when Ezra hurt Tru?"

Murrow stared down at me, his eyes squinting under his wavy hair.

"You should have done something." I adjusted his jacket, more roughly than was necessary.

But there wasn't any humor in his eyes. "Ezra did him a favor, Bryn."

I stepped back, giving him a look of sheer disbelief. They *were* crazy. All of them. "What does that even mean?"

His head tilted a little to one side and his voice lowered. "If Ezra hadn't given him that black eye, Henrik would have given him worse. Don't make assumptions about things you don't understand."

He fastened the last button of the jacket as the couturier returned and I stepped back, watching as he pinned the places in the fabric that needed adjusting.

You have no idea what you're talking about.

That was what Ezra had meant. He was protecting Tru by dealing with the mistake before Henrik had to. And he'd returned to the house with him. Maybe to report the mistake himself.

It hadn't occurred to me to ask myself why Murrow had come to Ezra with the problem in the ledger instead of going straight to Henrik. He'd gone to Ezra to protect Tru from whatever Henrik would dole out. And Ezra had been the one to make sure there was evidence of a punishment. That was the reason Tru wasn't angry with him. It was probably also the reason his father didn't seem bothered by what had happened. He might have even been grateful.

There were the rules and there were the consequences. A sharp line divided the two. But in this house, perhaps sometimes, violence was a mercy.

FOURTEEN

My uncles had grown quiet in the last few days leading up to the dinner at Simon's, all moving around Henrik's orders with careful attention. And though Henrik seemed himself, there was even something about him that was amiss. As if the stakes of the dinner were weighing on him. He was nervous.

We stood around the table, silently waiting until Henrik pulled out his chair and everyone else followed. Noel and Anthelia shared a look across the table as she tried to pull a wriggling Jameson into her lap and Noel reached out, taking the child from her. He settled in his father's arms, sticking a thumb into his mouth, instantly calm. They may be covered in other people's blood half the time, and I may not understand the dynamics that ran this family, but there was a kind of tenderness between them, making what happened with Tru even more confusing. To me, all of it was madness. To them, it was just the way of things.

I unfolded my napkin into my lap, my hands hitting the edge of the table when Henrik said my name.

"Now, Bryn." He drew in a breath, settling the lightness in the room that had been there only a moment ago. "What do we need to know for this dinner?"

I stared at him, unsure of his meaning.

"The dinner," he said, with less patience. "What do we need to know if we're not going to make fools of ourselves?"

"Oh." I looked between him and the others, shrinking under their attention. Even Ezra was waiting for my answer. I swallowed, studying the table. "Well, for starters, the napkins."

Henrik nodded. "All right, what about them?"

"You all leave them on the table while you're eating. They should be neatly folded in your lap until you get up."

"All right." He obeyed, picking up his napkin and setting it over his knees attentively. Everyone else shadowed him, doing the same. "What else?"

"The bread. You tear it, you don't cut it with your knife."

"Well, that doesn't make any sense," Murrow muttered beside me, but he shut his mouth when Henrik glared at him.

"And your elbows shouldn't touch the table," I continued, giving a fleeting glance to Ezra, who had his set on either side of his plate, as usual. When he didn't move, Henrik jerked his chin, ordering him to obey. He gave an irritated sigh before he sat back in his chair.

"You all eat too fast and take bites that are too big. And you shouldn't leave the plate completely empty or the host will think you left the table hungry."

Henrik listened intently, and I could see him thinking.

Going over the plan in his mind. But there was far more work to be done with this lot than dinner manners if they were going to be accepted into the society of the guilds. It was in everything they did. Everything they said.

We continued on like that throughout the meal and Sylvie watched from the hall, snickering into the corner of her apron. Her cheeks were rosy, watching like a clucking hen as I corrected them. Much to my surprise, I didn't get a single argument. Even Anthelia played along, helping Tru when he struggled to hold his knife in the correct hand.

After dinner, the soft haze of mullein smoke from my uncles' pipes drifted through the air, casting everything in a dreamlike glow. I was beginning to see the beauty in the house. Beneath its uneven papered walls and creaky floorboards, there was a history. Legends and myths. In the daylight, it was cold and dark, but at night, the home of the Roths came alive with warmth and candlelight, softening its jagged edges.

The ping of dice on the long counter in the kitchen ricocheted up the hall, followed by the collective roar of my uncles and cousins. When I came to stand in the doorway, they were gathered around the large rectangular butcher block that had been cleared for the game.

The counter along the wall was set with trays of little gooseberry jam cakes and small loaves of cardamom bread. In Nimsmire, they were considered to be rustic treats, never favored over the custard-filled pastries and gold-dusted chocolates that filled the extravagant shop windows. But here, they were treasures.

It was the dice that made me feel more at home. Three

Widows was a favorite of my great-aunt and everyone in the Merchant's District of Nimsmire. They'd gather in parlors and galleries of grand homes with bottles of cava and wine and play late into the night. That was the fine line edged between people like the Roths and the guild. Gambling was a guilty pleasure among the highbrow society, a kind of open secret. They all played, winning and losing coin, but only within the walls of private homes. Such things weren't for the daylight.

Noel picked up the three dice and cupped his hands, giving Anthelia a wink. She stood in front of the huge iron stove and when she smiled, she immediately looked years younger. Her face came alive. Noel threw the dice, letting them hit the wall before they scattered onto the counter. There was a holding of breath before shouting erupted again and Noel groaned, taking one of the cakes from the platter to soothe the sting.

I didn't know why the Roths never ate dessert at the table like any other normal family, but I supposed that was just it—they weren't normal. Whenever I'd attended family dinner, they'd retreated to the kitchen the way families in Nimsmire would have retreated to the salon.

Henrik stood leaning against the wall with his arms crossed over his chest, listening patiently as Tru recounted a story to him. From this angle, I couldn't see the bruise that marked his cheek, and I was glad. He looked like any other boy, with bright, wide eyes, his hands moving in the air as he described something that had happened down on the docks.

Henrik saw me watching from the doorway and scooted over to make a space for me against the wall. I took a cake from the tray and wedged myself between them. When Tru laughed, so did Henrik, and it was strange to see my uncle that way. Ezra and Murrow had thought it better to strike Tru across the face rather than send him to Henrik, but my uncle was a different person in that kitchen. As if the moment dinner ended, everyone finally exhaled.

Casimir had Jameson in his arms, talking over his mop of dark, unruly hair to Murrow until he became too fidgety to hold. He let him slide down to the floor and when his little hands reached up to the counter's edge for one of the cakes, Sylvie swatted him away gently.

Henrik watched from the corner of his eye until her back was turned, and he plucked one up from the tray, discreetly handing it to Jameson. The little boy's mouth opened into a perfect O and Henrik nudged him through the door, into the hallway. I found myself smiling as another round of clamor rang into the air and Murrow picked up the dice, shouting.

There was a rhythm to this family. A heartbeat. From the outside looking in, they were beastly. Monstrous, even. But I was beginning to see beneath their glittering scales.

"You ready for tomorrow?" Henrik said, turning so one shoulder was set against the wall beside me.

"Yes," I answered, almost instantly. I wasn't sure how true it was, but I didn't want to think too much about it.

Henrik gave me an approving smile. "Eden was that way." His voice drifted. "Always fearless."

I watched him carefully. It was the first time I'd heard him speak about my mother. The sound of her name on his lips made me feel a bit unsteady. "I'm not fearless," I said.

Henrik's empty gaze went past me, to the dark hallway,

and he gave no indication that he'd heard me. He seemed lost in thought. Or memories.

My parents had died not long after my grandfather, and Henrik had been the architect of the job they'd been on. Maybe that was why he didn't like talking about her.

I drew in a breath before I gathered up the courage to ask. "I saw the tea house in the Merchant's District when I went to see the couturier."

Henrik blinked several times before his eyes refocused on me. "Oh?" He suddenly looked a little uncomfortable and I was afraid it had been a mistake to mention it.

"How long has it been boarded up like that?"

His hands slid into his pockets, going a little stiff. "For years."

I understood now why Tru said Henrik didn't like talking about Eden. His whole manner changed, transforming him back into the man with bloodied knuckles I'd met the first day I arrived.

"Why didn't you ever open it?" I asked, more softly.

Henrik frowned. "The tea house was Eden's scheme. When the time came for her to have a stake of her own, I helped her purchase it. I thought it was a silly idea, but I gave it to her as a wedding gift and then she and Tomlin used their own coin to set it up."

"Why a tea house? Was it a front for something else?"

Henrik shook his head. "No, just a tea house. She wanted the family to venture into more respectable work. So did Sariah."

I watched his eyes, trying to see what danced in the light there. It pained him to talk about her. I could see that. Perhaps that's what all this was about—legitimizing the family with a merchant's ring. Maybe Henrik was fulfilling Eden's wishes, in a way.

"Didn't make much sense to open it once she was gone," he said.

"Why didn't you sell it?"

The air around him shifted and I held my breath. The problem with Henrik was that I didn't know where the edges of his moods were. There was a sharp melting point between his fury and his good nature.

"I was just thinking," I took a chance in saying it, "that it was a good idea. A tea house is the perfect way to endear the Roths to the guilds."

He puffed on the pipe in his hand, letting the smoke ripple from his lips.

"I would wager there isn't a merchant in Bastian who doesn't take meetings at a tea house. If you want the merchant's ring, it's a good place to start."

"That's what you think, is it?"

"I do."

"Sounds to me like you're making a pitch for your own stake."

"Why not? Everyone else in the family has one."

That made Henrik pause. "Everyone else has *earned* one," he corrected.

The implication was that I hadn't proven myself yet, and

he wasn't wrong. But if I could pull off this dinner and get Simon to offer his patronage, that would all change.

He turned back to the kitchen before I could answer, making it clear the conversation was over. But I could still see the thoughts illuminated behind his eyes. Getting the merchant's ring would give him everything he wanted. But if he was going to join the guild, he had to stop thinking like a criminal, gathering gossip in rye-soaked taverns, doing dirty deals, and stealing information from merchants' ledgers. At the very least he had to be better at hiding it.

"Are we really ready for tomorrow?" he asked, changing the subject.

I nodded. "We're ready."

He took the last puff on his pipe, staring into the ash-filled chamber as it blew out of his nostrils. Henrik would have to change if he wanted the family to change and I wasn't sure yet how to help him see that. But there was a pattern to Henrik like there was to any other man. I just had to be patient enough to dissect it.

"All right," Sylvie crooned, setting down the last tray. It was a tower of flaky, half-moon fruit pies with a golden crust. As soon as they hit the counter, Henrik joined the others, picking up the dice and shaking them in his fist.

The family swarmed around the butcher block like moths to a flame and Casimir poured another round of rye. The sound of their voices faded as I slipped out into the dark hallway, following the narrow passage to the workshop. I knocked three times and after a few moments, it opened.

Ezra stood inside, glancing over my head as if he had expected someone else to be standing there. "What is it?"

I reached into the pocket of my skirts, pulling out two hairpins. I held them up between us in answer and as soon as his eyes landed on them, he let the door swing open. He turned on his heel and I stepped inside, pushing the door closed behind me until the lock fell into place.

Ezra returned to his forge, going back to the anvil and picking up the mallet on the table. He was working on what looked like a cuffed bracelet, with delicate, intricate patterns hammered along its edge.

Down the hall, the shouting rang out. It sounded like Henrik was winning. "Don't you play?" I asked, coming around the table opposite of him where the locked chest was waiting. I'd been practicing every chance I got, spending late nights and early mornings in the workshop.

Ezra's eyes went to the closed door. "No."

"I saw the dice on your dressing table," I jibed, trying to thaw the ice between us. Whether I agreed with his treatment of Tru or not, I understood now that it wasn't barbarity that had made him do it. But Ezra was still keeping me at arm's length.

"I've lost enough with the toss of the dice," he said, more quietly.

The way he said it got beneath my skin. It wasn't a passing comment or a joke about coin. There was heaviness in the words. A truth.

I tilted my head. "You could have told me."

"What?"

"Why you hit Tru," I said. "You let me think you'd hurt him to be cruel."

His hand found the tiny pick in the pocket of his apron and he sat back down onto the stool. "What does it matter? I still hit him."

"It matters," I said, louder than I'd meant to.

Ezra stared at me, filling the space between us with a howling silence. He always seemed to be shifting between truth and lie. I didn't know which side of him was the real one.

"What did you mean when you said you weren't supposed to be at Arthur's?"

Ezra drew in a deep breath and his shirt pulled over his chest beneath the apron. The sound was like the brush of the waves against a ship. "If things had gotten out of hand, I would have stepped in."

I wanted to tell him that things did get out of hand. That I had the mark on my face to prove it. But I reminded myself that he lived in a world with a very different idea of what *out of hand* meant.

"What did you mean when you said you weren't supposed to be there?" I asked again, more quietly.

It took him a moment to decide if he would answer. "Henrik wanted to push Arthur out of the running for Simon's patronage, so he sent you there knowing what would happen. He wasn't happy that I followed you, but luckily his plan worked. Simon got wind of it and . . ."

"Murrow," I whispered. That's why he went to the tavern. To tell the story.

A tight feeling pulled at the center of my chest and my

fingers curled into a fist on the table. Murrow had been in on it, too. They all were. By the next morning, Simon had heard, and the invitation came.

I kept my eyes on the flames in the forge. I'd figured out what Henrik was up to, but Murrow playing along hurt. He was the one person in the house I'd thought was in my corner.

"If I had interfered, we'd probably be in a worse situation."

We. I wasn't sure what he meant by that. The family? Him and Henrik? Him and me?

He waited for me to say something, but I didn't. What was there to say? It was both infuriating and completely unsurprising. And there was absolutely nothing I could do about any of it.

Eventually the tapping started and I was grateful for the noise. The sound of Ezra's work was a constant resonance in the house, and it had become comforting. Now, it was the quiet that put my teeth on edge.

I got to work, bending the first pin the way he'd taught me. We didn't speak as I picked the lock over and over, resetting it each time it clicked open. I had the muscle memory now, but Simon's lock would be a little different. According to Ezra, they all were.

"Try it with your eyes closed," Ezra said.

I hadn't realized he'd stopped tapping. He stood on the other side of his table, leaning into it with both hands as he watched me.

When I hesitated, he lifted his chin toward the chest. "Try it."

I looked at the pins in my hands, turning them in the light

as I went through it in my mind once more. My eyes closed and I felt for the lock before me, my brow wrinkling as I worked. This time, they didn't release easily, and my hands fumbled for the right angle until I pulled them out and tried again, relying on only the feeling of the pins to guide me. It took longer and I had to go through the steps more slowly, but when the latch released, my eyes popped open.

I looked up at Ezra and he gave me a subtle nod, the slightest smile pulling at the corners of his mouth. There was a faint, delicate crack in the cold, hard exterior of the silversmith. And I was becoming more and more curious what lay beneath it.

A wide grin broke on my lips. That was all the approval I'd get from him, I thought.

He unclamped the piece of silver he was working and rotated it before the tapping resumed in a steady, calming rhythm. I started again, and as the night drew on, the rising moon filled the workshop with a pale blue light and the sound of dice in the kitchen faded.

The door to Henrik's study opened and closed and I sat up straighter, starting on the lock again. There'd been a different look in Henrik's eyes at dinner that night, an air of respect that hadn't been there before. He was a man who counted on no one. But in this, he was counting on me.

FIFTEEN

E ven I had to admit, the gown was perfect.

I stood in front of the long, framed mirror in my room, running my hands over the chiffon. The skirts swayed from my hips, where the waist was cinched up into a fitted silver bodice that bled into long, sheer sleeves. I buttoned the last of the closures at the back of my neck. The chiffon was embroidered with glittering thread that depicted drifting leaves. It was a gown that looked fit for a ball with sea nymphs. The couturier had done his best work and now I had to do mine.

The image I saw in the mirror was like looking back in time, to Nimsmire. I was exactly what Sariah had raised me to be. A finely dressed doll ready to play a role for my uncle. But the image was missing the brightly painted walls of Sariah's home. The polished wood furniture and the colorful rugs that covered the floor. The room that enveloped me was dark and shadowed and the candlelight played on my face until I was almost unrecognizable.

The girl in the mirror tonight wasn't me, I reminded my-self. She was a character in an elaborate stage play that had been going on for my entire life. Tonight, I was Bryn, the refinement of the Roths incarnate.

Beneath the shimmering gown, I was brimming with a dark excitement. There was a part of me that liked the idea of stepping into my mother's shoes. I'd never fit among the gilded shelf of pretty things in Nimsmire. I was a rose with one too many thorns. But here, I had a place. And the more time I spent with the Roths, the more hopeful I was that I could truly belong.

I clasped my shoes before putting up my hair, and then I carefully pulled down a few strands around my face. I didn't look like my mother in the portrait downstairs. I didn't have her curves, but the dress gave shape to where I had none. The color against my skin was like frost, and the raw-cut edges of the chiffon fluttered against my col-larbones, where three freckles were placed in a jagged constellation. I looked more like the woman I'd seen in Fig Alley. The one who'd appeared and disappeared like a specter. That woman was the kind of customer who would have made my mother's tea house an elegant, prestigious haunt among the guild. And if I played my cards right at Simon's, that was exactly what I planned to tell Henrik to sway him.

I draped my heavy, black velvet cloak over my arm and went downstairs. The doors to the study were open and the fire was blazing, as usual. But the man sitting behind the desk was new.

Henrik bent low over his ledger in his fine blue dinner jacket, scribbling with the quill.

"Careful," I said, smirking. "You get a blot of ink on that shirt and we'll never get it out."

His eyes flickered up, running over me, and for a moment, he seemed sad. But the frown on his face lifted as he spoke. "You look lovely."

I smiled. "Thank you."

He abandoned the quill and went to the mantel over the fireplace, taking a small case from between the candles. It opened in his hands and the light shimmered on what lay inside as he came around the desk, toward me.

My lips parted as I laid eyes on the earrings. They were made of a silver so smooth and polished that I could see my reflection in its surface. The metal was cast in the shape of two birds, their wings unfolded in flight and studded with star sapphires.

"They're beautiful," I whispered.

"Well, go ahead." He waited.

I reached inside, picking them up and holding them in my hands.

"They're part of the collection we'll be presenting to the guild at the exhibition."

My eyes widened in wonder. "Ezra made these?"

Henrik looked behind me and I turned to see Ezra standing there, framed in the doorway like a portrait. I stilled, my hands closing over the earrings. His coal-colored jacket fit him like a glove, making his dark features even more striking. He was somehow always buttoned up and clean-pressed, even after working entire days in front of the forge, but *this* Ezra was a masterpiece.

He gave me a side glance, tugging at the neck of his shirt. He was embarrassed and the thought delighted me. I liked seeing him that way.

"Well done." Henrik looked him over with satisfaction. "I think we just might pull this off."

He looked between us, but I was still staring at Ezra, waiting for him to look at me. He didn't give in, keeping his eyes on the desk until I opened my hand and fixed the earrings to my ears. The birds dangled from a delicate silver chain, hanging just below my jaw.

Finally, Ezra's gaze dragged over my shoulder, up my throat, and I turned, giving him my back before the color rushed to my cheeks.

"Bryn, you'll excuse yourself toward the end of dinner." Henrik went over the plan again. "The door to Simon's study is at the end of the hall off the salon. You'll see it when we come into the dining room."

I nodded as I listened, still heavily aware of Ezra's presence behind me.

"The desk is against the window, and from what Ezra's told me, you should have no problem with the lock."

Ezra said nothing, but I couldn't help but wonder how Ezra would know. Maybe it had something to do with the reason Henrik was bringing him along.

"You're looking for a name and a date, that's it. Don't worry about the sums. And don't take *anything*."

"I understand."

He came around the desk and sat on its edge, putting himself in front of Ezra and me. "One more thing." He paused.
"I want you to give special attention to Simon's son, Coen."

Ezra stiffened next to me and I blinked, confused. "What?"

"He has a good deal of influence over his father and he's
sure to inherit his merchant's ring when he dies. He'd make
a good match for you and an even better ally for this family."

I could feel the blood draining from my face, leaving me
cold. "You want me to . . ." I wasn't sure I understood. "You
want to match us?"

"Why not? If his son is infatuated with you, Simon will
agree to the patronage with the guild." He flung a hand at
my gown. "You should have no problem catching his notice
looking like that. And despite that temper of yours, I know
you can be amenable."

I was so stunned that I had no clue what to say. The idea
was humiliating. Insulting.

Heat crept up my neck, searing as it climbed. This wasn't
what I thought Henrik meant when he told me he wanted to
bring me into the family business. In fact, this was the very
reason I couldn't wait to leave Nimsmire.

Beside me, Ezra was like stone. The muscle in his jaw
ticked as he watched Henrik with stormy eyes.

Henrik clapped his hands together, as if to dismiss us, but
I stood glued to the floor as he made his way down the hallway. Ezra didn't move, and we stood there, shoulder to shoulder, staring into the fire without a word until he reached up,
fidgeting with his cravat again. He pulled at the satin so hard
that it looked as if it might tear.

"Stop it," I snapped, turning toward him and slapping his hand away.

He flinched as I reached up, tugging at the tie's ends, and when he tried to step backward, I pulled him to me more forcefully than I needed to. I was breathing too hard. My ribs pulled under the construction of the gown and I had to bite down on my lip to keep it from quivering. I was angry. Ashamed of myself. Embarrassed.

Ezra looked down into my face as I unraveled the poorly tied knot and started again, with practiced hands. I drew in a long, measured breath to slow the racing of my heart. I'd tied ties like this a hundred times because Sariah had made me. She'd been training me to dress a husband, and I'd played along because I thought it was an old woman's fantasy. That once I got to Bastian, it would be over. But here I was, being led by a leash to an auction block. Again.

"Did you know about this?" I kept my voice low.

I was terrified of his answer. And even more terrified of the reason it mattered to me.

For once, he didn't take his eyes from mine. "No." The word dragged on a deep rasp.

I blinked back the tears in my eyes and folded the gleaming satin around my finger, pulling the end through. I would throw myself into the fire before I let a single one fall.

When I was finished, I reached into the buttoned collar of Ezra's shirt to straighten the knot. But as my knuckles skimmed over the hollow of his throat, my hands stopped, and I let the back of my fingers move slowly over his skin. More slowly than was necessary.

He swallowed, his chest rising and falling beneath the shirt. I didn't dare look up then. I let my hands slip from his shirt and I brushed off the shoulders of the jacket, steadying myself.

The door to the street opened down the hallway, and the flames in the fireplace shifted violently, lighting Ezra's face. After what seemed like forever, he took a step back and this time, I didn't stop him. He turned on his heel, shoving his scarred hands into his pockets, and I stood there in the empty doorway, fingers tangled together so tightly at the top of my skirts that it felt as if the bones might break.

Henrik stood on the street when I came down the steps, holding open the door. There was no point in arguing. He had a plan and he'd see it through. Tonight, I was Bryn Roth. Henrik's lovely, refined niece who would make an eligible match with the watchmaker's son. Tomorrow, I'd have to dig myself out of that grave.

SIXTEEN

The watchmaker's door was set with a gold knocker cast in a circle of stars.

Henrik rapped four times and I took a deep, steadying breath. I drew my shoulders back and found Ezra's warmth unexpectedly close where he stood behind me on the lower step. Henrik wanted me front and center when that door opened and I put on my most elegant smile, the feeling souring in my gut.

Ezra hadn't spoken for the entire walk from Lower Vale to the Merchant's District. He'd trailed behind us at a clipped pace as Henrik rattled off information about Simon and his son for me to memorize. I pretended to listen, watching the gleam of light on the wet cobblestones and wrapping my arms around myself beneath my cloak.

Henrik straightened his arms, pulling his cuffs into place, and adjusted the hem of his dinner jacket. He didn't look nervous anymore. Excitement lit up his face, transforming his whole demeanor.

Henrik lived in a world made of glass, one that he had a tight grip on. He was always thinking ahead and preparing for different scenarios and it kept him from being surprised very often. Even now, as he waited, he was calm and cool, with no trace of the iron-fisted patriarch that ruled the family and its business. We were about to find out if Simon could be fooled.

The door opened and a servant in a smart black waistcoat stepped back to let us in.

Behind him, Simon was waiting with his hands clasped together and he gave me a genuinely warm smile. From where I stood, I couldn't even see so much as a shadow of the cutthroat man from North End that Murrow had spoken of.

"Henrik." He welcomed my uncle with a polite smile, stepping forward to shake his hand. "I'm very happy you accepted my invitation. Please, come in." He beckoned us inside and I took up my skirts to step over the threshold.

The marble floors were polished so brightly that the light reflected off of them like still water and a wooden staircase with a carved bannister wound up in a spiral above our heads. The home was a beautiful one, fit for the likes of the guild, but Ezra didn't look impressed. He came inside without so much as a glance at the extravagant entry.

"You've already met my niece," Henrik crooned, stepping back as if to present me. He'd been the one to send me to the watchmaker's shop and I wondered now if matching me with his son had been on his mind even then.

"We have." Simon nodded.

"She's recently arrived from Nimsmire where she's been living with my aunt," Henrik said. "You remember Sariah."

There was a brief but palpable pause at the mention of Sariah's name, and I watched the subtle change in Simon's face before the strange expression was lost to the shifting candlelight.

"Of course." He reached for my hand and I set my fingers into his, bowing my head a little. "It's lovely to see you again, Bryn. I trust your watch arrived and is to your satisfaction?"

"It did." I smiled sweetly. "It's such a beautiful piece that I'd be wearing it now if this gown had anywhere for me to put it."

Simon laughed. "Well, I do look forward to seeing it on you." He glanced to Henrik. "She has exquisite taste if I do say so myself."

"She does," Henrik agreed.

"I heard about that terrible business with the smith," Simon said quietly, his eyes running over my cheek. My face burned as he inspected me. I'd tried to cover the last remnants of the bruise so it was undetectable, but you could see it if you looked hard enough.

"Yes. A very unfortunate ordeal," Henrik tsked. "But I don't have to tell you that Arthur doesn't exactly do business like a gentleman."

Simon grunted in answer.

"And you know Ezra," Henrik went on.

"Of course I do. How are you, son?"

I looked at him, surprised. Ezra hadn't said anything about knowing Simon.

"I'm well," Ezra answered politely. He was playing along, too, but there was a stiffness in how he held himself. He was on edge.

"Never one to elaborate, is he?" Simon scoffed.

Henrik laughed. "No, he isn't."

Ezra didn't appear amused, looking between them with an unreadable expression.

"All right, shall we go in?" Simon turned without waiting for an answer, leading us along the wood-paneled hallway.

My eyes studied the closed doors we passed and when we reached a set of two doors with bronze knobs, Henrik made the slightest lift of his hand in their direction.

The study. My mark. By the time dinner ended, I'd need to find a way into it.

The room ahead was aglow with firelight and it spilled out into the corridor as we entered. Two enormous fireplaces sat at either end of a rectangular salon and the papered walls shimmered with a golden hue. Fine furnishings and the gleam of silver trimmings were tucked into every corner, the handwoven rug plush beneath my shoes. Henrik hadn't been exaggerating when he said that Simon had climbed the ranks of society. This home was as fine as any I'd seen in Nimsmire.

A cluster of men was gathered before the fire at the far end of the room, their conversation cutting short as we entered. I suspected Simon had invited them for a second opinion. He wasn't going to agree to a patronage unless he had support in the guild and thought he could win the vote at the exhibition. We were performing for an audience tonight.

Simon cleared his throat. "I'd like to introduce Henrik Roth, his niece Bryn Roth, and his silversmith, Ezra Finch."

My eyes cut to Ezra. *Finch*. I hadn't heard anyone say his full name before and I'd never thought to ask. My hand lifted to one of the earrings dangling from my ears as the realization set in. The birds—they were finches.

"Those are quite beautiful." The man with combed blond hair leaned in close to me, eyes narrowing as he inspected the earrings.

"They're Ezra's work," Henrik said, proudly.

They turned to him, but still, Ezra said nothing. He stood against the wall, looking as if he didn't like the attention.

"What he lacks in conversation, he makes up for in talent, I assure you." Henrik's mustache tilted in a devious grin.

The men laughed, their voices filling the warm room, and I shrank back a little, grimacing.

"I think we would all agree that talk isn't always the best judge of character," I said, looking to Henrik. I kept the smile on my face, but the laughter petered out.

Henrik's grin faltered as I met his eyes, confirming that he understood my meaning. I held more power in this room than I did anywhere else, and I wasn't afraid to use it. If he wanted to use me to get Simon in his pocket, so be it. He was using Ezra, too, putting him and his work on display. But he wasn't going to laugh at his expense.

"Very true." Henrik cleared his throat.

The blond man smiled down at me. "A nice change to have a lady among us."

"Agreed," Simon said. "Keeps us civilized."

The others seemed to almost enjoy my rebuke, but Henrik's eyes turned suspicious as he surveyed me. They drifted to Ezra and back, narrowing.

"I know your work well," one of the men said, reaching out a hand to Ezra. "I don't know if there's a merchant in Bastian who doesn't by now."

Ezra shook it, nodding appreciatively.

Technically, Henrik wasn't supposed to be producing pieces of any kind to be sold in Bastian. His trade was limited to Ceros in the Narrows. But obviously word had gotten around about his silversmith.

Simon snapped his fingers and a woman with a silver tray set with small etched glasses appeared beside us. Henrik took one and handed it to me, meeting my eyes coldly while Simon's back was turned. He was playing his part perfectly, taking care to remember everything I'd told him, but he didn't like being put in his place. It looked like his fangs would drop from his mouth and sink into me at any moment.

"Henrik, I'd like you to meet Peter." Simon waved him toward the fireplace and the smile returned to his lips as he stepped forward.

The sizing up had begun. We were being weighed.

I took a step back as Henrik fell into conversation, finding a place to stand beside Ezra. He had a glass of cava in his hand, and surprisingly, he didn't look completely out of place.

"Don't do that," he said under his breath.

"Do what?"

He took a drink. "You know what. I don't need you to protect me."

I lifted my glass to my lips, staring into the fire. I knew he didn't need protecting, but I didn't like the look in Henrik's eye when he'd spoken about Ezra. Maybe I was angry about what Henrik had said before we left the house. But it wasn't only that. I'd felt fiercely protective of Ezra in that moment.

The room shifted, falling quiet as a young man came in from the entry.

"Ah!" Simon said. "Coen."

The men stepped aside, and I laid eyes on Simon's son. He was handsome and lean, with wide blue eyes and light brown hair that was combed back from his face and tucked behind one ear.

I swallowed down the cava in three anxious gulps, leaving a burn in my throat.

Simon tilted his head toward me, leading his son across the room. I resisted the urge to fidget with my glass. "Coen, this is Bryn."

Coen stopped before me, his appraising gaze studying me from head to toe. It made me feel like a hundred eyes were on me. "I'm pleased to meet you." A small smile lifted on his lips as he raised an open hand between us.

I took it. "Pleased to meet you," I said, careful to keep my voice even.

He wasn't what I'd expected. When Henrik said we'd make a good match, I'd imagined an older man with enough coin to flood into Henrik's business. But from the looks of him, Coen couldn't have been more than a few years older than me.

"And you remember Ezra," Henrik said.

He stood behind me, his shoulders so straight in his jacket

that it looked like he might bust the seams. "Of course." Coen offered his hand to Ezra next.

Ezra hesitated before he relented, shaking.

Pain woke in my jaw from clenching my teeth. Ezra looked more than uncomfortable now, not bothering to fake a polite smile. He didn't want to be here, but deep down, I was glad he was.

"Coen, you'll escort Bryn, won't you?" Henrik interrupted my thoughts, and I realized the men were already moving to the dining room.

"It would be my pleasure," Coen answered, lifting his arm so I could take it.

I watched Ezra disappear through the archway ahead of us and as soon as he was out of sight, I forced another smile in Coen's direction.

Henrik was deep in conversation, his warm congeniality a useful skill in a situation like this. But I could feel half his attention still on me. He was playing the long game.

This was about more than catching Coen's attention. My uncle wanted to be tied to his influence by blood. All the pieces had been placed by him. In time, they'd be played by him, too.

SEVENTEEN

It was like coming home.

Simon's lavish dinner table was set and attended by a throng of servants beneath flickering candles atop crystal chandeliers. Their light danced, casting broken colors over the walls, and the warmth of the room grew with the booming voices as we gathered around the chairs.

Coen pulled mine out, waiting for me to sit, and I resisted the urge to laugh, thinking about my first night at the Roths, when no one could be bothered. The customs I'd grown up with in Nimsmire were everywhere in this house and they were familiar to me. They felt safe. But I was reminded of that caged feeling I'd always had beneath my great-aunt's roof. It wasn't until that moment I realized I hadn't felt it since I got to Bastian. Not until tonight.

"I've heard very good things about the development of your trade in Ceros." Simon kept his back against his chair as he turned the conversation toward Henrik.

Henrik looked comfortable with the attention, but it made my stomach twist into knots. The closer they looked at him, the more fearful I was that he would do or say something foolish. "I'm glad to hear it. I have no doubt it will do just as well in Bastian."

I grimaced. It was too forward. Too strong for leisurely business talk, but Simon seemed to forgive him the mistake. "It's been a tough business with Holland. I think we all agree that filling the hole she left behind will be a good thing. But there will be more than one candidate for her merchant's ring." He shot a glance to one of the other men and I took note. These men were going to hedge their bets and if Simon offered patronage, it would be to someone who could benefit them.

Henrik nodded as the servant filled the glass beside his plate. He exuded confidence. "Those jewels are only a glimpse of the collection we're curating for the exhibition."

"Working on a collection already." Simon smirked. "You must be very sure of yourself."

I looked for malice in the words, but there was none. Simon seemed to like Henrik's arrogance.

My uncle shrugged. "Ezra's skill gets stronger every year. He has a very bright future."

"Very lucky for you," Simon replied, lifting his glass. That time, I sensed an insult, but I didn't know what it was.

Coen leaned in beside me, taking my attention from their conversation. "My father says you've only just come to Bastian." I could hardly hear him over his father's booming voice.

"I have," I answered with a smile. "I grew up in Nimsmire with my great-aunt."

"To my knowledge, you're the first Roth not to be raised here in Bastian."

He was right. If he'd grown up in North End and Henrik and Simon had once moved in the same circles, he would know. But it struck me as bold that he was using my last name so informally. There wasn't even a hint of disapproval in it and I liked that. Coen had the same quality his father seemed to—sincerity.

He looked at me directly when he spoke, simultaneously putting me at ease and on my guard. "And how do you like it here?"

"It's . . . big. Much bigger than what I'm used to."

When the servant reached us, Coen fell quiet, allowing her to pour before he continued. "Why didn't you stay in Nimsmire?"

I picked up my glass, holding it before me. "Our family's business is here. My uncle needed me."

Coen liked my answer. He lifted an eyebrow, nodding. "Family is the only enduring legacy, isn't it?" He said it with such conviction that it made me look up.

The house and the decorum may have been familiar, but this watchmaker and his son weren't like the finely bred men I'd known. They were frank and to the point and I couldn't help but like them. Henrik, I thought, might actually do well among their ranks.

Coen spoke on about his father, recounting how he'd built their trade from nothing in North End. It was clear he respected Simon. Loved him, even. The thought made me feel regret for what Henrik was here to do, and for my part in it. But there was more at stake than my uncle's ring. If I was going to get out of a match and claim my stake, I didn't have the luxury of listening to a guilty conscience.

Ezra sat at the end of the table across from Henrik, cutting into his pheasant gently and taking small bites. He was the only thing out of place in the scene, answering the men's questions with one word here and there and going rigid every time he caught himself about to put his elbows on the table. He looked so miserable, I almost felt sorry for him. But more concerning was the fact that I couldn't stop looking at him. My eyes drifted in his direction every few minutes and though he pretended not to notice, he did. Every time my gaze landed on him, he rolled his shoulders or ran an anxious hand through his hair. By the end of the first course, it was falling into his eyes.

The chatter grew louder, and the merchants turned their focus to him. They asked questions about his latest work, a set of complicated molds he'd casted for diamond brooches that they'd heard about. He was polite, but wholly uninterested, and Henrik was growing visibly more frustrated by the minute. Ezra wasn't playing his part and I found myself cringing as I thought about what Henrik's reaction might be when we were done here.

"He's . . . an interesting fellow, isn't he?" Coen said suddenly, and I realized he'd caught me staring.

I dropped my eyes, pushing a roasted potato around on my plate. "I didn't realize you knew each other."

"Yes, for many years. He grew up in my father's workshop."

My fork scraped the plate. "He worked for Simon?"

Coen nodded. "Learned to cast in our forge. He apprenticed here until he was twelve or thirteen years old."

I'd put together that there was history between Ezra and Simon, but it had the air of a secret. "How did he end up with Henrik?" I asked, before thinking better of it. I was being too obvious, but I couldn't help myself. I knew next to nothing about Ezra.

My question appeared to make Coen curious. He eyed me, most likely wondering why I didn't already know. It was a misstep and he'd noticed. "Your uncle's cunning got the better of my father."

Simon's quip suddenly made sense. There was more to that story than anyone had let on, and this was all the explanation I would get. "I'm sorry," I said. "Simon seems like a good man."

Coen shot a look down the table. "He is. Our beginnings were humble, but he's made his own fate from a very unlikely set of stars."

The look in his eye was one of pride. I wondered if his mention of their humble origins was his way of putting the cards on the table. He had to know that Henrik had a match in mind. His father might even be in on it.

"I don't think I have to tell you about *our* stars," I said.

He smirked. "No, you don't. Everyone in this city knows your family's name." He leaned in closer. "But you don't look like a Roth."

I could feel my cheeks blooming red. "Is that why you agreed to sit beside me?"

Coen laughed. "I sat beside you because I was told to. But I'm glad I did."

He didn't hide his meaning. Henrik hadn't expected it to be difficult to catch Coen's attention, and he'd been right. Maybe the young women of the Merchant's District hadn't been willing to turn their eye to someone with his past. Or maybe the craftsman in him liked pretty things.

"Soon, I think." Henrik's voice broke the spell between us. "The tea house has been sitting for far too long. It's time."

My gaze moved back down the table. Henrik was relaxed in his chair, his plate empty except for a bite or two just like I'd instructed. He could take orders, after all.

"I'm thinking to open it in the next couple of weeks."

I could feel the glower on my face and even I was surprised by the storm it stirred in my chest.

"Couldn't hurt your chances with the guild," Simon said. "Every merchant in Bastian drinks tea."

I took care to divert my eyes, picking up my glass and taking a long sip. Henrik was going to open the tea house. My mother's tea house. I didn't know why it surprised me or why I was so angry. I'd been the one to suggest it, after all. But he'd brushed me off when I gave him the idea, and now he was taking the credit.

"Are you all right?" Coen noticed the change in my countenance, his brow wrinkling.

"I'm fine." I looked across the table. Ezra was looking at me for the first time since dinner began. He'd noticed, too.

"But I hear you've got your own bit of new business," Henrik said. "The *Serpent*."

I took another bite, listening. The *Serpent* was the ship he and my uncles had been talking about.

Simon leaned back in his chair, a smug look on his face. "Ah, yes. Violet Blake was set to take that contract, but you know we couldn't have that."

"Certainly not," Henrik agreed.

Recognizing the name, I leaned toward Coen, keeping my voice low. "Who's Violet Blake?"

He smiled as if he thought I was joking. "Really?"

"Really."

"She's a gem merchant on the rise in Bastian. Her trade has been taking up every spare coin to be had in this city and she's caught the disfavor of the other merchants because of it. If she'd secured that contract, she would have held more power than any member of the guild. But my father outbid her."

"I see." That was how the guilds worked—a teetering balance of alliance and competition.

"A good thing, too. People should know better than to get on my father's bad side." He said it with humor, but Murrow's account of Simon resurfaced in my mind. According to my cousin, anyone who crossed Simon found themselves floating in the harbor.

One of the men asked Coen a question, drawing his attention, and I set down my fork. If I was going to get to the study and back while the men were still eating, I needed to make my move. Now.

My hand tightened around my glass of cava, making its contents swish, and I tilted it just slightly, eyeing the edge of the table.

"Oh!" I tumbled the drink toward me, spilling it into my lap with a gasp.

Coen sprung from his chair, offering me his napkin, and I took it, pressing it against the chiffon firmly to soak it up. "Here." He reached for me, but I got to my feet, stepping out of his reach.

"I'm so sorry," I cried, trying to blot at the stains.

"Kit." Coen waved over a servant, but I lifted a hand, stopping her as she hurried toward me.

"I'll be fine."

"But your gown," the girl fussed. "Let me help you, miss."

"It's only a little bit of cava." I laughed. "Can you show me to the washroom? I just need to clean up a little."

Henrik watched me with a flicker of mirth in his eyes as I followed her out, my skirt clutched in my hands. She led me back the way we'd come, toward the salon, and I let out a relieved breath when I saw the doors of the study.

"Here you are." She stopped in front of the entrance to the washroom. "Are you sure you don't need my help? I'm happy to . . ."

"I'm sure." I waved her off. "Just a clumsy hand. Thank you."

She reluctantly gave me a small bow before she scurried back to the dining room, and I pushed the washroom door widely open, letting it close on its own with a loud creak.

When I could no longer hear footsteps, I moved down the hall-way silently. The study door was closed, but the handle turned easily, and I slipped inside without a sound.

Darkness enveloped the small room, the fireplace cold, but the full moon outside filled the window with a soft glow. I didn't waste any time, pulling the two extra pins from my hair and coming around the desk, my skirts swishing. I sat in the tufted leather chair and felt for the opening with the tip of my finger before fitting the pins inside.

The sound of my breath was loud in my ears, my pulse pounding. The pins inside the lock weren't as nimble as the ones in Henrik's chest. At the first attempt, they refused to slide into place.

I tried again. The pinheads scraped along the grooves as I moved them, and when I felt the first pin lift, I exhaled, going for the next. One after the other clicked and I bit my bottom lip as finally I turned it, opening the lock.

The bronze latch sprang open and I reached into the drawer, feeling for a ledger. I was careful not to shift the papers or sealing wax inside, my small hands delicate with the drawer's contents. But there was no book.

I dropped my hands into my lap, looking around until I saw a closed cabinet on the wall. It, too, was fit with a lock. But this one was different. It was round, with a bigger keyhole, and the latch looked more elaborate.

I closed the drawer softly and locked it, sliding the chair back into place before I crossed the room. I slipped one pin inside, feeling my way along the shaft of the lock. It was similar to the other, but there were more grooves. More mechanisms to manipulate. I swallowed down the pain in my throat, trying to even out my breaths. My hands were slick and shaking.

Once the hairpins were in place, I got to work, stretching my inhales to match my exhales as a sheen of cold sweat appeared on my skin. Any moment, the servant would come to check on me. If the door opened, there'd be no way to hide what I was doing.

I pinched my eyes closed, the way Ezra told me to, and worked the pins with no real rhythm. In fact, I couldn't be sure it wasn't the result of my trembling hands that finally did it, but when the lock opened, so did my eyes, and a small cry escaped my lips.

The cabinet door lifted and I reached inside, thumbing through the papers until I found it—a leather-bound book about the size of the one Henrik always carried. I pulled it out and tilted it toward the moonlight, flipping the pages and reading as fast as I could. I froze when I saw the name in the left-hand column. It repeated over and over in the same handwriting.

Holland.

A silence fell inside of me and I immediately closed the book, sliding it back into place. Henrik had everything he needed. An imminent patronage from Simon, a weapon to use against him, a silversmith to impress the guild, and a niece to use as a bargaining chip.

I closed the cabinet softly and let it lock, slipping the pins into my hair. My uncle knew what he was doing. He'd constructed his path to the guild with an expert hand. But now I had my own bit of leverage.

EIGHTEEN

The city had gone cold and I shivered, pulling my cloak tighter around me as we moved up the dark street. The three of us were no more than shadows shifting on the walls of the buildings, not a single word passing between us since we'd left Simon's. Henrik was walking so fast that I could hardly keep up, and he waited until we'd passed beneath the archway in Lower Vale before he finally asked.

"Well?" he said, not a single hitch in his step. "Did you find it?"

I clutched my skirts tighter and the sound of my shoes clapped, echoing. There was more than one way for me to draw my uncle's anger. The first was the reproach I'd given him for his comment about Ezra before dinner. I'd known the moment I saw his reaction that it would bear its own consequences, but I wasn't sure when they would come. The other was the ledger.

I'd practiced the words in my head for the remainder of

the evening as I pretended to listen to Coen. His voice had
been no more than a thrumming sound in the back of my
head as I lined up the pieces in my mind. I didn't like being
used, and that's all Henrik had done since I'd stepped into his
house. But the information about Holland gave me a small
bit of power—the first I'd run across since stepping off the
Jasper. And I was going to use it.

"It wasn't there," I said.

Henrik stopped in his tracks, whirling on me. "What?"

I kept myself composed, my fingers twisting into my
skirts beneath my cloak where he couldn't see them. I was
grateful for the darkness as his narrowed gaze found me. "I
found the ledger, but there was no mention of Holland."

Henrik stared at me, his mind clearly racing. One hand
came up, raking through his thick mustache before he pinned
his eyes on the ground. I liked seeing him like that—surprised.
"You must have missed it," he said, almost to himself.

"I checked more than once. If he's doing business with
Holland, he isn't keeping the numbers in the ledger."

Henrik was doing his best to keep his reaction in check,
and I wasn't sure whose benefit it was for. He let a long silence fall between us, but inside, my heart was pounding. Just
when I was sure his eyes would focus in suspicion, he sighed.

"Damn it," he muttered. His breath fogged in gusts as he
set his hands on his hips. He was reformulating. Finding a
new plan in the map of his tangled mind.

"I'm sorry," I breathed, trying to sound as if I meant it.
But this was the first time I had the upper hand and it felt
good to watch him be the one to squirm.

"It's all right. You did well tonight." He set a hand on my shoulder, catching me off guard with the brief show of affection. I stared at it until I realized he was waiting for me to look up. When I did, he gently touched the fading bruise on my cheek. There was a fatherly protectiveness in the gesture.

"I'm tougher than I look."

"I know that." He said it seriously. His eyes moved past me, to the darkness. "I think it's time she got the mark."

I turned, finding Ezra behind us. His suit was night itself, the collar of his shirt and his cuffs glowing. But his face was hidden in the shadow of the archway.

"I want it done. Tonight," Henrik said.

Ezra nodded.

The knot in my stomach returned as I looked between them. He was talking about the ouroboros. The tattoo that every Roth bore.

With that, Henrik turned on his heel, starting up the street ahead of us. Ezra followed after him without waiting for me. I pulled the hood of my cloak up against the wind, watching them grow small in the darkness as my heartbeat finally slowed. He'd believed me. Taken me at my word. And now, he was ready to give me the highest seal of his approval—the mark.

There was a finality in the decision. I could feel it. A point of no return.

When we got back to the house, Murrow was at the tavern and Casimir was at the docks. Even the kitchens were silent as I passed the open doors, heading toward the workshop where Ezra had disappeared. Henrik was already shut up in his study with the fire going, likely working out a new way to secure an advantage ahead of Simon's patronage.

The workshop was colder than it had been the night before, with the embers in the forge only faintly glowing, and when I looked over Ezra's worktable, I could see the finely shaped pieces of silver in what appeared to be delicate leaves.

He dropped his polishing rag over them, as if he didn't like me inspecting his work, and went to one of his shelves to retrieve a small wooden box.

"You sure about this?" he asked.

I untied the cloak from my shoulders, letting it fall into my arms. "Do I have a choice?"

"Probably not."

My pulse skipped unevenly, my eyes going to the inside of my elbow, where the mark would be. I'd imagined it there countless times, admiring the one Sariah had since I was little. It had always felt like a rite of passage. A claim. And that had made my heart swell as a child in a city where I had no clan of my own. I had never even had a future. But here, with the Roths, there was something to build. That's what I wanted to believe.

In a way, I'd longed for the day I'd bear the mark of the Roths. At least then I'd know who I was.

"What will it change, really?" I wondered aloud, my hand tracing where the ouroboros would soon be.

Ezra set down the box. "As far as protection goes in this city, it's the next best thing to a purse of coin."

I absently reached up, touching the cut on my lip that was still healing. The mark is what Arthur had been looking for when I went to collect payment for Henrik. If I'd had it, he wouldn't have dared lay a hand on me. Despite what Sariah had always told me about frocks and jewels, the mark of the Roths was the only real armor I had.

"Then yes. I'm sure," I said, unbuttoning the sleeve of my gown.

Ezra set down a burning candle before he opened the box. Inside, the contents were arranged neatly—a few different-sized needles with flat ends opposite their points, a bottle of ink, and a square wooden block.

He unrolled a clean cloth between us and set the items out in an orderly row, as if he'd done this a thousand times. But I was uneasy, watching his scarred, calloused hands pick up the small paintbrush. He unstoppered the ink, and a sharp smell filled the air as he dipped the little brush inside. He turned over the wooden block next, revealing the ouroboros carved into the other side. Two entwined snakes eating one another's tails in a kind of beautiful knot. He carefully painted the black ink over the design, avoiding the corners of the block, and when he was finished, he picked it up, holding his other hand out. His fingers unfurled before me, waiting.

"Your arm." His deep voice grated in the quiet.

I hesitated before I laid my arm into his open hand and I watched his jaw clench as his fingers wrapped around the place above my wrist. His grip tightened around my forearm as he turned it, and when my knuckles were flush against the table, he hovered the block over me, eyes narrowing before he pressed it to my skin. He rolled it from one side to the other, and when he lifted it, the mark was left behind in a perfect black stamp.

"Don't move," he said, taking time to wipe the block clean.

The ink glistened as it dried and he reached for a needle next, taking hold of my wrist. He leaned closer, studying the back mark and when I inhaled, I could smell him. Cloves and strong black tea.

He glanced up at me from the top of his gaze. "Relax."

"I am relaxed," I said, more sharply than I'd intended. But he was so close that I could feel his breath on my skin.

He gave me a knowing look. "I can feel your pulse."

I felt my face flush warm as I looked down at his thumb pressed firmly against my wrist to hold my arm in place. When I realized I wasn't breathing, I drew in a quick breath, and he suddenly let go.

"What are you doing?"

He didn't answer, walking to the other side of the work-table and crouching down to the crates beneath it. He rooted through a few tools before he stood, a dark corked bottle in one hand and a tiny green glass in the other. He set the glass next to me and opened the bottle, filling it. The smell of rye ignited in the air.

He said nothing as he sat down, but he was waiting, his hands folded in his lap.

I sighed before I picked up the glass and poured the rye into my mouth, managing to swallow without choking. But my eyes watered fiercely, my throat burning.

When I set the glass down, Ezra filled it again. He picked it up and took the rye in one swallow.

I eyed him. I wasn't the only one who needed to relax. Ezra had been wound tight all night. Ever since our conversation with Henrik in the study before dinner.

He set the glass down and picked up the needle. It glinted as he held it over the candle's flame, turning it slowly. Again, he took my wrist in his left hand, but more gently this time. Almost instantly, I could feel the rye bleeding into my veins, warming me against the chill of the workshop.

"It will sting for a few minutes and then your mind will sort of numb to it," he said.

He dipped the needle into the little pot of ink and poised it over the mark, as if deciding where to begin. I could see the moment he made the decision. His shoulders pulled away from his ears, his fingers tightening on my wrist. The first prick sent goose bumps running over my skin and I resisted the urge to pull away from him. He waited patiently for me to still before he continued, bringing the tip of the needle down in a steady rhythm.

I grit my teeth as the sting slowly grew into what felt like fire and I tried not to clench my fist. Ezra didn't seem to notice, so focused on his work that after a few minutes, it was almost as if he'd forgotten I was there.

I studied his face, watching the corners of his mouth. His sharp jaw was clean shaven, his hair perfectly trimmed around his ears. There was nothing unkempt about him, except for the scars that covered his hands and arms.

"Are those from the forge?" I asked softly, closing my eyes and trying not to think about the unrelenting bite of the needle.

"Yes," he answered, leaning closer.

I inhaled the smell of him again, this time, on purpose. My heart was still racing, but it wasn't the needle I feared. It was the fact that I liked him touching me. I liked that he was close.

But Ezra was as much a mystery to me as he was a magnet. He had the respect of the family. The adoration of Henrik. The loyalty of Murrow. But what I couldn't decipher was what Ezra thought about the new horizon of the family or my place within it.

I'd sat across the table from him at dinner, watching every time he stiffened, feeling it every time his eyes drifted to me. I knew when I had a man's attention, but this was different. Ezra had been careful to keep his distance and just when I thought I saw a glimmer of something in his eyes, it was replaced by the emptiness that seemed to live there.

"Coen said you used to work for Simon," I said, hoping that my curiosity wouldn't make him withdraw from me.

He took longer to answer this time, dipping the needle again. "I did."

Something warm slid down to the crook of my elbow, and I looked down to see blood pooling in the hollow. Ezra picked up the cloth and firmly wiped it clean before he started again. I stared at the bright red blot on the white fabric.

He was right. After a few minutes, the pain hadn't left me, but it didn't strike an ache in my stomach each time the needle came down, and I softened under his touch when I realized that he was doing his best not to hurt me. His movements were precise and deliberate, and he was quick about it.

"How did you end up here, then?" I asked.

"A game of dice."

"Dice?"

"Henrik won me off of Simon in a game of Three Widows."

My fingers curled into my palm and a soft burn ignited between my ribs where my heart was. That's what he'd meant when he told me he'd lost enough in a throw of the dice.

"How old were you?" I asked, more softly.

He sat up, dipping the needle. "Twelve, I think. Eleven? I don't know." He kept his attention on my skin, wiping the blood as it continued to drip.

He'd answered my questions easily, striking a different tone between us than the one I was used to. I didn't want to tempt fate with another.

He started again, and I barely noticed. My skin was mostly numb. I watched the dwindling flame on the candlestick as he worked in silence, so intently focused that it seemed as if he'd forgotten I was there once more. It was the same look he had when he was at the forge.

Once he was finished, he sat up, setting the needle down and wiping the length of my arm until the running ink and the last of the blood were gone. I winced at the burn, but when he turned the mark up to the light, my eyes widened. What had looked like a messy blot of black was a perfect rendering of the stamp. The snakes' eyes looked up at me, wide and open.

"It's . . ." I said, my voice drifting.

"What?" Ezra's brow furrowed.

I felt a smile pull at the corners of my mouth and I shrugged. I wasn't sure what I'd meant to say. There was a comfort I felt at having it there, despite the sting that was raging on my reddened skin. As if the last week had been a dream and I was only now waking in Bastian.

The ouroboros wasn't just the mark of the family or the thing that tied me to them. It was something more. Something I could feel inside me.

He dropped the rag, folding his arms on the table. "Why did you lie to Henrik about the ledger?"

I froze, every muscle in my body tensing. "What?"

"You lied. Why?" He waited. It didn't sound like an accusation, but I couldn't make out the look in his eye. He was calm. Too calm.

When I didn't answer, he guessed. "You feel guilty."

My mouth twisted to one side. The words were on the tip of my tongue. For some reason, I wanted to tell him the truth. But I couldn't bring myself to say it.

"You liked him—the watchmaker," he guessed again.

How did he do that? He always seemed to see beneath things.

"And the watchmaker's son?" he said.

My eyes snapped up, the heat flashing over my face.

The breath he'd inhaled poured from his lungs. He reached up, rubbing the heel of his hand over his jaw. "I'm sorry. I shouldn't have said that."

"Then why did you?" I asked, staring at him.

He didn't have to say it. The reason had been all over his face in the study before the dinner. He didn't like the idea of matching me with Coen. And he hadn't liked seeing us together at Simon's, either. But the most unnerving truth was that I was relieved that he didn't like it.

I stared at his hand on the table, my eyes running over

the pale silver scars that covered his skin. Almost every moment since I touched him in the study, I'd felt the echo of
him. Before I even thought about it, my hand lifted, moving
across the table.

Ezra went still, watching as I traced the pattern of scars on
his hand with the tip of my finger. When he didn't pull away
from me, I threaded my fingers into his. For a fleeting second,
a pained look broke the surface of his contained exterior. He
stared at our hands, a hundred thoughts passing over his face
in an instant.

"Bryn." He swallowed. "Henrik has plans for you." He
searched my eyes. "You understand that, don't you?"

I didn't care. The only thing I cared about right then was
the way my skin was set aflame every time he looked at me.

"That's part of all this." He looked around the room.
"That's how it is here."

Slowly, I stood up off the stool, sending my skirts cascading around my legs, and I didn't let him go as I leaned over
the table. Ezra stayed perfectly still as I moved closer and I
watched his lips part. His eyes dropped to my mouth and the
seconds pulled, dragging time until I couldn't breathe. Until
my heart was beating so hard that I could feel it in every inch
of my body. I wanted so badly for him to kiss me.

The hinges on the door creaked and Ezra pulled his hand
from mine, dropping it from the table. We turned to see Tru
standing in the doorway. "Henrik wants to see you."

Ezra looked stunned for a moment, closing the box of
inks clumsily and standing.

"Not you." Tru looked at me. "He wants *her.*"

NINETEEN

The warmth of Ezra's touch was still alive on my fingers, but now his hands were stuffed into the pockets of his trousers, the muscles in his arms clenched tight.

Tru had already disappeared, leaving the door to the workshop cracked open, and I could smell Henrik's pipe all the way from his study.

"Better go," Ezra said, but his voice was strained. He looked like he was about to come out of his skin.

I let my hand drop from the table, hurt curling between my ribs. I felt foolish suddenly, standing there in a glittering gown in the dim light of the workshop, my cards laid out on the table. Ezra still held all of his.

My slick palms clutched my skirts as I started toward the door, but Ezra's voice stopped me. "Wait."

I turned back, the tightness in my chest loosening just enough to let me breathe.

Ezra looked at me before he went to the shelf on the wall,

picking up a small round tin. He walked toward me, holding it in the air between us. "Twice a day until it's healed." His eyes dropped to my arm.

I looked down, only just remembering it was there—the ouroboros. It stained the inside of my arm, where the sleeve of my gown was still cinched up to my elbow. I could hardly feel the reddened skin, every inch of me humming with how close Ezra had been only seconds ago.

He turned away and went to the table along the wall, leaving me standing there alone. I wanted him to say something. Anything that would make it feel like he wasn't turning his back on *me*. When he didn't, I pressed the tin between my palms and left him in the workshop.

The house felt empty as I walked down the dark hallway, but Henrik's shadow moved in the crack of light on the floor.

His voice called out as I lifted my hand to knock. "Come in."

The door opened and Henrik stood beside the fire, puffing on his pipe. The room was filled with fragrant smoke, making it look like a scene from one of my great-aunt's oil paintings. His suit jacket was flung over one of the leather chairs, but his white shirt was still buttoned all the way to the neck.

A feeling of dread crept through me, slow and cold. I was afraid he knew, like Ezra, that I had lied. Or he wanted to reprimand me for what I'd said to him at the dinner. Or that somehow, he knew about the almost kiss in the workshop, and the wild tangle of vines around my heart that squeezed tight every time I thought about Ezra.

His attention went to the tattoo that marked my arm and he smiled, coming around the desk to take hold of my wrist. He held my arm toward the firelight so he could inspect it. "Very good," he said, almost to himself.

There was a kind of ownership in his eyes that I didn't like. Something possessive.

"I wanted to speak with you privately." He dropped my arm, going back to the fire.

"All right," I answered.

He motioned for me to sit in one of the chairs, but he remained standing. I couldn't help but wonder if it was so he could look down on me. But after a few silent moments, he changed his mind, taking the other chair and setting one foot atop his knee as he let another ripple of smoke trail from his lips.

"I wanted to tell you that I've thought about what you said."

I waited.

"The tea house. I think you're right."

I could feel a trap somewhere in the words. Something lingering behind what he was saying. He'd already told Simon about his plan to open it and until now, he hadn't said a word to me.

"And you're perfect for the job," he added, eyes sparkling.

I couldn't hide my surprise. "You want me to run it?"

"Yes." He laughed, his white teeth showing. "Of course I do. It was your idea."

My grip on the arm of the chair loosened and I sank back into it. He hadn't cut me out after all.

"You know far more about these things than I do, and it's a good way to get your face and name out there in the Merchant's District. You proved tonight that you're up to the task. You handled those merchants beautifully."

I stared at him, unsure of what to say. He was confusing. Rash. One minute he was angry and the next, he was proud. I couldn't keep up with him.

The tender skin on my arm stung as I ran my fingers over the mark. That was what this was about. He was bringing me into the family completely. No more tests.

He opened the drawer of the desk, pulling out a large purse full of coin, and set it down in front of me.

"What is that?"

"You wanted a stake, didn't you?"

"Yes," I said, my voice feeling far away.

"Well, now you have one. That's your copper to start. I expect you to manage it. We'll need the tea house up and running as soon as possible. I want every member of the guild through those doors by the time they vote at the exhibition. Can you do it?"

My eyes lifted. "I can do it." I felt a smile on my lips. It was getting easier and easier to say those words.

Henrik was beaming. "Seems fitting, doesn't it? After all, it was Eden's to begin with. Everyone in this family has a stake, and you're uniquely suited for this one. But most importantly, you've earned my trust, Bryn."

My eyes flickered up, a sick feeling souring in my gut. Behind his eyes, I could see he was thinking about the dinner, where I'd smiled in my pretty gown for the watchmaker's son. Like he'd told me to. I'd played his game and now he was giving me my prize.

I was getting what I wanted, but I wasn't proud of how I'd earned his approval.

He looked me in the eye. "We've had many legacies in this family, Bryn. Thieves, criminals, cheats. But *this* . . ." He paused. "This will be our last. Just like Eden wanted."

I stared at him as my mother's name filled the study around us. He really did want to legitimize the family. To scrub it clean of fake gems and bribes and dark deals. It wasn't only the family's legacy. It was Eden's. Was this all about her, in the end?

"I had a feeling, even when you were young, that you were special. That you would play a role in this family's destiny. The others weren't sure when you arrived from Nimsmire, but I was. And Ezra . . ." His voice trailed off.

"What about Ezra?" I tried not to let my voice take on an edge. I was learning that Henrik's ear was tuned to my moods. He didn't miss anything.

"He was convinced you wouldn't be able to pull this off. He took one look at you the night you arrived and said you were a waste. That you were too soft for this work." He shrugged. "He underestimated you."

I cringed. The words stung more than I wanted them to.

"It's nothing more than a little competition. I wouldn't worry," he said.

"I'm not competition."

"Sure you are." Henrik stood, going back to the mantel. I watched as he refilled his pipe with mullein and lit it. "He holds a powerful position in this family. It's no surprise that he doesn't want someone else coming in and taking what's his. He didn't want to cut you in. Told me I should send you back to Nimsmire. But he'll come around."

I swallowed hard, careful to not let a single emotion cross my face. I'd known that Ezra didn't want me here. That he didn't like the idea of me gaining any footing in the family business. But part of me had begun to think that had changed. I hadn't thought he'd go behind my back and try to sway Henrik against me.

"Be careful, Bryn," Henrik said, peering at me through the smoke. "Ezra is talented. And brilliant. Most importantly, he has no ambition. But there's one thing that will always be true." His gaze sharpened. "He's not blood."

"You don't trust him," I said, understanding.

"He's hiding something." Henrik leaned into the wall, thinking about it. "Could be a side job, a girl . . . wouldn't be the first time. Or it could be something that matters. Time will tell."

The coil of breath behind my ribs tightened, the seams of the gown making me sore. It hurt every time I drew air into my lungs.

"I just want you to be smart," he said again, more gently. "You are taking your place in this family, and Ezra has tried to undermine that. But I need him if I'm going to get that merchant's ring."

I breathed out slowly. I wanted to ask what he meant, but I was already on the edge of revealing how much I cared. And the last thing I wanted was for Henrik to know what hurt me. "I understand."

"Good." He looked relieved. "Now, you have a lot of work to do, starting tomorrow. You're going to be very busy. I'd like to hear your first report at family dinner."

I nodded dutifully, rising from the chair with my heart in my throat. Henrik went to the desk as I opened the door, but I paused, staring into the dark hallway. I turned back to him.

"And Coen?"

Henrik glanced up. "What about him?"

I let my eyes meet his, careful with the words. "I don't want to be matched."

Henrik half laughed. "You don't, do you?"

"No," I said. "I'll get the tea house up and running. I'll fill the coffers with coin and carve out a place for the Roths in the Merchant's District. But I *don't* want to be matched."

"Then show me," he said, simply.

"Show you what?"

"Show me that you're more valuable to me here than you are in Simon's house," he answered. "And then we'll talk."

I gritted my teeth, fury burning inside of me like the melted silver in the forge. My fingers dug into the soft leather of the coin purse.

"Although Ezra won't be too happy about that," he murmured to himself.

My eyes shot up. "What?"

Henrik rocked forward, standing from his chair with a grunt, as if his bones hurt. "It was his idea to match you with Coen."

All of a sudden, the room spun around me, making me

feel like there was a vicious wind. In my hair. Pouring down my throat. My head was light with it.

Ezra is the one he listens to.

That was what Murrow had said. Because Ezra *was* brilliant. He had a mind that knew how to bend and shape things, like his silver. In the last few days, I thought I'd found some kind of shelter in the silversmith. A hiding place. But he was making bets against me. He was using me like the rest of them.

"And Bryn?" Henrik looked up once more. A soft smile was on his lips. "You really did look beautiful tonight."

I clenched my teeth so hard that my jaw ached and I closed the door with the heavy purse clutched to my chest. The blackness of the hallway hid me as I climbed the stairs, back to my room. This was all a fixed game to Henrik. The guild. The tea house. The match with Coen. Like a trio of dice flung from his hands. And everyone in this house was playing. Even Ezra.

I pushed into my room and shut the door, too loudly. I paced, pressing my cold hands to my hot face, and when I caught my reflection in the mirror, I stopped short, sucking in a breath.

There, in the gilded frame, was the image of everything I was supposed to be. Beautiful. Useful. Bendable to everyone's will. The pale gold-and-silver gown had looked like the ethereal garments of a dream in the evening's candlelight. It had done its job, making me the creature of a fairy tale. Now, I looked like a ghost.

I was tired of being looked at. Assessed. Measured and weighed.

I pulled the chair from the table beside the window and clumsily took the quill from the inkpot, not caring if it dripped on my skirts. I scribbled, my heart racing, hand frozen as I signed my name. My eyes went to the ouroboros that now inked my skin. It looked up at me, the shape of it distorting through my tears.

No one was going to give me a place in this family. I had to claim it.

I folded up the parchment and sealed it with wax, turning it over to address the letter to the couturier. There was one more garment he would make for me.

TWENTY

It felt like every eye in the Merchant's District was on us. Murrow and I walked down the center of the street, shoulder to shoulder in the morning light. He was more than a head taller than me, hiding me in his shadow, but our boots hit the cobblestones in tandem, like the beat of a drum.

I could feel it—the quickening in my blood. I was finished trying to prove myself to Henrik. To all of them. But I still had something to prove to myself.

I belonged here. I didn't know if it was the tattoo on my arm or the secret about Holland I'd concealed from my uncle, but finally, I felt like one of the Roths.

Sharp gazes followed Murrow and me as we passed, more than one person averting their eyes when I returned their stares. I found that I liked the feeling of power it gave me. There was a delicate balance to be struck if we were going to find a place for ourselves in the guild—a fine line between influential and dangerous. We had to be both. The merchants of Bastian needed to fear us, and at the same time, want to be associated with us. And there was a chasm between where we stood and where we needed to get to if we were going to win the vote at the exhibition.

I'd spent my life pretending to be a soft thing with petals. A thing that grew in the sunlight. But I was beginning to wonder if I was a creature of darkness, like the faces that sat around my uncle's table. If that warmth beneath my skin when I saw eyes drop from mine had been there all along.

Ezra pushed his way into my mind like he had over and over since I'd opened my eyes that morning. The straight line of his mouth. The hardness of his jaw. He'd been gone before dawn and his seat at the breakfast table had been empty. But what Henrik had said still cut deep.

I replayed the moment, my fingers threaded into Ezra's, the brush of his breath over my skin as my mouth drifted toward his.

I'd wanted him to meet me halfway over that table and kiss me. To show me where he stood. But that was before Henrik offered me the tea house and before I knew that Ezra had been working against me.

I wasn't a fool. Henrik's claims could have been his attempt to keep me cradled in his palm. But something about it felt true. Since I'd arrived in Bastian, Ezra had made it clear he didn't want me there. And even if I'd caught his eyes on me more and more in the last few days and the space between us felt alive with hunger, I wasn't sure that meant I could trust him.

What I did know was that my growing feelings for Ezra had let me blur the lines between what I'd come here to do and what everyone else had planned for me. Now, I was glad he hadn't kissed me. I didn't know if there would have been any coming back from that.

"Where was Ezra this morning?" I asked, keeping my eyes ahead as we walked.

"Probably running an errand for Henrik." If Murrow had the same suspicions about Ezra that Henrik did, he didn't show it.

I caught a glimpse of us in a shop window as we passed. Murrow was watching me, but I couldn't help myself. "He disappears a lot."

The slightest hitch in Murrow's step revealed that he wasn't buying my attempt at sounding indifferent. "What exactly happened at that dinner last night?"

"What do you mean?"

He looked more amused than concerned, and I took that as a good sign. "When I got back, Ezra was in the workshop. He seemed off. I thought maybe something didn't go as planned. But Henrik didn't say anything at breakfast."

"Nothing happened." I kept my tone light. Murrow had lost what little trust I'd had in him when I learned he was in on Henrik's plot to send me to Arthur's. I liked him, but he wasn't on my side. None of them were. Now, he was mining me for information. The number of cards in my hand was growing by the minute and I liked that. I would need them all by the time I claimed my stake in the family.

We walked a few more steps before we reached the corner of Fig Alley and Murrow finally turned to face me. "Why are you so curious about him all of a sudden?"

"I don't know." I shrugged. "I just can't figure him out."

Murrow studied me with a trained eye. "We all have our secrets. I'd like to keep mine. I'm sure he'd like to keep his." He said it with humor, but there was an undertow of seriousness. It was a warning.

Perhaps he knew it was a strand that would unravel when pulled. Murrow cared about Ezra. He was protective, even. But I didn't doubt whose corner he'd be in if it came down to it. He would do exactly as he was told.

When we reached the tea house, the sun glinted off the seeded glass like a reflection on still water. The faded sign looked down at me and the scratched gold paint of my mother's name almost seemed to glow.

Murrow pulled his hand from his pocket and a short gold chain hung from his fingertip. On its end was strung a long, slender key that looked as if it hadn't seen the light of day in years. I watched it swing.

He extended his arm toward me, setting it into my hand with a mischievous grin. "Go ahead. It's yours."

The same smile pulled at my own lips as I fit it into the rusted lock. It creaked as I turned the key, but when I lifted the handle, it didn't budge.

"Let me." Murrow waited for me to step aside before he leaned into the jamb, jostling it on its hinges until the latch gave.

The bottom of the door scraped over the marble floor as I pushed it open. I held my breath as I stepped over the threshold, into the darkness of the tea house. It was cold but missing the damp air that hovered between the walls of the Roth house. A layer of dust covered every surface, softening the room, and I looked up to the ceiling. Gold chandeliers studded with quartz points hung over a long, carved wooden bar, backed with tall mirrors. Behind the glass, the silver was separating from the backing, and fine hand-painted teacups and teapots lined the shelves beyond the tables that covered the floor. It was as if the place had been frozen in time, untouched since the last time my mother stood between these walls.

I turned in a circle, a sense of awe consuming me.

"What do you think?" Murrow swept the dust from a nearby stool before he sat on it, crossing one ankle over the other as he watched me.

I grinned. "It's perfect."

And it was. I could see it—the candles lit and the steam pouring from the teapots. The colorful frocks and jackets and twinkle of crystal. The tea house was as beautiful as it was useful. There wasn't a sliver of gossip that didn't make its way through the doors of the tea houses in Nimsmire. If Henrik wanted to enter the society of the merchants, this was as good a door as any.

"I do remember Eden," Murrow said, suddenly. His voice wasn't humorous anymore. It matched the softness in his face. "I remember this place, too."

I slid onto the stool beside him, leaning into the counter. "No one ever talks about her."

"They don't like to talk about what happened."

"The uncles?"

He nodded. "Things changed when Eden died. Henrik, Noel, and my father changed, too. It's haunted Henrik for years, and I think he hoped you would replace her somehow. Fix what he couldn't."

I watched him fidget with his watch chain. He was being more candid than I would have expected.

"You think he feels responsible." I tried to get to the bottom of what he was saying.

"He *is* responsible. For all of us," Murrow said. "That's not a burden I would want to bear."

It occurred to me that Murrow wasn't just talking about Eden. In a way, he was defending Henrik. Trying to help me see why he did the things he did. Why Murrow followed his every command.

I had no doubt of Henrik's love for the family, or his sense of duty to its business. If I had to guess, I'd say he'd cut off his own hands before he let anyone harm us. But that didn't mean I wanted to be his puppet.

"What happened to the man who killed my parents?" I asked quietly. It was a question I had never asked, but I sensed that Murrow would give me the honest answer.

Murrow's voice lowered. "My father, Noel, and Henrik left that night after we got the news about what happened." He paused. "They didn't return until almost dawn. My father's shirt was soaked with blood. I didn't see it until I left on the rounds that morning—the door."

"The door?"

Murrow swallowed. "The door of the house. It was red."

I shifted uncomfortably on the stool.

"They'd painted it. With that man's blood." He swallowed. "People told the story for years. Everywhere I went— the tavern, the docks, North End, the piers . . . everyone told that story."

That sounded like the Roths I'd heard about. And it was probably the reason no one wanted to lay a hand on anyone with the tattoo. It was the family's reputation that protected us, the same way people feared going against Simon.

"People think they're heartless," he said, "I've heard more than one person say that Henrik has no soul. But his heart is this family. All of us."

"I guess that makes sense. He has no family of his own."

Murrow shrugged. He was holding back now.

"What? He does have a family?"

He hesitated. "There are rumors. Who knows if any of them are true."

But the look on his face told me that he didn't think it was just gossip.

"What about your mother?" I asked. "What happened to her?"

"Figured out pretty quickly that she wasn't cut out for this life."

I frowned. "I'm sorry."

"Can't really blame her," he said sincerely.

Murrow finally let go of his watch chain, crossing his arms over his chest as he drew in a tight breath. He looked over my head. "There's still one problem, you know."

I followed his gaze to the chandeliers. "What's that?"

"Who's going to take tea at a tea house run by the Roths?"

I'd had the same question spinning in my mind since I'd left Henrik's study the night before. It would take time for people to warm up to the idea of Henrik in their ranks, but he wanted the tea house open before the exhibition. More than that, he wanted the voting guild members in these seats before then. This tea house was my way out of a match with Coen and I'd told him I could do it. But I wasn't sure how.

My gaze skipped over the worn velvet backings of the chairs and the intricate mosaic floors until I caught my own eyes in the grand hanging mirrors. It didn't matter how much he tried, Henrik was never going to be one of them. Not really. His shadowed past would follow him for the rest of his life. But maybe that was where the opportunity lay. In that fine line between influential and dangerous.

"Maybe . . ." I murmured, my thoughts coming together as I spoke. When I looked at Murrow, his head tilted to the side inquisitively. "Maybe it's not *just* a tea house."

TWENTY-ONE

Y ou want to *what?*" Casimir gaped at me.

The people filing into the merchant's house stared at us, but behind him, Murrow stifled a laugh. He was enjoying this.

"Dice," I repeated.

It was perfect. Three Widows was the guilty pleasure of nearly every one of my great-aunt's high-society friends, and I'd watched from the darkened hallway many nights as her parlor filled with finely dressed merchants for a drunken night of throwing dice for coins and gems. It was the dirty little secret everyone knew about. And I was betting the highbrow merchants of Bastian were no different.

"It makes sense," I continued, perfecting my pitch. I would need it to be rock solid by the time I went to Henrik. "The tea house will be proper enough to entice them but just scandalous enough to keep them coming back. It will be . . . unexpected."

"How is that a good thing?" Casimir argued. "We need to give them what they know, Bryn. What they're comfortable with."

"If we do that, they won't come. They'll see it as low-landers trying to put on airs. But if we act like Roths, they will be intrigued. They won't be able to help themselves." I laid it out again. "It's a tea house. The finest of tea houses, with exotic brews and the hand-painted porcelain. But it's also a dice house. Right in the middle of the Merchant's District. No back rooms and secret games. It will be both. At the same time."

Casimir stared at me.

"They'll love it. Trust me."

"It's an insane idea." Casimir exhaled sharply. "Have you talked to Henrik about this?" He shot a glance to Murrow.

I squared my shoulders, drawing his gaze back to me. "He told *me* to get the tea house open and to get the guild members through the doors. This is how I'm going to do it."

Casimir's mouth twisted as he thought. He shook his head.

"This is *my* stake," I reminded him.

"You have to admit," Murrow said, surprising me. "It might be brilliant." I'd thought he had gone along with the idea because he liked it when things were shaken up, but he had my back with Casimir.

"And it might not," Casimir grumbled. "If you screw this up, it's on you." His tone was missing the bite that it usually had. He let his heavy gaze meet mine. A long, tense moment followed before he finally sighed. "What do you need?"

I smiled, excitedly pulling the parchment from the pocket

of my skirts and handing it to him. His eyes ran over the list quickly, his lips pursing.

"That's a lot of gems," he muttered, refolding it and tucking it into his pocket. "You'll spend half your coin on this. Why don't you have Henrik make fakes?"

"We can't do it that way," I said. "This has to be different."

He checked his watch. "Well, it better be quick. I'm meeting Ezra in North End for pickups. He'll be waiting."

He turned into the entrance and we followed until he broke off on the second aisle, where the gem merchants were housed. I watched him disappear into the crush of people and Murrow led me farther up the main artery of the merchant's house, looking back every few steps to keep an eye on me. The crowd parted before him, recognition in their eyes. Lower Vale and the Merchant's District weren't the only places the faces of the Roths were known.

When he turned again, he reached out, pulling me in front of him so I could make my way into the next aisle. The smell of earth and spices was thick in the sea air, the stalls filled with baskets and wooden bowls that carried everything from smoking herbs to medicines to barrels of infused vinegars.

When I found the stall I was looking for, I jerked my chin, signaling Murrow in my direction. The wide table was covered in muslin-lined baskets filled with tea leaves in every color. In each one, a wooden scoop was half-buried, and the fragrance filled my head with a thousand memories of Nimsmire.

The tea merchant was a frail-looking woman with hard

eyes rimmed in thick lashes. She blinked up at me, instantly
curious. "And what can I do for you?"

"Ten pounds of yearling, please." I pointed to the largest
of the baskets, where the black tea was nearly overflowing
onto the table.

She slid off her stool with a grunt, shuffling to the end
of the stall. She worked quickly, guessing the weight almost
exactly as she set the bag into the scale. When she had two
five-pound sacks, she tied them closed with a length of twine.
"Twenty coppers," she croaked.

"I'm not finished," I said, still looking over the baskets.
"Do you have any argon's whisper?"

Yearling was the favorite in Bastian, but it could be found
in anyone's kitchen at home. There had to be more than dice
to draw the snakes of the guild from their holes.

Her brows lifted, her hands stilling on the sacks of yearling. "Argon's whisper?"

"Yes." I took the lid off another basket, inspecting it. "It's
a red tea with—"

"I know what it is, child." She almost laughed. "What do
you want with a tea like that?"

I looked at her, confused. "I want to buy it. Five pounds.
And five pounds of white willow as well, if you have it."

She stared at me blankly for another moment before she
turned, giving us her back. "Argon's whisper and white willow." She hobbled to the table behind her, prying the sealed
lids off of two small black barrels that sat behind the others.
"Haven't had a request like that in quite some time. Usually
sell these to the traders headed up north."

That was exactly what I was counting on. Eden's Tea House would be unlike any other in the city. And if I was going to turn it into the heart of the merchants' society, I had to give people more than one reason to return.

Beyond the stall, I could see Casimir's head drifting through the crowd several aisles up. He was making his way from one gem merchant to the next, his trademark scowl heavy on his face. If Murrow hadn't spoken up for me, I wasn't sure he would have gone along with my plan. I could only hope that Henrik would, too.

I blinked, going still when a face drew my attention to the opposite wall of the merchant's house.

Ezra.

He walked quickly beneath the high windows, the collar of his jacket pulled up so it hid half of his face. But his gray eyes were stark in the muted light. He shouldered his way past the aisles, headed for the far wall.

My attention trailed back to Casimir, who was speaking with a merchant. Whatever Ezra was doing, he wasn't in North End like Casimir had thought. And he wouldn't expect to see any of us here, either. We'd all been given our duties for the day that morning and the merchant's house wasn't on anyone's list.

Ezra stopped at the end of the aisle, glancing back over his shoulder, and my eyes narrowed. His stern face was even darker than usual as his gaze darted over the crowd. As if he was looking for someone. He waited briefly before he made his way to the steps leading up to the balcony that overlooked the trading floor. When he reached the overhang, another figure was waiting. A man.

Curling black hair stuck out beneath a cap, but when he saw Ezra, the man's face turned slightly. My brow pulled. It was Arthur. The man from pier fourteen. The man who'd hit me.

An unsettled, sinking feeling woke in my stomach as I watched them. Why would he be meeting with Arthur?

Arthur gestured toward the door that led outside and Ezra followed him, disappearing. The bright windows glinted where they looked out over the water.

Maybe, I thought, he was on one of my uncle's errands. But Henrik had revealed he didn't trust Ezra and I doubted he'd send him to meet with Arthur on his behalf.

It was more likely Henrik was right. Ezra was up to something.

"Bryn." Murrow's voice lifted over the resounding noise of the merchant's house and I tore my eyes from the windows, looking up at him.

He was studying my face, half smirking. "You all right?" His gaze lifted to the balcony. "What is it?"

"Nothing." I swallowed, forcing a smile. I dug into the pocket of my jacket for the coin purse Henrik had given me, opening it.

I lied without thinking, and it took a second for me to realize what I was doing. Protecting Ezra. But if Henrik was telling the truth about him working against me, then Ezra didn't have any loyalty to me. I didn't owe him any in return.

Murrow looked confused, still scanning the scaffold overhead, but I kept my head down, counting the coins.

The woman held out a hand, waiting, and I dropped the copper into her palm. She checked them twice and when Murrow took up one of the sacks, she hissed. "No, no, boy. That's not how we do things." She dropped the coins into a chest behind her. "I'll have it brought over." She took a quill and a torn piece of parchment from the counter, looking at me. "Where should I have the tea delivered?"

"Eden's Tea House. In the Merchant's District," I answered, still distracted by the gleam of light on the windows overhead. "On Fig Alley."

Her brow furrowed and she lifted the quill from the parchment before she even began writing. "I don't know a tea house by that name."

I pulled up the hood of my cloak, smiling. "No. But you will."

TWENTY-TWO

Coen's reply to the message I'd sent him had been waiting for me at breakfast.

Ezra made an appearance at the table, but everyone was distracted that morning. Henrik, with the collection he was preparing for the guild; Murrow, with the extra work that Henrik had passed off to him.

Even Ezra was clearly preoccupied with something and I wondered if it had anything to do with him meeting Arthur. I'd kept what I witnessed at the merchant's house to myself, but I still wasn't sure why.

Ezra didn't acknowledge me as I took my seat and picked up the message sitting beside my plate. He had been more elusive than usual, returning home long after everyone was asleep and starting his work at the forge early each morning. I couldn't help but think he was avoiding me after what happened in the workshop.

I broke the seal of the message and opened it. As much as

I didn't want to admit it, the watchmaker and his son were the only real connection I had to the Merchant's District and its influential members. Somehow, Simon had climbed the rungs of society's ladder despite his less than pristine past, and if I was going to get Henrik to take my match with Coen off the table, I needed to ensure the same for the Roths.

Coen's invitation to tea was exactly what I'd hoped for when I wrote to him. But when I set the envelope down and Ezra saw Coen's seal in the wax, he stood from the table, not even finishing his food. I watched him disappear through the door and when I glanced back at Henrik, he was watching him.

I'd let Ezra distract me before, but there was too much on the line now. He'd caught Henrik's attention and that was a risk I couldn't take.

There was also the matter of him trying to match me with Coen. I didn't want to believe it was true, but if I was honest, it was my pride keeping me from considering it. If I were Ezra, maybe I'd have done the same. His place in the family was delicate and his lack of shared blood made him the most vulnerable. Another member of the Roths coming in was a threat. Maybe he thought it was one he couldn't weather.

So why was I keeping his secret about being at the merchant's house? I wasn't willing to answer that question, even to myself.

Simon's workshop was a stone-glazed building that was half-cloaked in morning fog and tucked inside the east corner of the Merchant's District. The streetlamps still glowed in the thick haze though the harbor bell had already rung. Coen had asked me to come to the workshop, and the request wasn't without intention. He, or perhaps Simon, wanted me to see the family business. It was all part of the same song and dance I'd seen play out before. Young, eligible woman available for a match, wooed on connection and potential. But I had no intention of marrying Coen or being the bridge between Simon and the Roths.

The door opened to a young woman in a waxed canvas apron. She had a monocle fit to her face and the gold chain glistened as she let it drop into the palm of her hand. "May I help you?"

"I'm here to see Coen," I answered.

She gave a hesitant nod and I climbed the steps, letting the hood of my cloak fall back. The girl waited for me to untie it before she took the cloak and hung it on a hook. "One moment."

The workshop was clean and organized, with bright light streaming through the high windows. It was nothing like the gloomy, tattered workshop at the Roths', where a film of soot from the forge and the furnace covered everything in sight. The sharp, high-pitched strike of metal echoed down the stone hallway and the sound of work being carried out behind the walls filled the building. On the wood paneling before the entrance hung a painted portrait of Simon in a brilliant red jacket, a gold watch clutched in his hand as if he was reading the time.

Coen appeared a few minutes later, still buttoning his jacket as he made his way up the hall. He was smartly dressed, but black ink stained his fingertips, like he'd spent the morning with a quill in hand.

"Bryn." He smiled warmly. "I was very happy to receive your message last night."

He turned, waiting for me to fall into step beside him as he showed me up the hallway. I slipped my hands into the pockets of my skirts, casting a glance through the open doorways we passed. Smiths and gem cutters were busy over worktables, shaping rounds of silver and gold that would become watch casings and finishing the chains that would attach to them. Simon's watches were traded at the finest shops and worn by important merchants even in Nimsmire. He had built a name for himself and it had been enough for the gem guild to forget his origins. But it was his son Coen who would inherit the kingdom he'd built.

He watched me as I inspected the workshop. It wasn't the burden shouldered by an unappreciative son, I thought. Coen was proud of who they were.

"I've had them set tea for us," he said, gesturing to the sunlit room ahead. "If you'd like to join me?"

"I would," I answered.

The sitting room was draped with luxurious silks on either side of the towering windows and the travertine mantel that framed the fireplace was an almost-translucent white. The room was likely used for meetings with other merchants and guild members. He wanted to impress me.

A beautiful tea set was already laid out on a low table before two plush chairs and I took one without it being offered. My informality seemed to put Coen at ease. He took the seat beside me and leaned back into it, dropping the rigidity of his posture.

"You said you had something to discuss with me," he said, lifting a hand to the woman standing in the corner of the room.

She immediately made her way to us, setting the small silver basket over the lip of my cup and pouring in one long, steady stream. The smell of the tea was pungent, an expensive heirloom leaf likely brought in from the crofters up north.

When she was finished, I picked up the saucer, setting it in my lap. "You've made quite a place for yourself here in the Merchant's District."

Coen was flattered. It was almost too easy. "We have. My father has a brilliant mind for business."

"You admire him," I observed. It was evident every time he brought him up. He worshipped Simon.

"What's not to admire? He built everything we have from nothing."

I'd made the right decision in lying to Henrik about the ledger. I was sure now. Simon was still feared and the stories about him proved him to be dangerous. Giving Henrik leverage against him would only put the Roths at risk. Simon was still doing dirty business on the side, but who wasn't? Coin was coin and we all needed it if we were going to keep the lives we'd built. For now, their secret was safe with me, but I'd use it if I had to. That, I realized, made me more like Henrik than I wanted to admit.

I stared into my tea, lost in the idea.

"You come from a family who takes pride in their name, too," he remarked.

I looked up at him. "I do."

"Except for Ezra, I mean."

I set my teacup onto the saucer, trying to read him. It wasn't the first time he'd brought Ezra up in conversation and that was strange. What did he care about the Roths' silversmith?

"Ezra told me Simon lost him in a game of dice." I said it offhandedly, but watched Coen's face carefully.

The faintest flicker of something passed over his expression, but it disappeared before it fully materialized. "That's how the story goes."

"Were the two of you friends?"

Coen's eyes shifted away from me. "Sure. We were the same age and he practically lived in my father's workshop while he was apprenticing. We grew up together, in a way."

"Do you think his work is enough to sway the guild on the merchant's ring?"

Coen thought about it. "There's one thing that's not up for debate. Ezra is a rare talent. It's a talent the gem guild needs if the Trade Council of the Unnamed Sea is going to hold its sway over the Narrows and everywhere else. They would be foolish not to give Henrik the merchant's ring." He paused. "There's not a day that goes by when my father doesn't regret that game of Three Widows." He said it on a laugh, but it was restrained and taut.

"Is that why he hasn't made a decision about Henrik's patronage?" I ventured into delicate territory, hoping my candor wouldn't put him off. We didn't have time for cordiality.

Coen only smiled wider. "He has yet to make a final decision."

I took a slow sip of tea, letting the silence drop between us. I wanted to know where he'd go with this thread of conversation. Eventually, he bit.

"I hope that doesn't disappoint you," he added, taking up his cup.

"That's not why I'm here, actually."

"It's not?" He looked genuinely surprised.

"No. I came to ask for your help with something."

Now he was curious. He leaned forward, setting his teacup down again before he propped his elbows up on his knees. "All right."

"I'm opening a tea house next week and I'd like you to come as my guest."

"Ah." He folded his hands together. "The infamous tea house."

My brows lifted. "You've heard about it?" That was good. Very good.

"Word about a tea house that throws dice isn't exactly a *boring* rumor. But I didn't know you were behind it."

"It was my mother's," I said. "Her stake in the family. Now it will be mine."

"Eden Roth." He said her name with a tone of reverence. "I've heard about her, too."

"And?"

He looked me in the eye. "My father admired her. More than admired her, I think."

"I didn't know he knew her so well."

Coen shrugged. "They were all in the same circles back then. A lot has changed."

I watched as he swirled the tea in his cup. "That's why I need your help," I said, turning to face him. "I won't dance around it. Your family's place in the guild has gained you the respect of the Merchant's District. And I need the tea house to be filled with those merchants when it opens if we're going to get their votes at the exhibition."

It was a bold thing to ask when there was no agreement about patronage or marriage made between our families. In fact, if anything, it would be a favor.

Coen studied me. "And what will I get in return?"

"My friendship." I leveled my eyes at him, not blinking.

Coen smiled, leaning into the arm of his chair conspiratorially. He considered for a moment before he looked up at me. "I suppose that's quite a fair trade."

TWENTY-THREE

I sat at the table in front of the single window in my room, writing by the waning light. The columns were already filling with numbers for the tea and gem purchases, and in the next few days, they would be joined by commissions for linen and art and candles, along with everything else that would be expected in a tea house.

I deducted them, one by one, from the coin Henrik had given me. I didn't just need to show him that I could open the tea house, I had to show him I could run the ledgers. In that regard, for once, Sariah's teachings were of use in this house. Watching her over the years, I'd learned how to keep books and handle trade. I'd even learned how to strike deals and talk down prices.

I eyed the stack of parchment beneath the ledger, where my handwriting was half-hidden beneath several sheets. I'd written pages and pages to Sariah since I'd arrived, but I had yet to send a single message to Nimsmire. I wasn't even sure if they were letters anymore. The writing was disjointed and confused, broken up by stories about Tru or questions I had never thought to ask. About my parents. Henrik. Her life in this house. But the longer the message became, the less sure I was that I would ever send it.

I set down the quill and leaned into the high back of the chair, watching the street below. The lamps had already been lit, the storefronts of Lower Vale shut up tight. My all-consuming work with the tea house had won me some freedom from my uncle's prying eyes and expectations. No one asked questions when I left the house or returned at odd hours. It was something earned, I'd realized. Henrik was giving me a length of rope to see what I'd do with it. If I wanted that rope to extend further, I needed to tread carefully.

The sound of steps trailed up the stairs and I watched the mirror, eyeing the darkness of the hallway behind me. I was beginning to recognize the sound of Ezra's gait. It was missing the lazy rhythm of Murrow's or the quick punch of Henrik's. Ezra moved in a deliberate, cautious manner and every time I caught the sound of it, I instinctively inhaled, searching the air for his scent.

I'd heard him return that afternoon from wherever he'd disappeared to, but I had yet to see him. The sound of his work downstairs had filled the house, and though I'd been tempted, I hadn't ventured into the workshop.

I watched the open door from the corner of my eye, turning slightly as his shadow moved in the hallway. I bit down onto my lip, changing my mind a hundred times before I finally said his name.

"Ezra?"

The shadow stopped. It stayed there for so long that I thought maybe I had imagined it. But then it was shifting again over the floorboards, in the opposite direction. A moment later, Ezra's face appeared in the open doorway. The top two buttons of his shirt were undone, his hair falling across his forehead. He looked tired.

"I haven't seen you in a couple of days," I said, closing the ledger in front of me. "Where have you been?"

He leaned one shoulder into the doorframe. "Working." It was as vague an answer as he could give. But I wasn't the only one who'd noticed Ezra's absence. Henrik had been asking questions, too.

The words were on the tip of my tongue—a warning. If Ezra wasn't careful, he was going to make Henrik his enemy. Maybe he already had. And that worried me more than what my uncle had said about Ezra trying to get rid of me. The sting of him playing me still smarted, but I didn't want him to be the recipient of Henrik's wrath.

"Murrow says the tea house is almost ready," he said, a little too formally. The ease we'd found with each other the night of the dinner was gone now. I supposed that was best, but I smiled unsteadily. I didn't like how uncomfortable he looked. How uncomfortable I felt.

"It is."

Ezra gave me a nod. "Good. That's good." But there was something bothering him. "I'll have the dice for you to look at in a day or two. They'll be ready in time."

I nodded, unsure of what else to say. He'd put a distance

between us since I'd almost kissed him and I didn't know how to cross it. Or if I wanted to.

We stared at each other in silence and his eyes ran over my face, like he was waiting for me to say something. When I didn't, he seemed to make up his mind, sliding his hands into his pockets. "I'll see you." He turned, taking the last few steps to his room before the door opened and closed.

I put my face into my hands, breathing through my fingers. I had questions. Many of them. I wanted to confront him about Coen. About his plans to get rid of me. But the more I considered, the more I couldn't deny that I was too afraid of the answers to ask a single one.

His door opened, and I watched in the mirror as the shape of him moved down the hallway. He was leaving again.

I leaned toward the window, watching as he appeared on the street below. The cold came through the glass, my breath fogging on its surface as he walked up the center of the alley with his jacket on and his cap pulled low over his eyes.

I pressed my lips together as he took the corner up the street. My jaw clenched painfully, the race of heat beneath my skin searing the way it had when I'd touched him.

I didn't know if the difference in Ezra over the last few days was because of what had been unspoken between us or because of whatever he'd been doing at the merchant's house. Maybe it was because Henrik was giving me a stake in the family. I couldn't trace the line between the Ezra who had looked into my eyes after the dinner and the Ezra who was shutting me out. One moment he seemed almost jealous of Coen and the next, he was ignoring me.

My fingers drummed on the cover of the ledger, my mind turning until I finally got up. Down the hallway, Murrow's room was dark, the candle blown out. To my left, Ezra's door was closed, but there weren't locks on the bedrooms. It was probably intentional on Henrik's part, but I'd picked up on the unspoken rule that the thresholds were a kind of boundary. The first words Ezra had ever spoken to me were a warning to stay out of his room.

I touched the cold handle and turned it slowly until the door opened. My heartbeat kicked up as I slipped inside and closed it behind me. The room was dark, the curtain drawn, with dappled moonlight speckling the floor beside the made bed in one corner. A rectangular mirror hung on the wall where a shelf held a comb and a straight razor beside a washbowl. Ezra's world was a small one. A simple one.

On top of the dressing table, the three dice still sat. I picked one up, turning it over in my fingers and feeling the grooves as I went to the wall of papers over the crude wooden desk. They were pinned with little brass tacks, overlapping like a tightly woven fabric.

I studied the writing, a subdued and practiced hand in black ink with almost no blots staining the paper. Ezra had notes on everything from accounts to commissions to ledger numbers. It was like looking at a map of his mind, and I wondered if this was the landscape behind his perpetually heavy gaze. Henrik had trusted him with the breadth of the family business, but somehow, Ezra had lost that trust. And if I was going to keep covering for him, I wanted to know why.

I opened the book on the desk, careful not to shift its

position, and thumbed through the pages gently. Numbers. For Henrik, for the workshop, even some payments for the barkeep at the tavern. Nothing about Simon or anything that could be construed as a secret. It was all information I'd heard discussed at family dinners and around the breakfast table each morning.

I dropped my hands into my lap with a sigh, staring at the circle of light painted on the wall. This room smelled like him, and I immediately pushed the thought from my mind. I didn't want to think about his hand entwined with mine or the feel of his breath on my skin. I didn't want to think about his thumb pressed to the soft hollow beneath my wrist. But I'd thought about almost nothing else in the days since.

I pinched the bridge of my nose and stood, but my eyes narrowed when I spotted a small wooden box on the shelf beside the desk. It was closed, but a corner of parchment was crushed beneath the lid. I reached up, taking it down and unhooking the small brass latch. Inside, a stack of letters was filed upright, the wax seals torn open. I took them out, reading the inscriptions until I found one with a name I recognized—Simon.

The letter was featherlight in my fingers as I lifted it from the others and opened it.

Ezra,

I agree that binding our families to protect our mutual interests is wise. I think we can come to an arrangement. I have extended an invitation to Henrik to join us for dinner on Tuesday next and I expect you to attend.

Simon

My lips parted as I read it again.

Bind our families.

The letter shook in my hand as the words carved them-selves into me. Henrik *had* been telling the truth. I hadn't wanted to believe it. A part of me was convinced my uncle had been manipulating me to keep control of everything and everyone. But the letter was addressed to Ezra. Not Henrik. And if he was talking about marriage, he was talking about me.

I refolded the letter and slipped it into the box, closing it with the burn of angry tears in my gaze. I'd looked into his eyes and asked him if he'd known about Henrik's plan to match me with Coen. And he'd lied.

The plan had been Ezra's all along.

TWENTY-FOUR

The couturier hadn't wasted any time with my request, and he hadn't asked any questions, either. The package sat on the center of my bed, where Sylvie had left it, and I stood before the box with a hollow feeling in my chest. The only side I was on now was my own.

The house was filled with the smell of dinner and my uncles were arriving downstairs, making the floorboards buzz with their deep voices as I stared at the package. I'd paid good coin to the couturier, the last of what I'd brought with me from Nimsmire. But it felt like so much more than a garment was inside that box.

I opened the lid, unfolding the thin, delicate paper. The rich, blue tweed looked up at me and I carefully lifted the jacket from inside, holding it out before me. The fabric had been brushed smooth, the stitching flawless along the seams. It was perfect.

Beneath it, a crisp white shirt with pearl buttons was

folded atop a pair of chestnut-colored trousers. I laid the
jacket over my bed and unbuttoned my frock, letting it fall to
the floor and not bothering to pick it up. The cold wind seep-
ing through the single-pane window danced over my skin as
I pulled on the trousers and the shirt, tucking it in neatly. The
suspenders were next, sliding over my shoulders in a perfect
fit, and I buttoned up the vest before reaching for the jacket.

The heavy wool hugged me and it wasn't until that
moment that I turned toward the long mirror. A shy smile
bloomed on my lips, the pink in my cheeks waking as I
studied the reflection. The warm colors and textures of the
clothes were alive in the candlelight. My dark hair was unraveling from its pins and I pulled them out, letting it fall
down over one shoulder.

I looked like a Roth, it was true. But the thing that made
my boots feel glued to the floorboards was that I looked
like . . . I looked like *myself*. Maybe for the first time ever.

There would be no more gowns for dinners and jewels
to catch the eyes of men. There would be no more rouged
cheeks and bashful smiles. I was tired of pretending.

I took my watch from the dressing table and tucked it into
my vest pocket before I opened the door and went down the
stairs. My steps were heavy. Sure. And when I came through
the door of the dining room, the voices snuffed out like the
flame on a wick, every eye landing on me.

I lifted my chin in challenge. My heart had been eaten
with rage since I'd found the letter in Ezra's room and I dared
them to say something. I wanted them to.

My uncles' eyes dragged over me in confusion as I took

my place behind my chair, waiting. Murrow's mouth was dropped open, but he said nothing, clearing his throat. It was the gaze coming from across the table that made me feel warm beneath my jacket. I willed myself to meet Ezra's dark eyes. His hands were gripped on the back of his chair, as if it were an anchor, and his gaze trailed over my hair, down the line of me.

I didn't look away from him, refusing to be the first to blink. I'd barely slept the last three nights, my mind pulling at the threads of everything I knew about the silversmith. It hadn't taken long to come to the conclusion that it was almost nothing. He was a tangled knot. A figure made of shadows. And I wasn't just finished with Henrik's schemes. I was finished with Ezra, too.

His were the hands that had given Henrik his only chance at the merchant's ring, and at times, I'd thought he was my only true ally in the house. But that was the foolish hope of a girl who wore a silly gown. One who laughed at dinners and charmed on behalf of others and followed orders.

I'd left that girl lying on the floor of my room along with her frock.

Beside me, I could feel Murrow watching us from the corner of his gaze. His eyes slid from me, across the table to Ezra in a question.

"Bryn?"

I sucked in a breath, realizing that Henrik was standing at the head of the table, his brow furrowed as he studied me.

"I *said*, what is this?" He grimaced, taking in my jacket and trousers.

I looked down at them. "They're clothes," I said, with more irritation than I should have.

Henrik didn't look fazed. "I can see that. But . . ." When I said nothing, he rubbed across his forehead with his hand. "Bryn—"

"You want me to open the tea house?" I cut him off. "You want me to sneak into studies and pick locks and woo the Merchant's District for you? Fine." I could hear the words coming out of my mouth, but I couldn't stop them. They rolled off my tongue bitterly. "But I'm not going to do any of it dressed up like a doll."

The stillness in the room pulled like a tight string, threatening to snap as Henrik and I locked eyes over the table. I swallowed hard, my heart racing in my chest as his eyes narrowed, the firelight gleaming in them. I was angry. At him. At Sariah. At Ezra. Most of all, I was angry with myself.

But right when I was sure Henrik was going to unleash his fury on me, his head tipped back and he laughed. Loudly. The sound filled the dining room, and it was followed by that of my uncles, who leaned over their chairs, snickering.

I looked up and down the table, confused. Ezra was the only one who wasn't laughing. His eyes were on my face, making me feel like the fire in the hearth was in my chest. Like he was seeing right through every single word I'd spoken.

Henrik pulled out his chair with the smile still plastered on his lips and he gave me an approving nod as he sat. "So be it," he said.

I pulled out my chair warily, sitting. But Henrik's ease had returned. "Now, tell me how it's going."

Still, I watched him, waiting for the mood to turn. I'd defied him. Maybe not outright, but in my own way. And it hadn't been lost on him. But he was all smiles and ease. All twinkling eyes. Not a single one of his perfectly combed feathers seemed ruffled. And that single fact made me angrier than anything else.

"The tea house," he said. "How's it going?"

"It's coming along," I answered, still unmistakably irritated. I wasn't sure what had just happened.

He took a sharp sip of rye. "You'll be open in time?"

"Plenty of time."

I'd set the opening of the tea house for six days and the tradesmen I'd hired were working around the clock to reupholster the seats and polish the chandeliers. In a matter of days, the doors would be open, and my uncle would decide whether I was worth more to him in a match or in the business.

"Good."

The warm light shifted over Ezra's face, making his features even more severe. The first night I'd eaten at this table, he'd been rude. Resentful. And I wondered if that was before or after he'd sold me to Simon as payment.

Simon wouldn't give Henrik his patronage without a price, and I'd been wondering what it was. The proper, silk-wrapped niece of a powerful man was a suitable prize for a merchant with a shadowy past. In fact, it couldn't have been easy to find a match for Coen with Simon's reputation, merchant ring or no.

My teeth clenched as the knife scraped against the plate. Again, Ezra's eyes found me from the top of his gaze. He didn't speak a word at dinner, except when Henrik addressed him directly, but every time I felt a burn trace my skin, I caught his eyes on me. They flitted away the moment they met mine.

When Henrik was finished, he took his glass into the kitchen and Casimir and Noel followed. As soon as they were gone, Ezra dropped his napkin on the table, getting to his feet. As if he'd been waiting for Henrik to leave.

I watched him with a narrow gaze, fury fuming in my gut. He buttoned his jacket and ran one hand through his dark hair, smoothing it back, before he started for the door. He was leaving. Again. And he didn't want Henrik noticing.

I waited for the door to the street to close before I shot up from my chair, leaving my dinner half-eaten on my plate.

"Where are you going?" Murrow spoke with a mouth full of food, his napkin clutched in one hand.

"The tea house. I've just remembered I forgot something." I tried to give him an easy smile, but it was stiff on my lips.

"Do you want me to go with you?"

"No," I said, too swiftly. "I'm all right. I'll be back before the streetlamps are lit."

Murrow hesitated before he took another bite, and I forced my steps to stay even and slow until I'd rounded the corner of the hallway. I snatched one of my uncles' hats from the hooks by the door and slipped out into the alley, closing the door softly behind me.

The street was empty. I looked up and down until I heard the faint echo of boots and I followed them in the direction of the main street that carved through Lower Vale. When I stepped onto the sidewalk, I saw him. Ezra's silhouette flashed before a lit store window ahead and he walked with quick steps, shoulders drawn back.

I waited three breaths before I followed, keeping close to the buildings from a far enough distance that I could duck into the shadow cast by a roof if his gaze drifted in my direction.

The city was changing in the dying light, with lanterns hung in doorways as the last of the wash lines were pulled in and carts were hauled from the market. Ezra didn't stray from the main street until we'd left Lower Vale. He took the turn toward the harbor and I followed, trying to keep sight of him amidst the crowds streaming up from the merchant's house.

Henrik had no business in this part of the piers that I knew of, but Ezra had the look of someone walking a well-worn path. One that was memorized. Wherever he was headed, it wasn't on my uncle's order.

Every few steps, his eyes shot up to the buildings overhead, like he was watching for something. The Roths were always watching for shadows. A lesson that would have served me well before I began to trust Ezra.

When he turned again, I stopped short, tucking myself between two open shutters. He was headed into the piers, where I'd gone the night that I'd knocked on Arthur's door. But Ezra did his pickups at the piers at the beginning of the week.

I let out a deep breath before I followed. The maze of buildings climbed the hill, dark-roofed structures in a tangle of tight alleyways and twisting roads. The farther we walked, the emptier they became, and I was forced to let Ezra pull farther ahead, worried he'd spot me.

He made turn after turn and I picked up my pace, trying to keep track of where we were. I looked back over my shoulder. The water was a cascade of black behind me, the city fading into a blanket of twinkling candle flames. When I turned to the street, a door flew open and a woman came barreling out with a bucket of water, slamming into me.

She screamed, almost tumbling to the cobblestones and I held onto her, keeping her on her feet. But as soon as she righted, she shoved me off. "What the hell are you doing?" She flung the dripping water from her hands and I scrambled around the open door, searching the street.

I shoved past her, my jacket soaked, to the next alley. Ezra wasn't there. The next, too, was empty.

I turned in a circle, my breath fogging in the cold. There was no one. Only the faint sounds of work within the piers and the harbor bell ringing in the distance. I groaned, pulling the hat from my head, and my hair came spilling down over my shoulder.

Ezra was gone.

TWENTY-FIVE

I didn't leave the tea house the next day until dark had fallen. Things were coming together, piece by piece, and with only two days left before the opening, I'd thrown myself into the work. It was a welcome distraction from the ache in my chest. Henrik. Coen.

Ezra.

The Roths liked to talk about family and blood ties, but the truth was that every one of its members was looking out for themselves. I was doing the same.

I stopped in the open doorway of the kitchens when I spotted Murrow. He had the collar of his shirt unbuttoned, his wild hair falling into his eyes—a sign that Henrik wasn't home. Behind him, Sylvie was vigorously kneading a round of dough on the butcher block.

"There you are," she crooned. "Have you eaten?" One of her eyebrows lifted, her lips pursing.

It sounded like an accusation. I hadn't been at a single

meal that day, and my appetite had vanished. Every moment not spent dreading my return to the house had been spent working. I had no desire to sit around a table with the people who'd pretended to care about me only to stuff their own pockets with coin. When the tea house was opened, that would become my home.

Murrow took a bite of an apple as he flipped the page of the ledger he was reading. "Ezra's looking for you." He gestured to the workshop door without taking his eyes from the sums.

I drew in a tight breath, willing myself to cross the hallway. I could hear him working at the forge, but I knocked on the locked door and the clanging instantly stopped. When it opened, Ezra bristled, stepping back.

"Hey." He opened the door wider, and I stepped inside without a word.

Hey. That's all he had to say for himself. I clenched my teeth to keep myself from replying with the string of curses dancing on my tongue.

"Murrow said you wanted to see me," I said flatly.

Ezra let the door swing shut. "Henrik asked me to show you the gems before I start the other sets."

I stared at him, waiting. I had no interest in a conversation. Every moment I stood in the same room with him was like breathing underwater. The only thing more infuriating than his lying was how much it had hurt. That was on me.

I wove between the tables behind him, stopping before the glowing forge. Ezra was working on a small silver box studded with diamonds. Or at least, they looked like diamonds. For all I knew, it was a batch of Henrik's fakes destined for Ceros.

He reached across the table for the small leather pouch that sat atop a stack of books and I flinched when his arm grazed mine. He noticed, holding out the pouch from a distance. I took it, not meeting his eyes, and when I turned it over, three dice tumbled into my palm. Amethyst, moonstone, and rose quartz.

I let out a long, soft breath. They were perfect. Exactly as I'd imagined them.

I picked up the amethyst die between two fingers and inspected it. The stone was polished so smooth that I could almost see my reflection in it, but the corners were sharp and the notches that marked the numbers perfectly round.

My eyes flitted up to meet his.

"Will they work?" He leaned into the table. Again, he was too close.

"Yes," I answered, dropping the dice back into his hand.

The look that flashed in his eyes almost looked like satisfaction. As if he was happy that I liked them. But I didn't care. At least, I didn't want to care. I just needed him to do his job.

"It's a good idea," he said. His voice was so deep that it sent a chill running up my spine. I hated that I felt that way. Like Ezra was an open flame. I could feel its heat anytime I was near him.

"We'll see," I murmured.

I didn't know what Ezra gained by pretending to be on my side, unless there was something he wanted from me. He already knew I'd lied to Henrik about Simon's ledger. Perhaps he thought that if he needed an ally against my uncle, I was it. He was wrong.

"What were you doing in the merchant's house the other day?" I asked.

Ezra's cool manner remained intact, but I could see I'd caught him off guard. He turned his back to me, busying himself with something on the worktable.

"How did you know I was at the merchant's house?" he asked.

"I saw you." I paused. "With Arthur."

"What were you doing at the piers last night?" he shot back. But it was calm. Missing the anger that laced my voice.

So, he *had* seen me.

"Whatever you're doing"—his eyes were as black as I'd ever seen them—"stop. Before you do something that can't be undone."

It was a threat, and the words drew a very clear line between us. We stood there, eyes locked, each of us waiting for the other to relent. But I refused.

It was Ezra who finally blinked. His jaw ticked slightly, but he gave away nothing. "I'll have them finished in time for the opening," he said, tossing the pouch of dice back to the table.

My gaze trailed over the shelves behind him. He spent hours in here every day with the door locked. Alone. I wondered for the first time if there was some clue between these walls about what exactly he'd been up to. Why he'd been going to the other side of the city on nights that he should have been at the tavern or somewhere else.

The words nearly made it to my lips. The questions. The accusations. But I couldn't say any of them aloud without him knowing how much he'd hurt me. And that was a price I wasn't willing to pay.

The door to the workshop flew open, making us jump, and Murrow appeared, out of breath.

"Better get your asses in here." He arched an eyebrow at us, tilting his head toward the study.

Ezra shot a look in my direction before he untied his apron and pulled it over his head. Beneath it, he was wearing his white shirt and suspenders. He worked the buttons at his throat closed as he made his way to the door and I followed.

Henrik's study was like a bright torch in the hallway, the doors open and the fire illuminating the darkness. I swallowed hard as soon as I saw him. He was pacing, one hand clamped on the back of his neck, his wild eyes searching the floor. Casimir and Noel were already waiting.

It wasn't until I found a place to stand in the corner that I saw the message on Henrik's desk. The corner of the parchment was crumpled, the envelope torn.

"That *bastard*." Henrik's voice sounded strange. Like the faraway hum of a storm before it made landfall.

Noel looked as if he was dreading whatever was about to unfold. "Who?"

"Arthur!" Henrik snapped.

"What about him?" Casimir asked, impatient.

"He's secured a patron from the gem guild," Henrik snarled. There wasn't a single face in the room that wasn't covered in shock at that news. A razor-thin silence settled, making the air cold despite the fire.

"Would anyone like to tell me how we didn't catch wind of this?" Henrik spoke through gritted teeth, nostrils flaring.

Casimir's eyes cut to Noel before they dropped.

"They clearly wanted to keep it hidden," Murrow muttered.

"Clearly," Henrik echoed sharply, turning to Ezra. "You were supposed to be watching him."

My gaze slid discreetly to Ezra. Only last night, I'd seen him at the piers. Maybe he was going to see Arthur. A painful twist ignited behind my ribs as the possible scenarios came together in my mind.

Ezra lifted his eyes from the rug. "I was. I am."

There wasn't the slightest trace of anything in Ezra's tone. He stood with a blank face, listening. It wasn't until I saw the hand tucked beneath one of his elbows that I blinked. His finger was nervously tapping against the seam of his jacket.

I'd been right. Ezra wasn't only working against me. He was working against Henrik. If that was true, the smartest thing he could do was ensure that Henrik didn't get the merchant's ring. Perhaps he'd helped Arthur find another patron.

"Then how the hell did this happen?" Henrik spoke so low that his voice cracked.

"I don't know," Ezra admitted.

"You don't know," Henrik scoffed. "Seems there's a lot you don't know lately."

Ezra went still, and for a moment, I thought I could see

fear in his usually composed expression. I could see whatever scheme he had going unraveling behind his eyes.

Noel finally broke the silence. "Who's the patron?"

"Roan," Henrik spat.

"Who's Roan?" I cut in.

"Gem merchant in North End," Murrow murmured beside me.

Henrik's knuckles were white, his grip on the back of the chair so tight that it looked as if he might snap the wood in two.

"We could just take care of him," Casimir said, flinging a hand into the air. "Arthur can't present at the exhibition if he isn't breathing."

My eyes widened as I looked between them. They all seemed to be seriously considering it. Killing him.

"It's too late for that," Henrik grumbled. "If we know about the patronage, then others know too. It will be too easy to pin on us."

Noel nodded in agreement. "You're right."

"No one sleeps until this is fixed," Henrik said slowly.

There was no argument to that. This wasn't just bad for Henrik. It was bad for them all. It was bad for me.

If Henrik didn't get that merchant's ring, he would never agree to forgo the match with Coen. He'd need it more than ever.

He pushed off the chair, turning toward the fire, and Casimir disappeared into the hallway, followed by Noel. Murrow and Ezra were next, and the door to the street opened and closed more than once. They'd been deployed and they'd make their rounds, finding out what they could.

But I had a feeling Ezra already knew what was going on. I also had a feeling it was too late to fix whatever he'd done.

When Henrik came back to the desk, he stopped short, surprised to see me still standing there. *"What?"*

My heart thumped heavily inside my chest as I looked at him. If I said it, there was no going back. There would be no shelter from Henrik's retribution, and there was still a small part of me that didn't want to see Ezra at the other end of Henrik's knife. That part of me needed to be cut out, like a sickness.

"I think . . ." I said, the words like poison on my tongue, "I think it was Ezra."

Every corner of the room suddenly seemed drenched in blackness, the fire reflecting in Henrik's eyes.

"I believe he somehow secured a patronage for Arthur."

"How? Why?" Henrik's rage made the hot room scorching.

I pulled at the neck of my shirt, shifting on my feet. "I followed him to the piers last night. It looked like he was headed to Arthur's." I was breathing so hard that my head was light. "And I saw him with Arthur at the merchant's house a few days ago."

Henrik went so still that he looked as if he were one of the statues in the Merchant's District.

"You were right. He's hiding something," I breathed.

He didn't look angry. He was thinking. The wheels of his mind were turning. And that was even scarier.

"Can you find out what it is?" he asked, his demeanor changing to an eerie calm.

I could feel it—the slow drip of his mind sifting through every scenario. Every possible plan. Each of them ended the same—with a noose around Ezra's throat. But Ezra had made his choices and I had made mine. The tea house was one thing. Loyalty was another. With this, I could slip the noose of a match with Coen. So, I gave him the only answer I could.

"Yes."

TWENTY-SIX

The man in the window had been watching me for hours. I stood with my shoulder tucked into the corner of the brick, watching the bottom of the hill. As the merchant's house closed and the work on the docks wound down, my post in the enclave of a boarded-up window grew cold, but I didn't move. I hadn't since I'd arrived that morning.

Across the street, the door to a smith's workshop was opened to the sea air and the man working inside eyed me. His gaze had grown more suspicious by the hour.

I'd managed to mostly avoid Ezra that morning, keeping my eyes on my plate at breakfast. I didn't want to think about what he would catch a glimpse of if I met his gaze. He always seemed to see beneath the surface. That's what had kept him valuable to Henrik and the others. But now his cunning had worked against him, and when I figured out what he was up to, I'd be the one at my uncle's right hand. A position that would require him to keep me unmatched.

It had taken only seconds to decide whether I'd give Henrik the proof he needed that Ezra was a traitor. To me and to the Roths. In turn, I'd ensure my freedom from the match with Coen and whatever else was planned for me.

I'd slipped out of the house as soon as he got to work at the forge, but it was only a matter of time before Ezra headed back to the piers, like he did almost every day. And when he did, I would be waiting.

My eyes strained in the waning light, fixed on the bottom of the hill. It was the only entrance to this side of the piers so Ezra would have to pass if he came this way. All day, I'd watched merchants and tradesmen and hucksters come and go, waiting for Ezra's tall, lean frame among them. His dark tweed cap, his pristine jacket and shined boots. I would be able to spot him anywhere. But if I was careful, he wouldn't spot me. Not this time.

It was nearly dark when finally, he showed. In a blink, Ezra appeared at the corner of the intersecting paths below, his steady, quick gait carrying him across the opening between buildings.

I sucked in a breath, jumping from my post and squinting as my vision refocused. He kept his eyes straight ahead as he crossed the cobblestones, but I knew the shape of him better than I wanted to admit. It was carved into my mind, the outline of him as he worked before the light of the forge.

I set out, cutting through the alley and walking parallel to his path. I held my breath every time he was hidden behind a building below and let it go every time he reappeared.

I wasn't going to make the same mistake I had last time. The Roths watched the streets and windows around them, but from here, I had a bird's-eye view of Ezra's path.

The streetlamps were like floating orbs in the thick fog that draped the streets of Bastian and I walked with the collar of my jacket pulled up against the wind. The black buildings were giants in the mist, towering over me as I followed the map etched into my mind. I'd studied it late into the night, trying to get my bearings on the intricate layout of the piers.

According to the assignments doled out at breakfast that morning, Ezra was supposed to be at his post in the tavern, but he was on the other side of town. He'd likely paid the barkeep to cover for him if any of the Roths came sniffing. It was the only explanation for how he'd gotten away with it under Henrik's watchful eye. But with Arthur securing a patronage, I could only guess that he'd worked out a deal. One where he wasn't only a silversmith and had a stake in the business.

The incline of the narrow street rose, and I climbed the hill as the sun disappeared over the horizon behind me. In the distance, the harbor was drenched in darkness, making the piers almost vanish against the sky, but I could hear the work carrying on within them.

There was no night for this part of the city. Gem merchants, sailmakers, smiths' workshops . . . the tradesmen and -women of Bastian worked on after the day ended, filling their quotas and inventories for the merchant's house and the traders that would be docked in the morning.

I reached the next opening, stopping short when Ezra

didn't appear on the street below. The swath of lamplight illuminated the alley between the buildings, but it was empty.
He couldn't have turned off without me seeing him, so that
could only mean one thing. He'd reached his destination.

But pier fourteen, Arthur's workshop, was farther up
the street, almost at the end of the claustrophobic cluster of
buildings.

I looked around me slowly, listening. No footsteps. No
voices. There was no one out except for the man with a ladder
on his shoulder, walking from streetlamp to streetlamp in the
distance.

When Ezra still didn't appear, I turned, setting out down
the hill where he should have been. The crossing was empty
when I reached it, but I kept to the shadows, studying the
street. Between this alley and the next, there was only one
building. One door.

Two chimneys lifted on either side of the roof, each
of them billowing smoke. But from the outside, I couldn't
tell what kind of workshop it was. I walked slowly, coming
around the corner until I saw the rusted sign.

PIER SIXTY-FOUR

It sat along the edge of the city wall that served as a
boundary before the foothills began. This wasn't the workshop of an influential merchant or a successful criminal. The
cornerstones were crumbling in places and it hadn't been
painted in my lifetime. No, this was something else.

I followed the tall, windowless exterior until I reached
the lone door. It was almost impossible to detect, covered in
the same chipped, black paint as the brick. There was no han-

dle. Only a row of iron rivets that ran along one side, where the hinges gave the passage away.

I pressed an ear to the cold metal, listening. It sounded like every other pier I'd passed, with the rumble of work going on inside, but the hum of voices was faint.

It wasn't unusual for tradesmen to have more than one workshop, so it could have been Arthur's. If Ezra was working with or for him, he was likely paying him a high sum. Or he'd offered something to Ezra that he couldn't refuse. Maybe even a partnership. Whatever it was, Henrik had been wrong when he said Ezra had no ambition. In fact, I suspected that my uncle had underestimated Ezra in more ways than one. Like I had.

A loud pop sounded behind the door and I jumped back as it flew open, almost knocking me down. A figure barreled out into the alley without looking up from the pipe in his hand and a soft glow lit its chamber as he puffed. I froze, pulling my cap down lower and pressing myself to the black wall, but he kept his eyes on the pipe, biting down on the stem before he started walking in the other direction.

The door slowly creaked closed beside me, but I didn't move as he disappeared into the fog, leaving only the scent of mullein trailing behind him. As soon as he turned the corner, I stuck one boot in the jamb before it could latch.

The sounds inside poured out into the alley and I watched through the crack in the door, trying to see what was inside. A long wall shielded the main floor of the warehouse from view, but lantern light crept down the long passage, painting the darkness in an amber glow.

I slipped inside, letting the door click softly before I followed the wall with my fingertips. The warehouse was warm and smelled of something familiar. Like oak or earth. Firewood, maybe. The passage curved and the lantern glow brightened with every step, until it dead-ended into an opening. I winced against the bright light as I peered around the corner of the wall, my lips parting as I laid eyes on what was inside.

Ahead, the enormous skeleton of a ship was perched up on rafters, like the bare bones of a giant whale.

My eyes jumped over the room frantically. Glass lanterns hung from nearly every post, lighting the long worktables of the men and women busy below. They were laborers, surrounded by metal tools and stacks of lumber and iron bolts in every size. And among them, a head of slicked black hair. A clean white shirt.

Ezra stood at the end of one of the tables, his sleeves rolled up to his elbows. He had a long, flat piece of metal in his hands, and he was scraping it along a slender cut of wood methodically.

He was . . . working. But this wasn't a gem merchant's workshop. Or a smith's. This pier belonged to a shipwright.

TWENTY-SEVEN

I stepped out from behind the wall, watching him with my heart lodged in my throat.

Ezra leaned over the long table, running one purposeful hand down the smooth side of the newly shaped wood. His eyes were focused, his mouth set the way it always was when he was at the forge. He was working. In a shipwright's workshop. It almost appeared as if he was . . . an apprentice.

The moment I thought it, his hands stilled on the wood and slowly, his gaze lifted. As if he could feel me standing there. Ezra's dark eyes were like polished, glinting tourmaline and his jaw tightened as he stared at me. There was something fearful in them. Like he'd been caught. But caught doing what?

I stood there, hands dropped to my sides, my stare unwavering. He set the tool down carefully, thinking. I could almost see his mind racing, but around the room, the work went on. No one seemed to notice me or the sea of cold silence that stretched between Ezra and me.

Behind him, the great frame of the ship towered up into the rafters. It looked like a clipper, the kind my great-aunt chartered from time to time on behalf of Nimsmire's merchants. But what was the most talented silversmith in Bastian doing building ships?

When I dropped my gaze back to the table, he was starting up the aisle toward me with slow steps. I held my breath until he reached me, but as soon as I opened my mouth, he took hold of my arm, leading me down the passage I'd come from. It wasn't until we were hidden in the shadows that he let me go. His pale skin was glistening, his shirt darkened with sweat at the center of his chest, and his cheeks were flushed.

"What are you doing here?" The words were clipped, riding on a tight breath.

I bristled, searching his wide eyes. I'd never seen him like that. He almost looked panicked.

"What are *you* doing here?" I snapped.

"I'm . . ." He ran both hands through his hair, pushing it back from his face. "I'm working."

"For a shipwright?" I said, hoarsely. None of it made sense.

Ezra finally looked at me. Really looked at me. His eyes jumped back and forth on mine, like he was making a decision. "Come on."

He pushed past me, up the passage, and I watched him disappear through the door before I followed. Outside, the man who'd been lighting the streetlamps was gone.

I followed closely as Ezra walked up the alley, toward

the black sparkling water beyond the next pier. His white shirt glowed in the moonlight, rippling around him, and his breath fogged, drifting into the air.

When he reached the bank's edge, he stopped, waiting. The water crashed on the rocks below, foaming white in a curved line. I came to stand beside him, but he was looking out to where the divide between the sea and the sky had vanished into darkness.

"You were the one in my room." He was calm now, the anxious look he'd had before replaced with something that resembled resolve.

I didn't answer. I didn't need to. He'd already begun to put it together. He'd probably connected the pieces the moment he saw me. But I was still lost.

"Ezra," I said his name softly, surprising myself. "What's going on?"

He kept his gaze pinned on the water. "I'm an apprentice for the shipwright. For almost a year now."

It was exactly what it had looked like. And there was only one reason for it. "You're getting out," I whispered. "Aren't you?" The thought pressed down on top of me, making me feel like the weight of the entire sea was on my chest.

He was leaving.

He nodded, falling into a long silence. "When Henrik got the merchant's ring to trade in Ceros," he finally began, "I knew it was only a matter of time before he got one in Bastian. When that happens, I won't have a way out."

In many ways, Ezra was already trapped, but once Henrik was relying on him to produce for the guild in Bastian, he wouldn't just be a silversmith anymore. He would be the Roths' prisoner. This wasn't about Arthur or betraying Henrik. This was about Ezra.

"I knew if I left, I had to have a trade."

"You have one. You're a silversmith."

"No," he said, heavily. "The day I first stepped in front of the forge is the day my life ended. I don't ever want to smith again. Not for anyone." He paused. "Building ships is as good a way to make coin as any. It's one of the few trades that doesn't often cross paths with Henrik."

That's what this was to him. There was no way he could have known as a child, when he first held a crucible in his hands, that he would turn out to be such a rare talent. That powerful men would gamble with his life and he'd be beholden to Henrik forever. To him, his gift was a curse.

"Where will you go?" I asked, my voice small.

"Somewhere that I'm no one."

I turned to look out at the water, pinching my eyes closed. This was a disaster. In the morning, Henrik would be waiting for me to report whatever I'd found out about what Ezra was doing at the piers. But I hadn't imagined it would lead here.

"Does Murrow know?" I asked.

"No one does."

"Well, Henrik suspects you're hiding something."

Ezra swallowed. He'd probably put that together, too.

"I told him . . ." I closed my eyes again. "I told him I thought you were the one who'd helped Arthur get a patronage."

"You *what?*" His voice rose suddenly.

I wiped a stray tear from my cheek. "I'm sorry." I didn't know why I was crying. What exactly the source of the pain inside of me was. I just knew that this hurt. All of it.

"Why? Why would you say that?"

"Because I saw you with Arthur. In the merchant's house," I stammered. "And I was angry with you for lying to me."

Ezra pinched the bridge of his nose as if his head hurt. "That wasn't about Henrik. That was about me."

"You? How?"

"Arthur got wind of my agreement with the shipwright. He was threatening to report it to Henrik and I had to pay him off to shut him up."

I bit down onto my lip, trying to keep it from quivering. If he wasn't behind what happened with Arthur, he was in a world of trouble. Trouble I'd landed him in.

"And when did I lie to you?" He still looked confused.

In an instant, the anger that had taken me across the city to the piers returned. "I know about Coen," I scoffed.

Ezra's brow pulled. "What about him?"

"I asked you if you knew about the match with him."

"I didn't."

I studied him. He looked like he was working hard to understand. Like he was genuinely baffled. "Henrik." My voice caught on his name. "He told me the match with Coen was your idea. That you were trying to get rid of me."

Ezra smiled suddenly, but it was bitter. "Of course he did."

"What is that supposed to mean?"

"He lied, Bryn. He's a liar." He flung a hand to the black, empty sky. "I didn't have anything to do with that. I didn't know about it until you did."

"I saw the letter!"

"What letter?"

"From Simon. He said you wanted to bind the families."

"With the *patronage*." Ezra was shouting now. "I'm the one who had a history with Simon, so Henrik asked me to approach him with the idea. So, I did. That letter had nothing to do with you."

The slow realization sunk in, drip by drip. *Bind our families*. He was talking about business. Not marriage.

"But Henrik said you wanted to get rid of me. That you didn't want me brought in."

"I didn't. I don't."

I stared at him, waiting for an explanation.

He sounded exhausted. "Bryn, you're not like them. You never should have come to Bastian."

"I didn't have a choice." Each word sounded less true as it left my mouth.

Ezra didn't speak, but I could see in his eyes what he was thinking. In a way, I did have a choice. Sariah had made her deal with Henrik, but I'd gone along with it. I'd longed to come here and be a part of the Roths. The truth was, I'd had no idea what I was getting myself into. Not really.

Henrik *had* lied. He'd known how I felt about Ezra. I'd given myself away at the dinner when I'd defended him. But my uncle needed my allegiance to be to him, not to his silversmith. I swallowed against the pain in my throat. He'd told me exactly what I needed to hear to get me to do what he wanted. And I'd believed him.

"You thought the match with Coen was my idea," Ezra said lowly, his hands sliding into his pockets.

I didn't answer. The coil of knots inside of me slowly unwound, making it easier to breathe than it had been in days.

"I'd rather see you leave Bastian than see you with him."

"With Coen?"

"With anyone." His eyes didn't leave mine. For once, they held my gaze, filling the darkness between us with the admission. "But I don't get to make decisions like that. That's not how my place in the family works."

It was the first time he'd acknowledged whatever it was between us. This aching, haunting thing that lived in my thoughts, day and night. It made sense now why he hadn't kissed me in the workshop. He was leaving. He was always going to be leaving.

I stared past him, to the black water. "I'm sorry," I said again. I was a fool. I'd walked right into Henrik's trap and Ezra was the one who would pay for it.

He was quiet for a long time, watching the ripple of moonlight on the water below. "Let's go."

I blinked. "Go where?"

He buttoned the top of his shirt, raking his hair back into place. "To Henrik."

I searched his face, trying to understand. "Why?"

"You're going to tell him the truth," he said.

"No, I'm not."

"Yes," Ezra said, more sternly. "You are. He already doesn't trust me. There's no fixing that. But you can use this to get what you want. Tell him the truth and that will earn you the leverage you need with him. It's worth more than you know." The last part, he said almost to himself.

"But what will he do to you?"

His jaw clenched. "I knew the risk I was taking, Bryn." He started back toward the pier, but I didn't move.

"I'm not going to tell him," I said.

Ezra's eyes narrowed when he turned to look at me. "That would be a mistake."

"I'm the only one who knows what you've been doing here. I'll go to him in the morning and tell him you have a girl in North End or something. He'll believe it. I'll keep your secret long enough for you to finish the apprenticeship and leave." The thought was almost unbearable.

"It might look that simple, but it's not." His focus on me grew sharp. "You don't want to be Henrik's enemy, Bryn."

"I already am." It was true. I'd lost. Henrik had used me in more ways than one to get what he wanted. And now I was going to use his own game against him.

The sound of the water crashed on the rocks in a steady beat and he stared at the shore below, silent for a long moment. "Why would you do that for me?"

"Because . . ." I said, the word hollow.

He took a step toward me. "Why?"

"Because I care about you." I met his eyes, the words swirling on my tongue. But I couldn't say them all. They already lived in the air between us. In every look. Every silence. And if he was leaving Bastian, I couldn't speak them aloud.

He knew the risks, but so did I. We would find a way to get Henrik his merchant's ring and I'd use the tea house to get out of the match with Coen. But in the end, Henrik would lose the only thing that gave him power—his silversmith. And I would lose him, too.

TWENTY-EIGHT

My eyes were open long before the sun began to swell beyond the sea.

I stared out the window, watching the color of the distant water turn from black to gray to blue. Sylvie could already be heard in the kitchen downstairs, but there was only one sound I was listening for: Henrik's study door.

I checked myself in the mirror, smoothing my hair back from my face and straightening the watch chain that dangled from my vest pocket. Ezra and I had agreed on a plan. Before the table was set for breakfast, I would report to Henrik that Ezra had been seeing a girl in North End for the last few months.

According to Ezra, members of the family discreetly entertaining companionship wasn't unusual, but it was something you were expected to disclose. It would put Henrik's suspicions to rest, and still satisfy his assumption that Ezra was lying. Between the tea house opening and the impending exhibition, there would be plenty to take Henrik's attention off of Ezra. I just hoped it would last long enough for him to get out of Bastian.

Ezra's room was silent beside mine, but he was probably awake. He'd returned home well past midnight, his footsteps stopping at my door for three agonizing seconds before they'd continued to his room.

I met my eyes in the reflection, blinking slowly. There was one thing I hadn't let myself think about for more than one moment at a time. If I did lie to my uncle, then Ezra really was leaving. And if he left, he would never return.

I put the thought away, turning toward the door. Ezra was the last thing I'd expected to find when I'd answered Henrik's letter and boarded the *Jasper,* but he felt like a vine that had grafted itself onto me. I didn't want to think about what would happen when it was torn out.

I followed the stairs down to the sunlit first floor and walked straight toward the closed study. I drew in a breath before I knocked and only a few seconds later, Henrik's voice answered.

"Come in."

I let the door swing open. Henrik sat behind his desk, quill in hand as he scribbled. He didn't look up as he finished writing the line of numbers he was working on. I let myself inside, coming to stand before him.

It looked like he was recording sums from one of Noel's reports. At breakfast, he'd hand the ledger off to Murrow, who would check the math. I realized I finally knew the order of things in this house. The inner cogs and wheels that turned were familiar now. Even my uncle's small movements and expressions had lost some of their mystery.

"Good morning," he said, after closing the book. He looked up at me with bright eyes and I immediately relaxed. He was in a good mood. "Looks like Sylvie will have breakfast set in a minute. Did you need something?"

I took great pains to keep my voice even and light. "I have good news."

His eyebrows arched. "You do?"

"I was wrong," I began. "It took some doing, but last night I followed Ezra to North End. He's got a girl there who works in a tailor's shop." Despite my best efforts, I was talking too fast. Smiling too much.

But Henrik's expression didn't change as the information settled in his mind. My heart pounded so loudly that I was sure he could hear it.

"I don't think he had anything to do with Arthur. It would only work against him for you to lose that ring from the guild. It was a stupid thought."

He folded his hands before him, setting his knuckles against his mouth. "That's a relief," he said, lowly.

I gave him a small smile. "It is. I admit, I was angry when you told me he didn't want me here. I may have let that anger get the better of me."

Henrik sighed. "I'm sure you can understand what he means to me. I've raised the boy as my own. Treated him like blood." He glanced up. "My father wouldn't have approved. He would have liked Ezra well enough, but he was never convinced that an outsider could truly be one of us. Still, I built a reputation in this city with Ezra's help. If it weren't for him, I wouldn't have this ring." He unfurled his fingers, staring at the tiger's-eye gem on his right hand. Slowly, he unfolded the other. "And without him, I know I will never be granted the other."

It was something I'd worked out already. Henrik cared about Ezra, but the bond between them was more about business than attachment. He'd had an instinct about the boy, and he'd gambled on that hunch. The dynasty he'd built was on Ezra's shoulders. My uncle's ability with the glass was a well-honed skill, but Ezra's work with the silver was a gift.

"I think you're beginning to understand what it means to be a part of this family, Bryn," he said, getting to his feet.

"I am," I said. And I meant it. I'd finally come to the conclusion that the only rules were the ones I made. I had to choose a side, and I was choosing Ezra's. Even if that meant being left to fend for myself among the Roths.

It gave me a sense of pride to hear Henrik say it though. Ever since I'd walked through that door, I'd wanted his approval. If nothing else, it was the thing I'd been taught to want. But now, he'd given me my own stake. My own destiny. And even if he was a liar and a cheat, for that, I was grateful.

"That's why I'm surprised you would think I'd leave a matter such as this in the hands of an eighteen-year-old girl enamored with my silversmith."

A swift prick lit on my skin as the words left his mouth. "What?" My voice was so thin that I could hardly hear it.

But Henrik's expression didn't change as he watched me. He looked the same as he always did. Calm. Settled. "I like things tidy and timely," he said, the sound of his voice warping in my mind.

The weight on my chest traveled down to my gut. I couldn't draw breath, waking a burn in my empty lungs.

"I don't blame you," he said. "Not really. This is a lesson best learned through failure." He came around the desk, going to the closed double doors that led to the small library.

Before they even opened, I knew what lay behind them.

The doors creaked and sunlight poured into the study, making my eyes sting. Inside, Ezra sat in one of the leather armchairs, his face drawn in a way I'd never seen it. His cheeks were flushed, his jaw clenched as he looked up at me. Behind him, Murrow stood silent, his eyes on the floor.

He knew. Henrik already knew.

He stood in the threshold between us, his arms crossed thoughtfully over his chest. "My silversmith seems to think he can take up an apprenticeship as a shipmaker without me knowing. That was his first mistake," he said. "The second was believing he would get away with it. But I think this little scheme has gone on long enough."

My breath was coming so fast now that my head felt light with it. I could feel the danger in the air, like spilled oil from a lamp. In a matter of moments, it would spark. And more than one of us would burn in the flames.

"Now, I believe this can be fixed," Henrik continued. "It's simply a matter of remembering your place."

The terrifying thing was that I believed every word. Henrik *meant* what he was saying. In his soul, this was who he was.

His eyes went to Murrow. "Leave his hands. He still needs to work."

My lips parted as I looked between Murrow and Ezra. Murrow's face was tense, his nostrils flared, but he gave Henrik a nod. He was the one who would carry out the punishment. A reminder for him, too, I thought.

Henrik took the three steps between us, stopping before me, and a tear slipped down my hot cheek as I looked up at him. "Please don't do this. It was my idea to lie. I—"

"Bryn." He gave me a genuine look of sympathy, setting one heavy hand on my shoulder. "He's not the only one who will pay for the mistake."

I blinked, and two more tears dripped from my chin.

"You will not move from this spot until Murrow is finished. Your punishment is to watch."

His hand squeezed my shoulder a little too hard before it dropped, and he walked out of the study without another word. The door closed softly behind me and when I looked up, Ezra was already getting to his feet. He unbuttoned his jacket and took it off before he threw it onto the chair. I watched in horror as he squared his shoulders to Murrow, who was rolling up the sleeves of his shirt.

Anger rippled beneath Murrow's subdued face. Anger at Henrik, at me, or at Ezra, I wasn't sure. All were justified. No matter which way you looked at it, Murrow had been pulled into the mess whether we'd intended it or not.

I sniffed, wiping at my face.

"Close your eyes." Ezra didn't look at me as he said it.

I obeyed, pinching them shut and sucking in a breath as

a horrible silence stretched out. I waited, a sickness brewing in my belly. When the first sound of a fist striking flesh broke the stillness, I wrapped my arms around myself, my fingers tangling into my shirtsleeves. I held on so tightly that I lost all feeling.

I listened as Murrow beat him, blow after blow landing against bone and muscle, the painful sound dragging in Ezra's throat like a whip stinging me every time I heard it.

All at once, I could feel every frailty. Every single crack in the stones I'd been built with. And there was no armor to protect against a wound like that.

TWENTY-NINE

I have one memory of Bastian *before*. Sometimes it surfaces in the last moments of a dream, sometimes while lost in thought, staring out a window.

In it, I'm small. I'm standing on the stairs and I know I'm barefoot because my feet are cold. I watch the shadows play over the floor as voices in the dining room drift in the silence. And then I see it. A flash of gold in the firelight as my father takes his polished pocket watch from his vest and opens it. It clicks softly as he closes it again, and that's it. There's nothing else.

I've asked myself many times if it's a memory at all. Often, I've wondered if it's the culmination of Sariah's stories, tangled up in the details of the little portraits that line her study shelf. Details that have come together in a kind of patchwork that lives in my mind. And though nothing about the image has ever felt real, it's still been the anchor that's held me to the Roths all these years.

The house down the alley in Lower Vale had lived in my memory as a place of warmth and belonging, even if it was the place responsible for my parents losing their lives. Now, I feared I might lose myself.

I curled up tighter beneath the quilts on my bed, hugging my knees to my chest. It had been a never-ending day, taking hours for the sun to start falling, and the meals at the dining table had come and gone without me there. No one knocked on my door.

I wasn't even there. Not really. I'd retreated in my mind to the night that Ezra came into my room and taught me how to pick a lock. The way his eyes had been focused, the candlelight dancing over his smooth skin. The flash of silver scars on his hands. I'd been angry that night, but it had been the first moment that I felt like someone had seen me. Not the girl I was so good at pretending to be. The one that lived inside of me. It had also been the first moment that the walls around Ezra Finch had begun to appear climbable.

He'd known even then that he was leaving Bastian. His plan had been in motion long before I'd joined the Roths. And even though it had made my heart ache to imagine him gone, it was nothing compared to the despair that tightened around me in knowing he would have to stay. He was a penned, treasured thing. Henrik's precious jewel. And he would never let him go. He would never let any of us go, I realized.

When moonlight finally cast through my window, I

pushed back the quilts and sat up slowly, lighting the candle beside my bed. I wished I had never come to Bastian. That I'd refused to board the *Jasper* and taken my chances with my uncle's retribution. I wondered what Sariah would have said if I'd asked her to keep me. To pass her enterprises into my hands and match me with a fine young man from the lower rung of the port city's merchant families.

The things I'd once dreaded sounded safe now. The allure of the Roths was poison in my veins and I felt withered by it. But Sariah had sent me off without so much as a tear. She'd only handed me that blasted letter.

My brow pulled as I remembered it. When I'd arrived in Lower Vale, I'd dropped it into a drawer, and after days of dreading the moment I would open it, I'd almost completely forgotten about the message altogether. My feet found their way across the cold floor and the top drawer of my dressing table squeaked as I pulled it open. Inside, the letter that Sariah had given me was nestled in the stack of blank parchments.

I picked it up and sank to the floor beside the bed, tearing open the wax seal. The thick paper unfolded and the smell of my great-aunt's potent ink filled my nose, making me so homesick for her house that tears threatened to fall again.

Her handwriting moved across the page unhurried. Steady, like her. But it wasn't the letter I'd imagined, a string of paragraphs that strung together a goodbye. The script was barely two sentences.

Bryn,

The day you were born a Roth is not the day your destiny
began. It began the day you stepped off that ship in Bastian.

Love,
Sariah

Emotion grew thick in my throat as I read the words, my fingers curling around the parchment so tightly that my grip creased the corners. Sariah had found her way out of this house, but only by the grace of her brother Felix. I couldn't help but wonder what price she had paid for her freedom. It was an escape the rest of us would never have. Not as long as Henrik was head of the family.

I glanced up to the closed window. The one Sariah's grandson Auster had climbed out of before he'd left and never looked back. I wondered what had happened to make him walk away with nothing. What had he seen? What had he done?

My eyes trailed across the room to the closed door. I got back to my feet and dried the tears from my face before I opened it. The hallway was dark except for the light coming from Murrow's room.

He was still dressed, poring over the ledgers he'd been asked to check, and he didn't give any indication that he heard me as I leaned into the frame, watching him. He looked younger. Softer, as he sat at his desk, a burning lamp casting its glow over him.

When he felt me there, his quill froze midair. He looked over his shoulder and I cringed when I saw his hands. Both sets of knuckles were raw and red, covered in busted, swollen skin that had been cleaned. Probably by Sylvie. Murrow hadn't bothered to wrap them, perhaps so as not to forget what he'd done. But the torture was heavy on his face. He looked as if he hadn't slept in days.

"He'd have done the same for me," he said, swallowing.

It was such a sad thought that I could hardly bear it. That's what this family did to you, I thought. Murrow had carried out Henrik's orders without question for the same reason that Ezra had struck Tru for ruining the coin count. I suspected it was also the reason Ezra had stood by and watched when Arthur hit me in that alley. There was always a trade being made.

If Murrow had refused to do as Henrik said, Casimir or Noel would have obliged. There was no shortage of respect for Ezra in this house, and even that would have been a mercy. But there was no worse possibility than Henrik doing it himself and Murrow knew that.

"I'm sorry for dragging you into this," I whispered hoarsely.

Murrow let out a long breath. "You didn't." His eyes returned to the ledger. "I knew."

"You knew?"

The quill turned in his fingers before he set it down. "I'd been following Ezra to the piers for a while before I figured it out." He shook his head. "I knew something was going on. And I was worried about him."

"You never said anything? Never asked him about it?"

Murrow shrugged. "Figured he would have told me if he wanted me to know."

That was how this worked. Not asking questions. Looking the other way. He'd kept his mouth shut for Ezra's sake, but he'd known exactly what would happen when Henrik found out. And from what I'd gathered, Henrik always found out.

"Henrik will be gone until morning," he said, quietly. "He's out trying to get to the bottom of this thing with Arthur." Murrow's gaze traveled past me, to Ezra's closed door. It lingered there before he turned back to the ledgers.

It was another unspoken conversation between us. I guessed he knew by now how I felt about Ezra. Murrow may not speak up, but he noticed things. He was always watching. And he might have even known before I did.

He got back to work, falling quiet, and I swallowed hard. He was as trapped as any of us, but Murrow would die a Roth. I had no doubt about that. And even if he was willing to look the other way, his loyalty would always be here. To this house and this family.

I walked slowly past my room, to Ezra's. My hand hovered over the knob for the length of a breath before I turned it, pushing the door open. The small room was dark, but I could see the form of him beneath the quilts on the bed, turned toward the window. He was always this brooding, pensive presence, but here between these walls, Ezra was just a broken body.

He didn't move as I stepped inside, closing his door behind me. His bloodstained shirt was draped neatly over the chair in the corner, where the washbowl was filled with pink water. I could already see the bruises that covered the bare skin of his arms and back, even in the darkness.

The floorboards creaked as I crossed the room and pulled back the corner of the quilt, but he didn't move. I slipped beneath them, into Ezra's warmth, and tucked myself behind him. I could see that his eyes weren't closed as I pressed the line of my body to his. He didn't argue. He didn't shift away from me or stiffen under my touch.

He was still for a long time before he finally reached back, finding my hand. His fingers laced into mine before they closed and he pulled my hand around him, moving my palm to his chest, where his heart was beating hard.

This was what lay beneath the frozen surface of him, only visible in the dark. I'd felt the shadow of it the first time I saw him. The first time he'd looked at me. And now, we were tangled together in a grim, looming fate.

In the days leading up to the dinner at Simon's, I'd been drawn to him like a moth to flame. When Henrik told me that Ezra wanted to trade me like coin to Simon, it wasn't just the deal that had crushed me. Deep down, I'd wanted to believe that Ezra wouldn't give me away. That he'd want to keep me for himself, the way I wanted to keep him.

I pressed my lips to the groove between his shoulder blades and he drew in a deep, measured breath as I closed my eyes. The tears slipped silently over the bridge of my nose, disappearing into my hair.

"I'm sorry," I whispered, my voice fading.

He said nothing, but as the minutes passed, his heartbeat

slowed under my palm. His breaths began to stretch, pulling long until his muscles relaxed against me. I counted them until his grip on my hand loosened and he fell into sleep. The kind of deep, black sleep that let the mind unravel.

I exhaled, closing my eyes. If we were stuck, at least we were together.

THIRTY

That night, family dinner was like any other. And that was the problem.

Everyone arrived before the harbor bell sounded, like always. We stood behind our chairs, the fire roaring in the hearth as Sylvie brought out platters of food and jugs of rye, placing everything in their usual positions on the table. Even the conversations as we waited were the same. Noel relaying a discussion with a merchant to Casimir. A whispered joke soliciting snickers between Murrow and Tru. Anthelia bribing Jameson out from under the table with one of the grapes from the plate of cheese.

When I'd woken that morning in Ezra's bed, he was gone, the linens where he'd slept cold beside me. I came down to breakfast and he was already working. He hadn't left the workshop since before dawn.

I'd listened all day with my stomach in knots as the sound of the hammer on the anvil rang out hour after hour after hour. The sound was an echoing reminder. Ezra had been placed back in his cage, wings clipped.

Henrik appeared at the head of the table and everyone took their seats quietly. I watched, numb, as my uncle unfolded his napkin in his lap. Correctly, I noticed. He was learning.

Ezra was wearing clean clothes with his jacket on, hiding nearly all the cuts and bruises that covered him, but they still marked his face. His silver-scarred hands had been left untouched, as Henrik requested. After all, he needed them if he was going to complete the pieces being added to the collection that would be presented to the guild. The only true evidence of what had happened that I could see was in the way Ezra winced when he leaned into the wall. As if it hurt to touch anything. But his demeanor was the same quiet, withdrawn presence it always was.

Even Murrow seemed back to himself, despite the bright red knuckles that covered his hands. He hovered over his plate as he scarfed down Sylvie's stew, the bites too big for his mouth. My plate went almost untouched.

The rye was poured, and the reports began, starting with Casimir. I stared at one of the lit candles at the center of the table, unblinking as the conversation drew on about merchants and informants and pages of ledgers that had been passed along. An update about Simon's new contract with the *Serpent*. Noel was next, giving Henrik a report on cargo inventories coming in from the Narrows. Murrow relayed rumors overheard at the tavern, only one of which caught Henrik's interest with any real noticeability. Ezra offered accounts of his progress on the pieces he was working on. Some were commissioned by merchants in Ceros, others would be added to Henrik's collection for the exhibition. As each of them spoke, Henrik made note after note in his ledger, planning and scheming, his mind turning.

It was always turning.

"And Bryn?" Henrik said, making my eyes snap up suddenly.

Somehow, the minutes had ticked by and everyone's plates and glasses were empty except mine. I glanced at my fork, realizing I hadn't even taken my first bite of food.

My fingers curled around my fork as I studied my uncle's smug expression. He was sitting on his throne. In control. And we were all playing along.

Across the table, Ezra watched me with a measured gaze. He was perfectly still, but there was a warning in his eyes. A plead to behave.

Temper, Bryn.

Sariah's words echoed the look on his face.

"Your report?" Noel said beside me. He touched his elbow to mine, a discreet gesture that was unlike him. Even he was nervous that I was about to say or do something stupid.

"Yes." I cleared my throat, pulling my small leather book from inside my vest and laying it on the table before me. My voice was uneven as I began, my fingers trembling as I turned the pages. Murrow seemed to notice, leaning forward just enough to half hide me from Henrik's view.

Maybe I could count on him after all.

"We're set to open in two days. I've already ordered the

next shipment of tea and the dice are ready. The tea house itself has come together beautifully, and it being on the cusp of the Merchant's District has already helped to get the word out." I rattled off my rehearsed report. "I spoke with Coen and he said the rumors are flying."

"You spoke to Coen?" Henrik looked intrigued.

"I wanted to invite him to the opening in person. He'll be there and hopefully that will draw others, as well."

He smirked. "Seems the two of you make decent partners after all."

I tried to keep myself from looking at Ezra, but I couldn't help myself. He was staring at the table, his mouth set in a straight line.

"Very good." Henrik nodded. "The more talk there is, the sooner Simon will formally offer his patronage. That bastard won't be able to resist being caught up in the excitement. He's always been one for fanfare."

Casimir made a grunt, catching Henrik's attention.

"What is it?"

Casimir set his elbows on the table, thinking before he spoke. "It's just a lot of coin to invest for something with no guarantee of a payoff. If we want information, we know where to get it. The tavern."

I let the ledger close over my hand, holding my place. "The tavern is filled with traders and ship crews. If you want information about the docks or inventories, that's the place to get it. But if you want the kind of social rumors and indiscretions that give you power over the guild, you have to go to the places they spend their time. Turning this family's business away from fake gems and into a legitimate trade will require you, *all* of you, to become one of *them*—the merchants. This is how you do that." I set a finger on the ledger.

Casimir turned his attention on me. "You really think it can be done?"

"I do," I answered. "I know it can."

I needed this if I was going to get out of the match with Coen. And I'd seen it. Sariah had carved out a place for herself in Nimsmire, and Simon had done it here in Bastian. If they could do it, so could we.

"If she says she can do it, she'll do it," Henrik said, matter-of-factly. But when I looked at him, the expression on his face was cold and distant. It soured in me, knowing what my uncle's disapproval looked like. He wasn't saying he believed in me. He was saying I would do it because I *had* to. Because if I didn't, there would be consequences.

"Simon's patronage will come. I'm sure of it. And then the guild will vote."

"And if they vote for Arthur instead?" Noel asked.

"I'm working on that. But in the end, I will be holding that merchant's ring," he said evenly. "Then a new chapter begins for this family. Are we all clear?"

His eyes moved over the table and one by one, each of them nodded. Even Anthelia.

I understood now why she always seemed to be on the fringes, hiding behind her children and hovering just outside of any responsibility in the family. It was the safest place she could exist, and I wondered if maybe Noel had been the one to put her there. Maybe he'd kept his wife from his brother's reach.

Murrow interjected with something about the barkeep at the tavern, and the conversation drifted away from me. Ezra chimed in here and there, and I could see that there was no tension between him and Murrow. No harbored anger about what had happened the day before. It just was. The thought made me feel sick inside.

I had watched the entire scene of the dinner play out in a kind of petrified awe. In the short amount of time I'd spent in the Roth house, this was by far the most surreal. They'd collectively turned on one of their own who had betrayed them. And now, they'd brought him back into the fold with warmth and care. There was something so twisted about it that I couldn't even think to give it a name.

I'd done exactly what my uncle had asked of me since I came to Bastian, like everyone else. And I'd seen what happened when you didn't. But that only made me more confused about what it meant to sit at this table.

When dinner was finished and my uncles made their way to the kitchens, I stayed behind, watching the fire die down. In only two days, I'd open the doors of the tea house and usher my family into the world of the Merchant's District. If I succeeded, I had to believe that I'd win my freedom. Temporarily, at least. If I failed, I'd find myself married off to Coen in a trade deal between the two families. Either way, Henrik would get what he wanted. That was the only thing I was sure of.

When I finally stood from the table, I headed for the stairs. I didn't want to stand with them in the kitchen and eat cake and play round after round of Three Widows. I didn't want to pretend to be one of them. If the last few days had shown me anything, it was that. But I was also afraid that deep down, I already was.

I set my foot on the first step and froze when I spotted Henrik. He stood in the shadow cast by the kitchen's bright light, leaning into the wall beside the closed workshop door. He stared at it, listening to the sharp ping that rang out every time Ezra's hammer came down on the anvil.

"His focus is back," he said, glancing up at me. "That's good." He nodded.

I didn't know if it was supposed to justify what had happened or if Henrik was just reassuring himself. It didn't seem possible that he could feel guilty. If the words were for me or him, there was no way to tell.

"Now we can get back to work," he said, shoving off the wall. "Whatever that was last night, it's over. Understand?"

The blood drained from my face, making me shiver. So, he did know I'd spent the night in Ezra's room. And that was a complication he didn't want. One he wouldn't allow.

"I made you a deal, and I never break my word," he continued. "You pull this off with the tea house, and we'll talk about the match. But that"—he gestured to the workshop door—"that's not on the list of options."

I clenched my teeth so hard that they felt like they might crack.

"Are we clear?"

He focused his sharp eyes on me until Jameson came running down the hallway and Henrik caught him, lifting the small boy into the air with a wide smile. Jameson squealed, wriggling in his uncle's arms, and I watched as they disappeared into the kitchen, where Murrow's laughter was echoing. But inside the workshop, the strike of the hammer went on.

THIRTY-ONE

It was a magnificent thing to behold.

In only two weeks, the dust-covered tea house was a sparkling, twinkling jewel at the end of a brick-lined alleyway off the main thoroughfare of the Merchant's District. Tucked away just enough to be out of sight but still firmly planted within the boundaries of acceptable society. I couldn't have chosen a more perfect location myself, and I could only assume that had been my mother's thought when she purchased it. It was exactly the kind of thing Sariah would have done. Maybe it had been a plot schemed up between the two of them. I liked that idea.

I stood behind the counter, checking the teacups one more time. The gold rim along the ivory porcelain was hand-painted with tiny bouquets and inside, a single blue flower was unfolded at the bottom of the cup. They were a one-of-a-kind set, likely ordered from one of the port cities in the Unnamed Sea that specialized in such pieces. And after all these years hidden away in a forgotten tea house, they would finally see the light of day.

I set it down onto the saucer and looked out across the floor, where pristine white linens were draped over the round tables and the chandeliers hung like clusters of stars overhead. It was beautiful. So beautiful that even Sariah would be impressed, and that was no small feat.

A soft ache bloomed in my chest when I thought of her. She'd never been a tender caregiver, but I trusted her. And I was realizing more by the day what a truly rare thing that was. Here in my ancestral home, in a house with my own flesh and blood, I felt alone. But I'd always known that in her own way, Sariah was in my corner.

Outside, more than one passerby stopped to look through the windows, where the name of the tea house was painted on the glass in a bright gold. EDEN'S TEA HOUSE. But every time I saw a figure appear, I had the briefest thought that maybe it was Ezra.

I hadn't spoken to him since the night I'd climbed into his bed. After Henrik's warning, I'd kept my distance. He'd kept his distance from me, too. Over the last several days, he had put his hands back to work and was doing as he was told. And every time I almost knocked on his bedroom door or went into the workshop to catch a glimpse of him, I reminded myself what it had sounded like in the library as I stood there and listened to Murrow beat him.

The bell on the door jingled and I startled, nearly knocking the teacup from the saucer. Murrow came barreling in out of the wind and I exhaled, disappointed. Everyone in the family had come for the opening. Everyone except Ezra.

"How're we doing?" Murrow panted, taking off his wet jacket. His eyes were bright with excitement as he joined Henrik, Casimir, and Noel in a back booth.

"Just fine," Henrik answered. "Get over here, Bryn."

I braced myself as I came around the counter, catching my reflection in the mirrors behind the bar. My suit was finely tailored with sharp seams and horn buttons that were polished to a shine. The tweed was a deep amber and my dark hair fell over one shoulder in a tumble of loose waves.

It was an odd picture to see myself like that against the backdrop of the refined, gilded room. Weeks ago, I would have been dressed head to toe in the finest gown the couturier could make. But I was through putting on other people's skins. And soon, Henrik would know it.

He slid a glass to the edge of the table and filled it as I walked toward them. It was a tea house, but my uncles were drinking a bottle of rye, and I couldn't think of a better picture that would encapsulate them as they sat there in their beautiful suits with perfectly combed hair.

Henrik lifted his glass into the air, a glimmer of pride in his eyes. For a moment, it looked as if he was hesitant to speak. "To Eden."

A soft silence fell between us, and Casimir and Noel met eyes across the table in one of their silent exchanges.

"To Eden," I echoed, raising my glass higher.

I tipped my head back and swallowed the rye in one gulp, wincing as it lit my throat on fire.

Casimir clapped me on the back, laughing, and then poured himself another. Tonight, they weren't working. They were spectators. And it was up to me to give them a good show.

"Open her up!" Henrik clapped his hands together, taking the bottle from Cass.

The servers unlocked the door right as the harbor bell began to chime and a stream of hooded cloaks in the glow of the streetlamps began to appear outside the curtain-draped windows. All over the city, tea houses would begin to fill and in moments, I'd know my fate. If I succeeded, I'd be closer to winning my autonomy from Henrik. If I didn't, he'd find better employment for me in a match with Coen.

I returned to the bar as the servers pushed the doors open to find three women waiting, their wide eyes moving over the tea house from beneath their hoods. Two men rushed forward to take their cloaks, and I sighed with relief when I saw them slip from their shoulders. Beneath, extravagant frocks and jewelry glistened around their throats and wrists, revealing them to be not just the shop runners that catered to the merchants. These were the kind of guests that could be the wives and sisters of the merchants themselves.

One after the other, they filed in. Men and women of the Merchant's District in their glamorous jackets and hats and rouge-painted cheeks. There was a wonder in their eyes. A mischievous light that flickered in their gazes as they trailed across the room. It was the feeling that they shouldn't be here. That it wasn't proper. And yet, it was just proper enough to be acceptable. The teetering balance of the two was what I'd placed my bets on.

Only minutes after the doors opened, I spotted a tall young man towering among them, a stroke of light brown hair slicked to one side.

Coen.

He was with a group of young men and I smiled when he caught my eyes and broke away from them, crossing the room toward me. From the back booth, I could feel my uncle's scrutinizing attention on me.

Coen inspected my clothing with an amused grin. "I must say, you're very strange, Bryn Roth," he said, with an edge of humor.

I smiled back. I may not want to marry him, but there was something I liked about Coen. He had a grounded countenance that high-society men never had and wasn't afraid to laugh at himself. Probably because he'd grown up with a father from North End. But he was also naive enough to believe that a strange wife wouldn't cost him with the Merchant's District when he inherited his father's place in the guild. And in that way, I was doing us both a favor by avoiding the match my uncle had his heart set on.

But his eyes lingered on me a little too long and I realized they were more glossy than usual. When I inhaled, I could smell rye. He and his friends had obviously already started their evening with a few drinks.

"Well done," he said, surveying the tea house around us. "Very well done."

"Thank you." I stood taller beside him, watching as the guests took their chairs.

Already, ladies were pulling their gloves from their

hands and servers scurried around the tables with pots of tea hovering in the air. Freshly arranged flowers spilled from gold vases at their centers and I caught one woman admiring them—hothouse blooms I'd specially requested from a greenhouse in North End.

"Silly, isn't it?"

I looked up at him. "What?"

"This." He motioned to the room. "These people. Nearly every purse of coin in this city hangs from the belt of a fool who thinks they're scandalous for taking tea under the roof of the Roths. It's all a game."

I smirked. The rye had loosed his tongue. "Well, right now, I think I'm winning."

He nodded. "I think you are, too."

I wondered if there was more to those words than what I could hear. If maybe he knew that I needed the advantage of the tea house to keep from marrying him. But he watched the room around us, his expression still light until his gaze found the door.

"My, my . . ." he said, surprised.

It opened with a gust of rain-soaked wind and a woman in a velvet jacket ducked inside, her ruby satin hat tipped low over her brow. All at once, the commotion of the tea house vanished, and a room of wide eyes landed on her.

"Who is that?" I whispered, eyes narrowing.

She reached up, unpinning her hat, and a pair of red lips was tilted in a smile. I knew her face, but I couldn't place it.

Coen smirked. "That's Violet Blake."

My mouth dropped open as I remembered. It was the woman who'd been there in the alley the day I first saw the tea house. She'd never given me her name.

"Did you do this?" I whispered, looking up at Coen.

He laughed. "Violet Blake wouldn't so much as glance in my direction. And she hates my father since he outbid her on that contract with the *Serpent*. You clearly have friends in much higher places than me."

But I didn't. Simon and Coen were the only real link Henrik had to the merchant class.

Violet cast a warm smile on the women waiting for seats, and they instantly parted, making way for her. But she wasn't headed to a table. Her eyes moved over the room slowly until they settled on me. Her grin pulled wider, and she made her way up the bar until she reached us.

A single gloved hand extended from the fur stole draped over her arm. "You must be Bryn." Her eyes raked over me, studying my suit with fascination.

I stood up straighter, hesitating before I took her hand. "I am," I answered. "I'm honored to have you, Ms. Blake."

"I am the one who is honored." Her head tipped to one side. "Your great-aunt wrote to inform me that I was to be at the opening of her niece's tea house. There aren't many people who can give me orders, but Sariah is one of them." Her smooth voice was laced in warm humor, the way it had been the day I'd met her in the empty alley.

Sariah. I hadn't even sent her a letter yet, but she was keeping tabs on me. Maybe through Henrik.

"You know my great-aunt," I said.

"I do." Her thin, crimson-painted lips curled. "She was the one who taught me to play Three Widows, if I remember correctly." She leaned in closely. "That's not the only thing I learned from her."

From the back corner booth, Henrik looked as if his eyes were going to drop right out of his head. Another full glass of rye dangled from his fingertips as he watched us, but he had the good sense to stay put. The last thing I needed was for him to mess this up with his indelicate decorum.

"Now, I didn't come for the tea," Violet said, pulling the gloves from her small hands. "And I suppose someone has to throw the first die."

I smiled, giving a nod to the man standing behind the bar, and he sprung forward with a velvet pouch on a silver tray. I picked it up, dropping it into Violet's hand.

"Thank you, dear." She winked at me. "Haven't had the best of luck lately." Her eyes cut knowingly to Coen. She was talking about the contract she'd lost to Simon. "Let's see if I can change it."

I stepped aside, motioning for one of the servers to pull out an open chair, and Violet sat, her skirts cascading around her like a plume of feathers. Everyone fell silent as the server lifted the flower arrangement from the table and Violet reached into the small purse around her wrist, pulling out four coppers. She set them at the center and the man beside her followed suit, placing his bet.

She raised both hands into the air, closing them over the

dice, and the entire tea house quieted once more. She unfurled her fingers, and the dice tumbled across the linen, followed by an eruption of cheers. Triple stars.

Violet laughed, scraping the coin toward her, and the
tea house came to life with voices and clinking teacups and
the jingle of coin. It was exactly as I'd imagined it, filled to
the brim with stories that would be told over tomorrow's
breakfasts.

I found myself smiling, eyes moving over the candlelit
room. I'd done it. I'd actually done it.

"The silversmith couldn't make it?" Coen said, eyeing the
booth where the Roths sat.

The question pulled me from thought, replacing the pride
I'd felt with the sting of remembering Ezra's battered face.

"No," I answered. I didn't know if I was relieved or disappointed that he hadn't come. I didn't like the idea of Ezra
watching me play Henrik's games, but he was the only sense
of gravity I had in Bastian. "Doesn't have much luck with
Three Widows, as you know." I tried to make light of it.

Coen laughed, a little too loudly. It wasn't the congenial
laugh I recognized. This one was sharp and jagged. Maybe
he'd had more to drink than I'd realized. "Luck had nothing
to do with it."

I tore my gaze from Violet Blake, searching Coen's face.
"What do you mean?"

He propped one arm on the counter beside me. "Sometimes what looks like chance is actually just a stacked deck."

I turned toward him. "I'm afraid I don't follow."

Coen leaned closer, a conspiratorial look in his eye. "I gave him the dice. Henrik."

I stared at him, still trying to understand.

"I liked Ezra, sure. I didn't have any siblings, and in a way, he'd become one. But his talent garnered far too much attention from my father. He'd wanted me to have that gift with the forge, but I'd never shown the promise Ezra did," he said. "I could see it from the time I was very young—he wished that Ezra had been his son."

My eyes narrowed at him. "What are you saying?"

"That night, my father and Henrik were drunk. They weren't friends, but they did business together and they'd just finished up a job they'd been planning for months. They were celebrating. And when Henrik proposed a game of Three Widows, he had his prize already named. My father sent me to fetch the dice and I did."

"You gave him weighted dice." I breathed.

One side of Coen's mouth lifted. "The next day, Ezra was gone." His eyes glinted like a wolf's. "Sometimes we have to make our own fate."

I let the counter hold up my weight as I stared at the floor, a heavy feeling threatening to bring me crashing down into it. That was it. That single moment brought everything into line, the pieces clicking. A wide, gaping hollow opened in my chest, where Sariah's words swirled like an eddy.

The day you were born a Roth is not the day your destiny began. It began the day you stepped off that ship in Bastian.

My gaze lifted to the booth in the corner, where Henrik and my uncles sat with Murrow. From the moment I was born, I thought my future had been fixed. I'd waited for that letter every day and when it came, I answered without question.

My gaze drifted down to the sleeve of my jacket and I pulled it up, revealing the wide snake's eye on the ouroboros.

I was one of them. Made in their image. And it was time I started acting like it.

THIRTY-TWO

My uncles and Murrow left the tea house for the tavern, but I stayed behind, sitting in the empty booth at the back as the servers cleaned up. I let myself disappear into the shadows of the quiet with each candle that was blown out, and when it was dark and silent, I finally drained my glass of rye and started the walk home.

Somehow, I'd pulled it off. And most surprising, it had felt like second nature. Sariah hadn't known what lay ahead when she sent me to Bastian, and I'd long thought she'd spent the years grooming me for her own purposes. But she had, in fact, sent me with everything I needed. She had been sure that I'd set my own course. And as I stood on the dark street looking up at the lone lit window of the Roth house, I knew there was more than one path I wanted to forge.

I climbed the stairs slowly, stopping on the top step when I saw that the door to Ezra's room was cracked open. I hoped, secretly, that it had been left open for me. But there was more unspoken than spoken in this house. More questions than answers.

Moving past my own room, I crept into that bit of light. Inside, Ezra sat at the desk with an open bottle of rye, lit by a single candle that was nearing the end of its wick. I leaned into the wall outside of his room, watching him for a long, silent moment. The light cast his usually pale skin in a warm amber and his freshly cut hair was almost the color of ink. On the dressing table against the wall sat the three dice.

"I heard it went well," he said, without looking up.

I smiled to myself, wondering if there was ever anything that went on in this house that he *didn't* know. "I thought maybe you'd come," I admitted. I didn't care anymore what that may sound like to him. The time for pretending had long passed.

"Henrik had things for me to do here."

"I thought maybe you were hiding from me." I gave him a playful smile, but I meant it.

He exhaled, running one hand through his hair. A habit of his when he didn't know what to say. "Maybe a little."

My smile dropped slightly. So, he was being honest, too.

I stepped inside, closing the door behind me with a click and making my way to the dressing table. I picked up one of the dice and set it into the center of my palm, studying it. It looked like any other die and it had probably seemed like any other game that night. Henrik hadn't even known when he threw them that they were rigged in his favor.

When I looked up, Ezra's eyes were drifting from me, to the die, and back. Maybe I'd tell him one day what Coen had done, but not tonight. There would be a cost to that truth and Ezra had paid enough for the time being.

He stood from the stool and went to the window, pushing back the curtain so he could watch the street below. "You shouldn't be in here. Henrik wouldn't like it."

I followed the line of bruises on his skin with my eyes until they disappeared beneath his shirt. "Henrik doesn't like a lot of things."

"I'm serious," he said, more heavily. "You need to be careful with him. He's watching you."

"I know."

He leaned into the wall with his arms crossed over his chest. "I don't think you do. You still believe you can get what you want."

"No. I'm just done *asking* for what I want."

"It doesn't work that way."

"That's what you did," I argued. "You got the apprenticeship on your own. You—"

"And look where it got me," he interrupted. "I was stupid for thinking I could leave. That he would ever let me."

"So, you're giving up?"

"I know when I've lost, Bryn," he answered.

I set the die down, staring at the three of them. My life had been decided by a deal. So had Ezra's. But I was finished letting other people decide for me. The power of Henrik Roth was no more than lifting smoke. He was the sum of beliefs and myths and tales told. I was ready to tell my own stories.

"I'm not going to be matched with Coen. I'm going to stay here and run the tea house."

He stared at me. "If you stay here, he will always control you. Everything about you."

"Are you saying I should take the match with Coen?"

He sighed. "I don't know what I'm saying."

I came to stand in front of him, the toes of my boots almost touching his. Outside, the black sky was glittering with stars strung over a night-shrouded sea. The cool air seeped in through the window and the glass fogged along the corners of the pane. Out there lay a world beyond the walls of this house and life suddenly felt like a cage that had accidentally been left open.

"Tru told me Auster climbed out that window." I pointed to the window of my bedroom. You could see it from here. "And he never came back."

At the mention of Auster's name, Ezra stiffened. The muscle in his jaw ticked. "I know. I saw him."

"You did?"

"I think that's why I got it into my head that I could leave. Auster came back last year, and he'd made this whole other life for himself. Like all those years in this house had never happened and . . ." He swallowed. "I started thinking I could leave, too."

"You still can."

Ezra's gaze returned to the dark street below. "That was before."

"Before what?"

He swallowed. "Before I had a reason to stay."

I looked up at him, but he kept his gaze fixed out the window. The pain that had been in my chest rose to my throat and the sting of tears lit behind my eyes.

"In a way, Henrik finding out about the apprenticeship made that decision for me."

"Ezra . . ." I said his name with a tenderness that I hadn't been brave enough to use before. But something about what Coen had said to me had stripped me of my fear. The world was suddenly a stark black-and-white, separated into the things I wanted and didn't want. And the most blazing, bright thing in that world stood before me.

"Look, Bryn," he said. "Henrik—"

I lifted up onto my toes and pressed my mouth to his, drawing in what felt like the very first breath I'd ever taken. It filled my lungs with the smell of him and I parted his lips with mine. The taste of rye lit on my tongue and Ezra froze, pulling back and putting inches of space between us.

He stared at me, and the look on his face was something I hadn't seen there before. Shock. Or confusion. I couldn't tell. His chest rose and fell with heavy breaths, his eyes fixed on mine. But I didn't want to give him the chance to think better of it. Or to push me away. I wanted to bind my destiny to his.

Without taking my eyes from Ezra's, I pulled open my jacket and let it slide down my shoulders. I wasn't afraid anymore. The thing I felt in the center of my gut when I was with him was the only thing that had ever felt real. More real than Henrik's letter. More real than the agreement he'd made with Sariah. More real than the stake with the tea house or the match with Coen. This belonged to me. It was the only thing that belonged to me.

Ezra watched as I unbuttoned my vest. "Bryn . . ."

He looked terrified, a darkness falling over his face. But that didn't scare me anymore, either. I let the vest drop to the floor and pulled my shirt from where it was tucked into my trousers.

He reached out, taking hold of my wrists to stop me. His voice was ragged. "What are you doing?"

I closed the space between us until I could feel the warmth coming off of his body. His breath kissed my skin as I shrugged off the shirt. His eyes were searching mine, the thoughts racing through them so fast, I could almost hear them swirling in the air around us.

"I'm making my own fate," I said, tears filling my eyes again as I spoke Coen's words. But these tears weren't sad. They were ones of deep relief. "If we stay, we stay together."

It was a question. A hope. And as I stood there in front of him with my heart bared between us, I waited for his answer.

His gaze dropped to my mouth and I waited, hoping with everything inside of me that this time, he would be brave enough to cross the invisible line between us.

"This is a really bad idea." He moved closer, and my heartbeat grew louder as slowly, his hands came to my face. His fingertips slid into the hair at the nape of my neck and my head tipped back before his mouth met mine. And the deep emptiness within me was flooded, filling with him. I pulled at his shirt until the buttons were undone and my hands moved over the rippling shape of his stomach. He reached back with stiff arms and a shudder went through him as I tugged his shirt off. When I looked up, his face was pinched in pain.

"Am I hurting you?"

"Yes," he said, but it was on a laugh.

He reached for me again, and this time, he wasn't gentle. He held me to him tightly, as if he was afraid I would disappear. I pulled him into me until I couldn't get any closer and then we were only skin and hands and breath. I didn't want him to stop. I didn't want even a sliver of space between us.

My feet followed his away from the window, his mouth still pressed to mine, and I pulled him down onto the bed, letting his weight come over me. I wasn't thinking anymore about what would happen or when. This was the only moment that existed. Here, between us.

I pushed the waist of his trousers down so I could follow the line of his hips with my hands and Ezra stilled, staring at me in the dark.

The candle's flame had finally snuffed, leaving only a twisting trail of disintegrating smoke in the air. The room gave way to darkness, painting half his face with silver moonlight.

"Have you ever been with someone before?" His voice was a crackling fire.

I hadn't, though I guessed that maybe he had. And instead of embarrassing me, I was happy. My body wouldn't be auctioned off to a husband like the girls in Nimsmire. It was mine. It was mine to give.

I traced the Roth tattoo on the inside of his arm. "No," I answered, my heartbeat slowing. "But I want to be with you."

It was so true that the words were strangled in my throat. They became solid between us.

I melted into the darkness, with only the sound of his breath and the feel of his skin to guide me. For the first time, I was truly choosing. In the empty house at the end of an alley in Bastian's Lower Vale, I threw the dice. And on the other side, I didn't care what was waiting.

THIRTY-THREE

I woke to silence. Not the hollow quiet of emptiness. It was the kind of silence that made me feel heavy. Safe.

My eyes didn't open. I didn't want to see that the sun had risen or that the harbor bell would soon ring. Instead, I pulled in a slow, deep breath. The scent of Ezra's quilts swirled inside of me and I tucked my face into the crook of his shoulder.

I had never been so still inside. This was a quiet that was full of tomorrows and I smiled quietly to myself, the thought warming me. I could find a way to chart my destiny within the Roths, like Sariah had said. I already was. The tea house was one thing, but *this* . . . these arms around me were another.

A distant knocking sounded somewhere in the house and deep in the corner of my sluggish thoughts, I remembered where we were. My eyes finally opened, and Ezra's bruised, pale skin came into focus with the soft drift of dust in the beams of light coming through the window.

I tipped up my chin, blinking, but Ezra's eyes looked focused. He was perfectly still, and I realized he was listening. Slowly, his grip on me went rigid and a wave of cold dread crept through me. Footsteps. They were coming up the stairs.

"*Shit.*" The word was a rumble in Ezra's throat as he sat up and I followed, searching for my shirt on the floor.

I was pulling it over my head when Murrow burst through the door, ducking so he didn't hit his head. "Ez—" But he stopped short when he saw me, his mouth dropping open. "What the . . ."

Ezra and I froze, standing together half-dressed in front of the window, and a look of pure shock transfigured Murrow's handsome face into something contorted.

"I . . . uh . . ." His lips moved around unintelligible words. "Simon's here," he finally managed. "And Coen. Henrik wants you downstairs. Both of you." He stifled a laugh, looking from me to Ezra.

"Get out," Ezra rasped, buttoning his trousers.

Murrow closed the door and disappeared, the sound of his boots trailing down the stairs as I shook out my hair and braided it with frantic fingers. I wrapped it around the crown of my head and pinned it into place. Over my shoulder, I could see Ezra wincing in the mirror. He cursed as he pulled on his shirt, the pain visible on his face with every quick movement. But once he had it buttoned up, most of the evidence of Henrik's punishment was covered. The only remnants were the cut on his lip and the bruise on his cheek.

I looked up at him as I laced up my boots, catching a

grin at the corner of his mouth and I smiled, too. "Good morning."

He laughed, and my hands froze on the laces. I didn't know if I'd ever seen him actually laugh. A slice of white teeth stretched up one cheek and I stared at him in awe.

He snatched his pocket watch up from where it sat on the dressing table. "What?"

"Nothing." I smiled, but it faded as I finished tying my boots. That glimpse of him was what he could be. What he might have been if he'd been able to escape this house.

I wanted to believe that we could make our own rules under this roof. Ones that made it easier to live. I wanted to believe that there was some bit of light to be found in the way Ezra had touched me the night before, but grief had risen in me when I saw him smile like that. I didn't want to wonder if I'd ever see it again.

He waited with one hand on the doorknob and I came to stand before him, listening to the hallway. When I didn't hear anything, I stepped back so he could open it. But Ezra leaned down, catching my mouth with his and he kissed me softly.

He was gone in the next breath and I let myself smile then. There *was* some light to be had. And I was going to hold onto it. No matter what.

I waited a full minute before I went downstairs. Henrik's smooth voice was coming from the library and I could hear Simon, too. They prattled on about something to do with a trader in Ceros and the sound was relaxed. Happy, even. I hoped that meant Simon was here with the good news we'd been waiting for.

But as I passed the breakfast room, Sylvie was beginning to set the table and it occurred to me that such an early visit was strange. The fleeting thought conjured to life a faint warning in the back of my mind, but I dismissed it.

I came through the doors to find Henrik and Simon sitting in the leather armchairs. Coen stood against the bookcase behind his father's seat and gave me a warm smile when he saw me. His eyes were clearer than they'd been last night.

It made me recoil inside, knowing what he'd done to Ezra. It wasn't all that shocking though. He'd grown up with the customs of Lower Vale and North End and a father who knew how to get what he wanted. Coen had found a way to deal with Ezra and I guessed he didn't have the slightest bit of regret about it.

"Ah, there she is." Simon gave me a small nod in greeting and I returned it.

"Good morning. I'm sorry to keep you waiting."

Ezra was in his usual place, tucked into the corner like a silent observer and I took the wall opposite, resisting the urge to look at him. This was either going to be the moment Henrik had been waiting for, or the one he'd dreaded. The fallout of the latter would affect us all.

"Nonsense," Simon said. "It's a beautiful morning. And I wanted you both here for the occasion."

Beneath Henrik's cool expression, I could see his excitement. If Simon called it an occasion, it could only mean one thing.

Simon clapped his hands together before him as he turned to my uncle. "I've decided to offer you my patronage to the gem guild."

A smile broke on Henrik's lips and he leaned forward in his chair, shaking Simon's hand more firmly than necessary. "Thank you, old friend."

Henrik's gaze immediately went to Ezra behind me, a beaming look of pride in his eyes. This is what he'd waited for. Everything he'd worked for. And the first person he'd looked to was Ezra. There was more in that single look than a proud man. There was affection there. This wasn't only his achievement and he knew it.

That was the scary thing about Henrik. What he did, he did out of love.

"You've earned it," Simon said. "I think we can all agree on that. And you'll have the collection to present to the guild to prove it."

"Congratulations, uncle," I said, unable to truly mean it.

Henrik's success meant my success, but he'd used Ezra to get it. And when Ezra had tried to mark his own path, he'd beaten him back down. It didn't matter what was in my uncle's heart or what his reasons were. I would never, ever forgive him for that moment in the study. I would never trust him again.

"Sylvie!" Henrik called out, rising from the chair. He leaned out of the open doors. "Rye!"

The small woman scurried up the hallway in a frenzy and the chime of glass clinking sounded in the kitchen.

"You won't regret this, Simon," Henrik began. "Ezra will have the collection ready before—"

"I have no doubt." Simon raised a hand to silence him as Sylvie poured the rye and handed out glasses.

I held mine before me, the smell making me feel sick so early in the morning. When Henrik lifted his glass, so did Simon, and the rest of us followed suit.

"To the exhibition!" Henrik crowed.

"The exhibition!" The voices resounded in the tiny room.

Henrik was visibly lighter with the news and I hated how the sight of him like that made me relax. Being at the whims of his caprice was exhausting.

I snuck a look in Ezra's direction, wanting to steady myself, but he was looking into his glass with an empty expression. He didn't appear to be happy or relieved. He didn't look disappointed, either. He was more experienced in Henrik's changing winds than I was. He was an expert.

"There is still the matter of Arthur." Henrik leaned forward, trying to be delicate. But there was nothing delicate about him. He had the smoothness of a sea urchin. "I'm sure you've heard he's also secured a patronage."

"I have." Simon sipped his rye slowly, taking his time. Something about the deliberate movement made the hair stand up on the back of my neck. "I arranged it."

Henrik's hand stalled as he raised his glass to his lips again. "What?" He laughed awkwardly.

Behind Simon, Coen was studying his father with a pensive brow. Whatever the watchmaker was talking about, it was news to his son.

"I arranged the patron for Arthur," he said again. "Of course I did."

The corners of Henrik's mouth turned down. "Why would you do that?"

Simon scoffed. "Henrik, you can't honestly think I've agreed to the patronage out of my own goodwill."

"I"—Henrik stumbled over the words—"I don't understand."

Sylvie glided into the room with a silver tray, placing it on the low table. It was set with fruit and cheese, a platter meant for the breakfast table. Simon helped himself, picking a few of the grapes from the stem before he refilled Henrik's glass. My uncle sat there motionless, like he was unsure of what else to do.

"If you want my patronage, I will require something in return." Simon popped one of the grapes into his mouth and chewed. His eyes went past me, to the corner of the library, where Ezra watched silently.

Henrik's nostrils flared, the glass shaking in his hand.

"Ezra will come back to work for me," Simon said, taking another shot of rye in one swallow.

Coen's eyes were wide, his mouth dropped half-open. He shifted on his feet uncomfortably. This was clearly a plan Simon had kept to himself. And Coen wouldn't be happy to be saddled with Ezra as competition for his father's admiration and respect again.

I looked to Henrik, who was fuming. He was trapped and he knew it. If Simon didn't agree to be his patron and left Henrik without one, Arthur would get the ring as the only candidate at the exhibition.

"Ezra will come back to where he belongs, and you will get your ring." Simon held a hand toward Henrik, offering to shake on it.

"What does that guarantee me if you've ensured Arthur has a patronage, too? The guild could select him for the ring. Then what do I have?"

"Oh!" Simon dropped his hand, shaking his head. "Of course, I've forgotten that detail. The patronage is one thing. Securing the votes in your favor is another. That will require a separate payment." His eyes lifted to me. "Bryn and Coen will be matched, as previously discussed."

Coen's eyes cut to Simon. *"Father."* The word was heavy with rebuke, but Simon's fiery gaze found his son and at that, Coen shut his mouth.

I couldn't keep myself from looking at Ezra. He was still as stone, his jaw clenched. There was something rippling beneath the surface of him. He was like the edge of a knife pressed to skin.

"The tea house will fall under our business," Simon added. "Seems fitting it would come back to dice, don't you think?" He laughed.

Henrik snarled, fixing Simon with a poisonous stare. "That's what this is about, Simon? That game of Three Widows all those years ago?"

Behind Simon, Coen was nervous. He looked at me, his cheeks flushed. He and I were the only ones who knew the game Henrik spoke of had been fixed.

Simon stared into his glass before he lifted it to his mouth. A cold, unsettling silence fell over the room before he set it down onto the tray again. He let the tension expand before he answered. "This isn't about him," he said. His head tilted to one side, the bitterness in his voice melting away. "This is about *her*." He breathed out roughly, glancing up to the portrait on the wall.

Eden.

Simon hadn't been friends with my mother. He'd loved her. And by the way he was looking at Henrik, it was clear that he blamed him for her death. For everything.

Simon stood, jerking his chin toward his son, who fell into step behind his father as he stalked out of the room. The three of us stood there silent, listening to the door to the street open and close. And then there was nothing.

The color drained from Henrik's face and he suddenly looked smaller in that decadent chair. Frailer. The sight was almost nauseating. He was a man cut down, a toppled king. And though everything within me was writhing with the words Simon had spoken, I liked seeing my uncle fall.

THIRTY-FOUR

The Roth family sat around the table, but tonight, there was no dinner.

The fire blazed at Henrik's back as he sat erect in the chair. Everyone waited. For what, I wasn't sure. My uncle had proved to be an unpredictable creature, but one thing I'd never seen on him was surprise. Pure, uninhibited surprise. And that's exactly what had marked his face as he'd sat in the library, listening to Simon's demands. It made the room feel as if it were paved with a thin layer of brittle ice. We were all balancing on its precarious surface, wondering not *if* it would crack, but *when*.

Everyone had been called, even Anthelia and Tru. Sylvie had Jameson in the kitchens, stuffing him with sliced apricots, and Anthelia had tucked herself behind Noel at the farthest seat at the table. As if she was ready to shield herself from Henrik's wrath. This wasn't the first time a plan had unraveled, and it wouldn't be the last. At least in this instance, no one had lost their lives. Not yet anyway.

Henrik set a fist on top of the polished wood surface, pulling in a slow, measured breath. "I want to know how this happened."

My uncles and cousin shot each other glances, as if wordlessly deciding who would be the one to speak. But Ezra only stared out the window, arms crossed over his chest. He would let the others take the lead, like he usually did, and I was glad.

In the end, it was Casimir who answered. "Simon must have set up Arthur's patronage before he made his demands to ensure we would be forced to comply. The patron is a trade partner of Simon's, though their business isn't well known in Bastian. That's why we didn't connect them before."

"Has Simon announced his patronage of me to the guild?" Henrik stared at the table with dead eyes.

"Not yet," Casimir answered. "He's waiting for you to accept his terms." He pulled a message from his pocket and slid it down the table, but Henrik didn't bother picking it up. "We have until the evening harbor bell tomorrow to answer him."

I swallowed hard, lifting my gaze to Ezra again. The implications of this weren't only his freedom and mine. We had already been trapped in Henrik's snare before Simon knocked on the door that morning. But I could think of few worse things than being forced to marry Coen when I was in love with the silversmith working downstairs in his father's workshop. The thought was like swallowing broken glass.

I couldn't tell if Ezra was thinking the same thing. He was unreadable, his dark irises focused on something in the distance.

"Maybe there's a way we can get a new patron," I said, my voice giving away my desperation.

Henrik shook his head. "It's too late for that."

"The guild vote is in three days," Noel chimed in. "Simon was already a long shot and securing a new patronage in that time would be impossible. I don't know of a merchant who'd go against him. If we don't accept, word will spread, and no one will touch us."

"Then we don't accept and wait for the next ring," I said. "Eventually someone will die or fall from grace. If we're patient . . ."

Henrik snorted. "You don't know the first thing about any of this."

"That's not true," I said, carefully. "I was raised in this world. I know how the guilds work."

"You know how to charm. How to make connections. You don't know anything about doing what needs to be done or getting your hands dirty." The words were sharp. He looked at me with utter contempt, revealing how he really felt. "I never should have agreed to let Sariah take you to Nimsmire in the first place. That was a mistake."

"What does it matter if I was here or in Nimsmire if either way I'd be sold in a match?" My voice rose.

"Your match is the least of my concerns!" Henrik snapped, "Our prospects with the merchants rely on Ezra's work. Without him, we have *nothing*."

I watched Ezra swallow and his eyes finally dropped to the table. This is why he'd said he never wanted to smith again. He'd built himself a set of shackles with this gift. But what was more illuminating about what Henrik said was that my part of this was of next to no consequence to him. He'd already been prepared to hand me over to Coen and the only reason he'd reconsidered was because I was set to fill his pockets with more coin.

"We have no choice," Henrik finally said, his fist clenching tighter. "Ezra will return to Simon's workshop. Bryn will marry Coen. Once I have the merchant's ring, I'll find a way to get you back." He was speaking to Ezra.

"And me?" I said, a sharp sting burning behind my eyes.

Henrik glared at me. "You want to be *saved* from a good match with a powerful family?"

"Yes." I hated to admit it. But I *was* asking to be saved. By him.

"We have bigger problems, Bryn." Henrik scooted his chair back, dismissing me. "Ezra, come with me."

I clenched my teeth, staring into the blinding light of the fire until my eyes watered. The others followed him out, leaving me to drown in the racing beat of my own heart. I was no freer than I'd been in Nimsmire. I already knew that. And it didn't matter if I wanted to take control over my own fate. Sariah's letter was a fantasy. A false promise. And in that moment, I hated her for it.

Even she hadn't been free. She'd left Bastian, but the distance between her and her nephews hadn't cut her ties to them or the family of Roth. She'd been as bound as the rest of us, raising a calf in a pretty dress for slaughter.

"She was in love with him." A soft voice cut through the

silence and I blinked, sending two heavy tears rolling down my cheeks. "Simon."

Anthelia still sat at the other end of the table, a strand of hair absently slipping through her fingers. She hadn't gotten up when the others had left.

"What?" I said, the word cracking.

"Eden," she said. It was the first time she'd really looked me in the eyes since I'd arrived at this house. "She was in love with Simon, but her brothers forbade their being together. Too much competition for the business in Lower Vale, they said. Instead, she accepted a match with Tomlin."

More tears welled in my eyes as I listened. I didn't know the woman she spoke of. My mother was a stranger to me. But it still cut deep. I didn't like knowing that she had gone along with their schemes, like I had. In the end, they were the same ones that killed her.

"She wanted to do her duty to the family. But she was also afraid of what might happen to Simon if she didn't listen to her brothers." Anthelia spoke softly. When she glanced up to the doorway, I realized she didn't want to be overheard.

"Why did you do it?" I said, angry.

"Do what?"

"Become part of this family. Raise children among them."

She wound her finger into the ends of her hair, taking her time before she spoke. "I loved Noel, so I didn't feel like I had a choice." She paused. "But I did. And there isn't a day that goes by that I don't wonder if I made the wrong one."

"You did." I swallowed. "You did make the wrong one."

I didn't know why she'd chosen now to say what she'd said or why I felt the need to punish her. I wondered if they were words she'd ever spoken aloud to anyone. But I hated her for choosing this path when the rest of us had been born to it.

"Did they love each other? My parents?" I whispered, afraid of the answer.

She sighed. "They made good partners."

"That's not the same thing."

She smiled sadly. "No, it's not."

The sharp ping of the silver hammer rang out suddenly and I closed my eyes, breathing through the pain in my throat. Ezra was in the workshop. Back to work. What else was he going to do?

I stood, following the sound and leaving Anthelia behind in the empty dining room. The workshop door was propped open. The cold air rippled out into the warm house, the sound growing louder as Ezra brought the hammer down in angry strikes. When I peered inside, he was a stiff form in front of the forge, his profile in sharp focus against its glow.

I locked the door behind me and went to him. But he didn't look at me as I came around the table. He didn't stop swinging the hammer until I reached up, taking hold of his arm. The muscles under the skin were carved from stone, his pulse racing under my fingertips. It took a moment for him to finally turn to me, but when he did, he wasn't really there. The thaw I'd seen the night before was gone, replaced with the Ezra I'd met the first night I came to Bastian.

"Don't worry about the match," he said hollowly, dropping the hammer to the table.

"What do you mean? You heard Henrik."

He took a step back from me, busying himself with the vise on the anvil. "I know Simon. I can make a deal with him."

"What kind of deal?"

He shook his head, not answering.

"Ezra." I took hold of his arm again, my grip on him tightening.

"I'll take care of it," he said. He wasn't going to tell me, whatever it was.

I watched helplessly as he went back to the worktable. He was unraveling inside. I could see it. But on the outside, he was stone. "What about the shipwright?"

"What about him?" He sounded exhausted.

"Maybe he would help you. Help *us*."

Ezra shook his head. "It took doing just to get him to take me on. He would never cross Henrik. Or Simon."

"Maybe . . ."

"Bryn," he cut me off sharply. "*This*." He gestured to the workshop around us. "This is my life. This has always been my life. Whether I'm swinging a hammer here in Lower Vale or in the Merchant's District, it's all the same. But you with Coen . . ." He shook his head, dragging one hand over his face. "I won't survive that."

When he looked at me then, he was defeated. Afraid. He took slow, measured breaths, like he was trying to keep whatever was inside from escaping. Like he was about to come apart at the seams.

I closed the space between us and wrapped my arms around him tightly, trying to feel that calm quiet I'd felt when I awoke in his room. But it was gone. His hands came around me and there was pain in the way he held onto me. An anguish in his breath.

I didn't let go of him, holding him there until he pressed his face into the hollow of my neck and finally let out the tight breath he'd been holding. Slowly, he softened.

This was the only safe place in the city. This small space that we fit into. And I wasn't Eden. I wasn't going to let it go. Not for anything. If there wasn't a way out of this, I would make one.

When I pulled away to look at him, there was a single glistening streak on his cheek. It disappeared beneath the line of his jaw.

I wiped it with my thumb, meeting his eyes. "Are we still in this together?"

He thought about his answer before he gave it. His eyes seared into mine. "Yes."

As soon as he said it, I exhaled. "Then I have an idea."

THIRTY-FIVE

For the two days that the tea house had been opened, it had been filled to the brim.

I sat in the booth at the back corner, watching from behind the thick velvet curtain. The seats were full, but still, the door kept opening, pushing small crowds around the tables where games of Three Widows were already entire coin purses deep.

The most disturbing thing about the scene was that in Lower Vale, there would be knives drawn over losses so large and accusations of cheating. But here, among the merchants, there was so much copper in the purses that it was just . . . fun. A kind of sick, forbidden fun.

They held their dainty teacups filled with rare heirloom teas with jeweled ring fingers, throwing their coin away round after round. And yet, there was nothing but smiles. Laughter and cheer.

Back in the Roth house, my very small world was coming

apart, but here, mayhem was merriment. Silly, Coen had called it. But in this moment, it was revolting.

My plan was, admittedly, a very thin one. And it required a specific set of stars to align. But I had very few threads to weave together in this city and I didn't have enough time to take the chance of asking Sariah for help. I wasn't sure I was willing to pull her into this mess, anyway. She'd built her own ship to sail away from this family. I wasn't going to be the one to sink it.

I pulled my pocket watch from my vest, checking the time. I'd hung every hope on this meeting and the later the hour drew on, the more foolish I felt for thinking it would work. But right when I'd become convinced that she wouldn't show, Violet Blake appeared at the door of the tea house.

Her brilliant purple frock drew the attention of every soul in the room and she watched them all with a hungry gaze from beneath her hat. She enjoyed the attention. And she didn't care who knew it. That would be an important detail if I was going to convince her to help me.

She pulled the black lace gloves from her hands, holding them delicately in the air until a server took them. When she'd had her fill of onlookers and whispers, her eyes moved over the tea house slowly until they found me. She glided through the room with a dancer's steps as I slid from the booth.

"Bryn." She greeted me with a smile, her perfect lips like the strokes of a paintbrush.

"I'm glad you came." I gestured toward the booth and she sat, spreading her skirts over the velvet seat so they wouldn't wrinkle.

"An invitation from the most scandalous member of the merchants' circle is hard to resist."

I eyed her. "You've heard."

"About the patronage? Of course I've heard."

I studied her. That didn't make sense. Henrik had agreed to Simon's terms, but the guild wouldn't announce the patronages to the merchants until the exhibition.

"I keep a close eye on things, Bryn. Which is why I know this isn't a social call," she said.

I was glad she wasn't interested in tiptoeing around it. She may have had the manners of the guilds in her blood, but she wasn't above stepping out of line. I picked up the pot of tea from the table and set the sieve into her cup.

"I smell argon's whisper," she said, leaning forward to breathe in the steam as I poured. "That's a rare brew. Trying to impress me?"

I set down the pot between us. "I couldn't decide whether to offer you cava or tea."

"Whatever's most expensive." She grinned, picking up the small spoon and stirring. "Now, what is it you need, my dear? I assume you need *something* from me."

I folded my hands on the table, sitting up straighter. I'd only get one chance to ask and there was no delicate way to do it. "I'd like you to take on the patronage for Henrik."

She instantly winced, as if it hurt to swallow the tea. Her hand was pressing the napkin to her lips before she'd even gotten it down and the white linen came away with a smear of pink. "*What?*"

I didn't react. I kept my voice even and confident. "Simon's patronage hasn't been announced yet. I'd like you to take it over before it is."

Violet's blue eyes were so bright that they looked as if they were carved from sapphire. "Why on earth would I do that?" She spoke very slowly.

I leaned back into the booth, not breaking her gaze. "The merchant's ring isn't the only part of Henrik's deal with Simon. So is the silversmith."

"Ezra." She frowned. Her demeanor suddenly changed as she placed her cup on the saucer.

I knew she wouldn't like that. She and Simon were already at odds and having Ezra in his workshop was only going to make him more of a competitor. Giving him the most talented silversmith would only cement her place beneath him in both coin and renown.

"The tea house is also to come under Simon's business."

That caught her attention. "Why would Henrik agree to that?"

"I'm to be matched with Coen," I answered.

"Of course you are." Violet sneered. "Ask any man in the guild and they'd tell you the answer to any problem is as simple as putting someone in their bed." She sighed. "So. Simon gives Henrik the patronage, and in return, Henrik gives him his silversmith *and* his niece, along with her holdings." She laid out the pieces of the puzzle, examining them. "I admit, I don't like the sound of that at all. And Sariah will not be happy when she hears Henrik has married you off the first chance he's gotten."

"No, she won't. But there's not much she can do about it from Nimsmire," I said. "If you take on the patronage, you'll keep Simon from holding those cards."

Violet seemed to think about it, still stirring her tea even after the sugar was dissolved.

"And maybe you'll find some favor with my great-aunt as well."

She grinned. "Not an easy thing to come by."

"No, it's not."

Whatever Violet was thinking, it didn't show on her face. She knew how to keep her thoughts to herself.

"And the silversmith?" she asked, one eyebrow arching. "Do I get him, too?"

The words carved an edge into me and she noticed. "He's not part of any deal," I answered.

"Then it doesn't do me much good, does it?" She paused, assessing me. "You know, your great-aunt was something of a mentor to me. She's the one who taught me how to survive in this world and I have a feeling she did the same for you. So, I don't think I have to tell you that if I make Henrik a candidate to the guild, I keep Simon from gaining something. That's all well and good, but if I gain nothing myself, that's not very good business."

I set my elbows onto the table, not caring that it was vulgar. In fact, I had a feeling vulgarity would serve me well in this instance. "What do you want, Ms. Blake?"

"I want the thing that Simon cheated me out of. I want the contract with the *Serpent*."

I stared at her, my heart sinking. I had very limited power in this city, and none of it lay with traders. "The *Serpent*? What makes you think I could get you something like that?"

"Either you can, or you can't, Ms. Roth." She enunciated my name, her eyes flashing.

"You'd have a much better chance of getting that contract than I would."

"True. But my name can't be anywhere near this. I know you're new here, but Simon's reputation for revenge precedes him. It doesn't matter how many ships I have sailing for me. I can't very well collect my coin if someone's cut my throat, can I?"

No, she couldn't. If Simon got wind of her involvement in this, she would pay a price. It didn't matter what kind of loyalty she had to Sariah; she wasn't going to stick her neck out that far for me.

"You find a way to get me that contract and I'll give Henrik my patronage." She took one last sip of her tea and stood, smoothing her frock with her delicate hands. "Thank you for the invitation. I hope to receive another very soon."

I gave her a tight smile.

Her attention floated over the room and heads were already turning toward her. She wound the chain of her necklace around her finger, her eyes sparkling. "It really is a pretty little tea house." Her skirts swayed as she turned and walked away.

I watched her go, cursing under my breath. I'd known it was a long shot, but it was the only bet I'd had to make. And what she'd asked was impossible. I knew how contracts worked and I'd spent enough time around traders to know that they cared about one thing, and one thing only—copper. Simon had outbid Violet. It was that simple. Getting the helmsman of the *Serpent* to change his mind *and* keep his mouth shut was impossible. I had a better chance of getting Simon to agree to the deal himself.

My brow pulled as I stared into the teacup, my reflection rippling in the amber liquid. The only way to change the contract now was to cancel it, and that required a signature and a seal. But maybe it wasn't Simon's that I needed.

THIRTY-SIX

There were only two places I could think that Coen would be at this hour, and he wasn't at Simon's workshop.

Ezra and I stood at the mouth of the harbor, watching the ships below. Coen had been down on one of the farthest slips, supervising the load of one of the traders' inventories for the last hour and he kept checking his watch, as if he had somewhere else to be.

He wouldn't be on the docks if the cargo hadn't been important, so I guessed it was some of their most valuable pieces headed to Nimsmire or some other port city with high-paying customers in need of pretty things. Simon wouldn't trust the task to anyone else, and with Ezra headed back into their ranks, Coen would be on his best behavior. When it came to his father, he always was.

Every time he pulled the timepiece from his vest, the knot in my stomach wound tighter. This was the only way

I could think of to get what we needed, but I didn't know Coen well enough to guess what he'd do. The only thing I was sure about was that he loved his father. Worshipped him, even. And Violet Blake was our only hope of escaping Simon's scheme.

I knew how to listen to the words people weren't saying in order to work out who they were and what they wanted. And I'd known very soon after I met Coen that he wanted only one thing—his father's approval.

When the last crate was loaded onto the ship, Coen lifted a hand into the air, waving to the helmsman up on deck. He started up the dock, pulling his collar up and his hat low, but he had no chance of blending in. He was handsome and striking, with a jacket that drew the eye of everyone he passed. He may not be the most important man in the Merchant's District yet, but I had a feeling that eventually, he could be.

"You really think this will work?" Ezra asked, keeping his back to the stairs.

I looked into his eyes. The bruising on his face was beginning to fade, but there'd be invisible scars left behind. "I don't know." I told him the truth.

"If it doesn't?"

I didn't have an answer to that question. If I couldn't give Violet what she wanted, she wouldn't give Henrik her patronage. He would take Simon's instead, and Ezra and I would be traded in the deal. The only other option was to risk running, but my uncle would follow. Simon, too. Being one dangerous man's enemy was one thing. Two was another.

Coen started up the steps and Ezra stood up off the

streetlamp, pulling his hat down low over his eyes. I did the same, watching from the corner of my eye until I saw Coen's red leather boots come into view. I immediately started walking, falling into step beside him.

It took him a second to notice me, but when he did, his steps faltered. "Bryn." He said my name in a gasp.

He spotted Ezra on the other side of him and his hands lifted into the air, as if he was bracing for one of us to swing. It didn't sound like such a terrible idea after everything that had happened.

"*Walk,*" Ezra said, his voice a rumble.

Coen looked around us before he obeyed, starting up the street, away from the harbor. We passed under the entrance, rounding the corner of the merchant's house before he finally spoke.

"Look, Bryn." He pulled off his hat, running one hand through his hair nervously. "I didn't know what he was doing with the patronage. I swear. He didn't tell me."

"I know." Coen may have been a cheat, but I had never gotten the sense that he'd lied to me.

His relief at my answer was all over his face. It had been obvious that morning in Henrik's library that Coen was as shocked as the rest of us. In a way, his father had played him, too. And most important, he cared what I thought of him. That would work in my favor.

"But that doesn't change that we have a serious problem. You as much as the rest of us."

Coen stopped. "Me?"

I leveled my gaze at him. "You want Ezra back in your father's workshop?"

Coen's eyes slid to Ezra, who stood motionless beside him. "Not particularly."

"Then you'd better listen to me." I started walking again and it was a few steps before I heard him follow, his boots slapping the cobblestones.

"All right. What?" he said between breaths.

"I know Simon is working with Holland," I began. "Trading her pieces under his own seal." The details, I was only guessing at. But his reaction confirmed it.

Coen's eyes went ablaze, his lips pursed. "You don't know anything."

"I've seen the ledger," I said.

"What? How?"

I gave him an irritated look. "That night when I spilled the cava on my dress, I snuck into your father's study and picked the lock on his cabinet. Her name is in there a hundred times. And I would bet most of those transactions took place after she lost her merchant's ring."

Coen looked horrified but not shocked. That was an indiscretion he *did* know about.

"And there's more than one merchant in this city who would help me find the proof. If that happens, the guild will turn on Simon. And then we won't need a patronage because there will be enough rings to go around for all of us."

Coen fumed, but he'd already given himself away. He was antsy and anxious, checking over his shoulder every few seconds. As if he was afraid someone would overhear us. "What the hell do you want from me?" he growled.

I jerked my chin to the lamppost ahead, where the street opened up to another. Ezra shoved Coen toward it. We slipped into the narrow passage.

"I want you to cancel your contract with the *Serpent*."

Coen scoffed, looking between us. "You can't be serious." When we said nothing, he scowled. *"No."*

"Do it or I report your father to the gem guild." My voice didn't even sound like my own. My anger was like hot rye in my veins. I felt nothing as I watched his panicked face. His frantic shifting. I was the one with the power now.

Coen looked up and down the alley, his breath fogging in the evening cold. "Even if I wanted to, I couldn't do that."

Ezra watched him with a look of satisfaction. He was enjoying this—seeing Coen squirm. "You're a partner in Simon's business. You signed the contract."

"The helmsman of the *Serpent* would never buy it. He would insist on speaking to my father and you know what he would say. He'd sooner see both your bodies floating in the harbor than give up that contract. He would never agree. I don't care what you have on him."

"He might not care," I said. "But you do."

Coen settled his eyes on me then.

"Maybe because you really do love him. Maybe because you know you'll inherit whatever he leaves behind. It doesn't really matter to me. I just need you to do this."

Coen was struggling to keep himself at bay. His hands clenched into fists at his sides, his face turning red.

"Void the contract or I take Simon down. Either way, Henrik will get that ring. It's just a matter of whether you'll still be left standing at your father's side at the end of this."

I could hardly believe my own words. Because I meant them. I was completely willing to burn them to the ground and walk away with the flames at my back. There was nothing inside of me that even flinched at the thought.

"When?" Coen spat.

I arched an eyebrow at him.

"When do you need it canceled by?"

"Now," I answered. "By sunset at the latest. But no one can know. Not yet."

That part would be up to Violet to handle. I didn't care how she did it, as long as she kept her word.

"If you do this," Coen said, some of the anger bleeding out of him, "there will be no escaping him. Even if I don't tell him, he will find out. And my father will kill you." He was looking at me, and they weren't empty words. He was worried. For a split second, I almost believed that he cared.

"He won't be able to find us," I said.

Coen's brow furrowed before a look of understanding settled in his expression. "'Us'?" He glanced between Ezra and me, and after a moment, he looked like he was going to laugh. "Of course." He shook his head.

He ran both hands over his face, exhaling. "Fine. I'll do it."

I let out a ragged breath, feeling like I was going to fall to the ground with relief. "Thank you."

The wind blew Coen's hair over his forehead as he looked down at me. More than once, he reconsidered whatever he was about to say. In the end, it was only a warning. "Be careful, Bryn. I mean it."

I gave him one last look before I started toward the main street, but when Ezra didn't follow, I stopped. He took one slow step toward Coen until they were almost nose to nose.

"Now you're the one holding weighted dice," Ezra said.

Coen's eyes widened and I watched his mouth open, ready to deny it.

But Ezra didn't blink. He didn't speak. Beneath the anger in his face, there was sadness. It was painful to look at.

He turned his back to Coen, pulling his cap down low again, and when he reached me, I took his hand. His fingers closed over mine as we walked, but he watched the street around us warily.

"You knew?" I breathed.

Ezra nodded. "I always knew."

THIRTY-SEVEN

The Roths were dressed in their finest, boots shined and watches sparkling, as we stood before the gem guild commission. It would be Henrik's first time crossing that threshold, and if Coen and Violet came through, it wouldn't be his last.

Casimir carried the carved wooden chest in his arms, balancing it against his broad frame. The sides and tops were decorated in pearl and abalone inlay that mimicked the tales of the sea demons, with rolling waves and bones on the sea floor. Its gold lock was polished so brightly that it reflected the sunlight like a mirror.

Inside was everything Henrik had worked for since that fateful night when he threw the dice at Simon's. It was also everything forged by Ezra's hands. His best work. His most valuable creations.

Everything Ezra wanted to leave behind.

The heavy doors opened and a man in an emerald-green

suit looked down at us from the top of the steps. We didn't look like the crude cuts of stone from Lower Vale anymore, cleaned of the outer rock and cut for weighing. No, we were the faceted, brilliant gems of the Merchant's District now.

The man waved us inside and Ezra stayed close to me as I climbed the stairs, his arm brushing mine. The only safety we had from what was about to happen was that neither Henrik nor Simon would risk their place with the guild by drawing a knife inside the commission. At least, I hoped they wouldn't. I'd underestimated Henrik before.

The wide corridor was lined with richly oiled wood panels and a glass ceiling overhead cast the entire interior of the commission in bright light. The panes were spotless, and the blue sky looked like it had been painted there.

Voices swelled around us as the corridor opened up to a great hall, where the men and women of the guild were gathered, cava glasses in hand. They had donned their best garments and jewels for the occasion, sure to maintain appearances in front of the two candidates for the ring. It would be Henrik's job to impress them with the collection if he wanted their votes.

More than one of the merchants watched me with a curious, attentive gaze, their eyes roaming over my suit, down to my polished leather shoes.

"Over here." A woman motioned us forward, to a long, narrow table that was covered in a black silk drape.

This was where the collection would be viewed, each member of the guild making their own pass and assessment before the votes were cast. It was a delicate thing. The merchants would choose based not only on the beauty of the pieces, but on the candidate. The collection that was most impressive would add to the gem guild's renown and power, keeping the Trade Council of the Unnamed Sea with the upper hand over the Narrows. But adding a merchant to the guild with that much talent also meant competition. And there was a very cutthroat hierarchy to be maintained.

I had no doubt that Henrik would navigate those treacherous waters beautifully. He knew how to charm, and he knew how to lie. Most important, he knew how to get what he wanted.

Across the room, Arthur's collection was set out and ready for the exhibition. Gilded hand mirrors and silver combs and diamond-studded goblets were on display. He stood along the wall with his companions, his suit jacket a bit too tight. But he looked smug.

Casimir set down the case and Ezra pulled the gold key from his pocket, unlocking it. There was a quiet hush that dropped in the room as he lifted the lid. Inside, a neatly organized tray held the pieces that would be displayed. The silver was so bright that more than one whisper sounded behind us.

Henrik looked like a cat; his wrinkle-framed eyes squinted with delight. He was confident, and he had every reason to be. He'd also made peace with this loss to Simon, a slight that wouldn't go unanswered. He'd have to play the long game, but in his mind, he would find a way to get Ezra back. I, on the other hand, would be left to fend for myself.

Ezra handled the pieces with care, setting them out along the table in a specific order to be viewed. When he got to the bird earrings, a little twist ignited in my gut. The night I'd worn them was the night I became a Roth, and I'd wager it was also the night I fell in love with Ezra Finch.

The conversation around us picked up and I looked to the entrance, where Coen's suit was washed in the sunlight cascading down from the ceiling. He was in a black jacket and a silver cravat that made his eyes appear an even deeper shade of blue. Simon was at his side, a warm smile on his face as he greeted his fellow merchants. This charade was as much for the candidates as it was for the patrons. Today, all eyes would be on him.

Once the gem guild master called the exhibition to order, Simon's patronage would be formally announced, and that made him the man of the hour. Little did the gem guild know that it was a deal struck with Henrik as the loser.

When Coen spotted me, his placid smile faded, and he slipped from his father's side. He made his way toward me, weaving in and out of the attendants until he stood only inches away.

"Take my arm," he said, lifting his elbow.

I obeyed, hooking my hand around it, and he started walking, leading us around the back of the room. Dozens of eyes followed us and I knew why. We made a handsome pair. One that would give our families an advantage against the purebred members of the gem guild. But I was no longer even the slightest bit interested in doing my duty to the Roths.

"Is it done?" I asked.

Coen took a glass of cava from one of the servers and handed it to me before he took one for himself. He was still smiling, being sure to put on airs for his father, who watched us from a distance.

He lifted the glass to his lips. "It's done."

I closed my eyes, breathing deep. When I opened them, Coen was studying me. If I didn't know better, I'd think there was hurt in his eyes.

"Thank you," I said, pulling away from him.

But he caught my hand, holding me there. "Bryn." He hesitated.

"What is it?" I spoke under my breath, trying to keep from drawing the curiosity of the people around us.

"Don't ever come back," he said, seriously. "If you do, he *will* kill you."

I was sure he was going to say something more. Maybe a heartfelt goodbye of some kind. But he only looked at me once more before he let go, his hand slipping from mine. Then he was disappearing into the crowd.

I pushed my way back toward Ezra, but another hand caught hold of me, making the cava swish from the lip of my glass. It dripped over my hand, falling to the floor.

"Careful." Violet Blake's honey-laced voice was suddenly beside me. She had a soft smile, her eyes rimmed in shimmering powder. "I hope you have good news for me," she purred.

"Simon's contract with the *Serpent* has been canceled. He doesn't know it yet, but he's finished with them."

She batted her eyelashes at me. "And how exactly did you manage that, little Roth?"

"Does it matter?"

Violet looked around us, tucking a strand of shiny hair

behind her ear. "I suppose I'd better get ready for the big announcement then. It's a good thing I wore the red, don't you think?"

I looked down at her beautiful frock. The fabric was the color of blood and it was perfect. She was perfect.

"There's a ship in the harbor waiting for two more passengers. The *Mystic*." She sipped her cava, tapping her diamond ring on the belly of the glass as she emptied it.

"What?" I stared at her.

"I don't need you hanging around to complicate things once the sun sets on this little arrangement."

"Thank you," I said, hoping that she could hear in my words how much I meant it. She'd done it for herself, I knew that. But I would still owe her for it. I'd owe her forever.

Her lips pursed with pleasure and she lifted her chin, looking down her nose at me as she plucked the glass from my hand. I smiled when she began to drink from it. "You'd better get going. The master will start soon."

I gave her one last smile before I shouldered through the merchants. When I reached the table, my uncles were lined up in a handsome trio and the sight reminded me of that portrait in the study. They were only missing my mother.

I caught Ezra's eyes and he walked toward me, leaving Murrow's side.

Henrik watched the room, his hands folded behind his back. He stood up straight, his perfectly groomed mustache hiding the grin on his mouth, but it was visible in his eyes.

"You have to decide now," I said, keeping my voice low as I took the place beside him.

He looked down at me. "What?"

I shoved my hands into my pockets to keep them from trembling. "In a few minutes, the master will announce your patronage from Violet Blake. If you want it."

Henrik turned his back to the room slowly, his eyes widening. "Bryn, what are you talking about?" There was still excitement in his voice. He didn't understand what was happening yet. How could he?

"Violet has agreed to be your patron. You'll have a powerful ally in the guild, and you won't be beholden to Simon."

"Why would she do that?" Now he sounded suspicious.

"You have to agree . . ." My voice wavered and I swallowed, clearing my throat. "You have to agree to let us go."

"Who?" His brow wrinkled, his mustache going lopsided.

"Ezra." I breathed. "And me."

Slowly, the look in Henrik's eyes turned vicious.

"If you take Simon's patronage, Ezra will belong to him. You might think you can get him back, but you can't. And you'll never hold sway over the gem trade if Simon has Ezra working for him." I paused. "If you take Violet's patronage, you'll still lose Ezra, but so does Simon. The playing field will be equal."

Beside me, Ezra was listening, but his eyes were on the room around us.

"Simon is your enemy. He will always be your enemy. But Violet can be an ally."

"And you?" Henrik growled.

"You've lost me either way, too."

He stared at me, waiting for an explanation.

"You lost me the moment you tried to sell me to Coen," I said, my voice lowering. "Even if you find a way to keep me here, you'll never be able to trust me again."

Henrik looked as if he'd swallowed fire. His chest was pumping beneath his jacket, the red in his skin boiling. "Arthur still has a patronage. It's still me or him. What if the vote doesn't go in my favor?"

I shrugged. "That's up to fate," I said. "It was always going to be up to fate."

He was quiet. Behind him, Casimir, Noel, and Murrow were lost in conversation, drinking cava and unaware of the silent war being waged only feet away.

I reached into the pocket of my vest, pulling a thick envelope free. He stared at it before he took it and opened the flap. Inside was the key and the deed to the tea house, along with the ledger. As soon as he realized what it was, he discreetly pulled it into his jacket, concealing it.

"You can still do it. You can still finish what she started," I said, my throat tight.

He was quiet for a long moment before he turned back to the room and I watched as slowly, he pulled himself together. Piece by piece, he recomposed himself, his cool manner returning.

"If you walk away, you walk away with nothing." He was talking to Ezra now.

"I know." There was almost a tenderness in the way Ezra looked at him. As if there was some part of him that was grieving. And maybe there was. From what little I knew, Henrik had been the closest thing to a father that Ezra had ever had. The Roth house had been his home, even if it had been one with steep costs.

Henrik swallowed, smoothing over the look on his face until he looked like himself again. "Gotta hand it to you," he said, a bit of slyness reaching his voice. "For a girl who was raised on a gold platter in Nimsmire, you sure look a lot like a Roth to me."

He didn't take his eyes off me and I found that my heart hurt at the words. It was the only approval I'd ever get from my uncle. I wondered if to him, it was a parting gift.

I looked past him, to where Murrow was standing at the table. He was watching us, the smile missing from his face. He looked at me with a question in his eyes, but I couldn't answer. I didn't know how to say goodbye to him. This was where he belonged. Where he would always belong.

As I thought it, he gave me a small smile and turned back to his father. It was a kind farewell. A gentle one.

The feel of Ezra's hand was suddenly at my back, making me blink, and then we were walking. Toward the light. The hum of the room bled away as we glided through the corridor, and when we stepped out onto the street, I drew in the deepest breath I'd ever taken. Air laced with salt and freedom poured into my lungs and our boots hit the cobblestones in tandem, making my heart race.

Ezra reached up, untying the green silk cravat knotted around his neck. He dropped it to the street, and it fluttered behind us as he unbuttoned the top of his shirt, pulling it open with his scarred hands. I could almost feel the ropes loosening around him. No more *tidy and timely*. No more clenched fists and swallowed words at family dinners and orders to be followed.

Behind us, the commission was being called to order. In moments, the exhibition would begin, and the guild would inspect Ezra's collection, with no idea that he was gone. That he was never coming back. The votes would be cast and either my uncle would leave that building with a ring on his finger, or he wouldn't. Maybe I would never know.

The entrance to the harbor appeared ahead and I stopped at the top step, searching the bows until I saw it. The crew of the *Mystic* was scrambling over the deck, the sails unrolling on the masts as they readied the ship to set sail.

"Where is it going?" Ezra spoke beside me. The way he looked with his unkempt hair blowing over his face in the wind was like looking at a different person. One I'd only glimpsed that night in his room when I kissed him in the dark and he unwound in my arms.

"I don't know," I said. "Do you care?"

Ezra grinned. It wasn't heavy and restrained like before. This time, there was light in his eyes as he answered. "No." He breathed. "I don't."

ACKNOWLEDGMENTS

This book was such a wild ride from start to finish, and I am very lucky that I had so many amazing people in my corner to make it come to life.

Most deserving of my gratitude, as always, is my family. Joel, Ethan, Josiah, Finley, and River, thank you for keeping my world filled with love and laughter.

Thank you to Barbara Poelle, who worked her best agent magic to make sure this book saw the light of day. And to my editor, Eileen Rothschild, whom the Roths were named after. Thank you for your unflinching belief that I could do this.

Thank you to Vicki Lame, who donned the editor superhero cape for this project. What a lovely twist of fate it was!

Another book, another thank-you to the rest of my Wednesday Books team: Sara Goodman, Lisa Bonvissuto, DJ DeSmyter, Alexis Neuville, Mary Moates, Brant Janeway, and cover designer Kerri Resnick for setting her hands to yet another amazing cover.

Thank you to Kristin Dwyer, who convinced me to throw caution to the wind and call my agent about this project when it would not. Stop. Haunting me. I don't know if I can really put into print, for eternal record, that you were "right" . . . but I will say I'm glad I listened to you.

An enormous thank-you to Carolyn Schweitz, my right hand and also the only functioning part of my brain. Without you, I literally would not have finished this novel and I am so grateful to have you on my team.

Thank you to Natalie Faria, my beta reader who is always one of the first sets of eyes on any story I write.

I count myself very lucky to have such an amazing support system that cheers me on, celebrates my wins, and keeps my head on straight. Thank you to my entire family, my amazing friends, and my incredible writing community for going on this adventure with me.